THE FOURTH LAST

By Ben Osborne

CHAPTER 1

THE BLOOD WAS EVERYWHERE. A claret wash over ceramic basin and floor tiles.

With fistfuls of grey paper towels, Danny Rawlings mopped feverishly. Taps gushing hot and cold.

He wasn't religious but felt the need to pray.

Distant screaming sirens came and went. He caught a flash of fish-white skin, dead eyes. It felt like a stranger staring back in that bank of mirrors; the portrait of a ghost. *This can't be happening.*

The nauseous waves sparked some forgotten memory of a school trip, gripping a canteen table as the Dover-Calais ferry was tossed by rough seas. Is this what they meant by the moment life flashes before your eyes? He wasn't ready for *that* moment. He had so much more to do. And there was Sara and little Jack to protect, provide for.

Feeling his mind slowly shut down, he chanted, 'I'm Danny Rawlings, done nothing wrong, I'm Danny Rawlings …'

He turned. *Need to sit.* He eyed the line of cubicles, four doors open. He staggered over and summoned the energy to kick the other three. He was alone. He entered the end stall and slumped down. He lowered his hand, heavy and tingly, letting blood drip into the skid-marked toilet bowl, life slowly seeping from him.

A ringing in his ears drowned out the sirens. He bit down on his bottom lip until a metallic taste filled his mouth as he peeled away his shirt sleeve, blackened and soggy. He sucked in loudly, inspecting the damage. It was deeper than he feared. The gash ran from just above his wrist to not far from the crook of his elbow, showing bone, flesh and flapping skin. It was bleeding though not profusely enough to suggest a main artery had been severed. Would already be dead if it had, Danny reckoned.

He began farming for tiny shards of glass embedded in open flesh. He ripped off his other sleeve and tied a crude tourniquet to stem the flow. He felt woozy and forced a few painfully dry swallows.

He glanced at his wedding band and the 6342 inked in broken black on the back of his swollen right hand, skin white as the toilet rim. And the teeth marks crimped onto the flesh of his left, resembling a savage animal bite.

'Fit for the knacker's yard,' he mumbled smiling inanely, now drunk on hysteria.

He felt himself go and let the cistern take his weight. Slowly the lights went out.

CHAPTER 2

FOUR MONTHS EARLIER

Danny's right hand gripped a cold railing four rows back in the stands, the other acted as a steadier to binoculars tracking a runner toiling in eighth.

'No … he's stuffed,' Danny muttered through grinding teeth. 'Don't beat him up Rhys, there'll be other days. Be a good boy, put the stick down!'

He felt something pull at his khaki padded jacket. He hoped it wasn't the disgruntled owner asking why his promising French import had barely lifted a leg over the hurdles and was now out with the washing. He put off responding, ready with the age-old adage 'got bogged down in the ground'.

'Excuse me,' came from his right. Didn't sound like the owner. Younger voice, cut-glass English accent. 'Can I have a word?'

Danny dropped the bins to hang loose from his neck; he'd seen more than enough. The grey brooding skies mirrored his mood. 'What?' he asked, turning to face the man. A wave of blonde hair swept to the right on a fresh, clean-cut face with lagoon-blue eyes. He wore a tweed jacket over matching waistcoat on a slim figure, and moleskin trousers. He held eye contact confidently. Probably got lost straying from his rich daddy over in the Premier enclosure, Danny thought.

'Daniel Rawlings?'

'Who's asking?'

'Ethan Player,' he replied, offering his hand.

Danny responded more with suspicion than conviction, as if shaking the hand of a stranger in the street.

'I appreciate you're a busy man but I have something that will interest you, a business proposal.'

'If you're selling something, go swing for it.'

Get enough aggro with cold calls at home, he thought, even had some 'lucky' heather shoved in my face in the car park just now, fat lot of good it did.

'Far from it,' Ethan said, hand now lost in the lining of his jacket. 'It's more a case of what we can offer you.'

'Go on,' Danny said, attention grabbed.

'Can we discuss this someplace quieter?'

'Tell me here, won't change my answer. Any road, got a runner in the next, need to meet connections down there.' Danny's eyes flicked from Ethan to the oval of green alongside the betting ring.

'Very well,' Ethan said, 'I represent a businessman looking to invest in a burgeoning yard with a view to, in time, take on the big boys … and yours fits the bill.'

Danny worked hard to hold the poker face, trying to play it cool. 'Keep talking.'

'We'll inject cash into the yard, so you'll be working with stronger talent, both horses and staff, and facilities.'

'Who's the businessman?' Danny asked. Can Google the name later, he thought.

'An extremely private individual, a recluse you might say. And wishes to stay that way. This is where I come in. I oversee how much is spent and where, act as an agent if you will.'

'No free lunches in this game,' Danny said. 'What do you expect in return?'

'Quite,' Ethan said, hand combing through his fine hair. 'We'll obviously need results.' He stopped as a white-haired man, led by a gut stretching the weave of a green sweater, pushed between them. He clasped a crumpled ticket in one hand, off to go collect in the betting ring below no doubt. 'Set campaign targets and goals, we'll reassesses on an ongoing basis, though we realise it's like any other business and downturns are par for the course.'

'As long as you know the score,' Danny said. 'Too many go into this game green as that grass over there, expecting the next Best Mate or Desert Orchid. Dreamers. Any return's a bonus, should only spend disposable income. Talking of money, what sort of figures we talking?'

'We're no Russian billionaire,' Ethan said, flashing a white smile. 'But then, as I'm sure you know, don't need to fork out millions to make a mark in the jumping game, just a shrewd man at the helm and in you, I believe we may have found him.'

Danny couldn't help but be lifted by the well-timed compliment. He'd made a promising start since being granted a full licence and putting down a deposit on Samuel House nestled in the deep-green foothills, shadowed by the north face of Caerphilly Mountain. He'd waved goodbye to former boss Roger Crane, who retired ungracefully to someplace on the North Devon coast with dog Racket. Danny hadn't heard from him since but reports suggested he was still hitting the bottle hard.

'We're a very small outfit, one of the minnows,' Danny said. 'Just so you don't get the wrong idea, fifteen boxes.'

'I know,' Ethan said, 'we've done our homework, it's not a problem.'

The chimes of the PA blared from speakers dotted in the rafters of the stands. 'Weighed in … weighed in. Horses away … horses away.'

'If things go well, we can always increase capacity. For now, it's about getting results with our handful of new recruits, all will be sound and capable. To give them the best start, we'll add a horse-walk and all-weather gallop strip.'

'How do ya know I haven't already got those?' Danny said, arching eyebrows. 'Not even got the website up and running.'

'Hope you don't mind, I paid the yard a visit last week. Saw no one was home and didn't want a wasted journey, so took a brief tour myself.'

Danny felt like shouting him down. Who the hell does he think he is? *Got a wife and young child. A stranger roaming the remote yard, scare them half to death.* But he watered down his response, not wanting to spurn this golden carrot. 'Bit previous?'

'I'll ring before visits in future,' Ethan said. 'That is, if you think we have a future.'

'Perhaps,' Danny said, accepting the business card being shown to him.

'Don't stall on this Danny, the offer is on the table for forty-eight hours. We need to move quick, the jumping season will soon be in full stride.'

'I'll call,' Danny said. 'Got to run it by the wife.' He was mindful of his rash decisions and cavalier approach of the past and his promise to make joint decisions from now on. He felt certain she'd back him on this, too good to turn down given the recession. Owners were like gold dust. Beggars can't be choosers.

There was more strength behind their farewell handshake.

'I look forward to hearing from you,' Ethan said and was swallowed by the milling crowds.

Danny remained on course to watch his other runner finish third before setting off on the short trip home to Samuel House.

CHAPTER 3

Danny tossed the van keys in a fruit bowl on a Welsh dresser hogging the hallway of Samuel House, a three-bedroom red-bricked farmhouse with the stables out the back and standing on nearly twenty acres of sloping fields. There was an extension housing a second kitchen and utility room for stable staff to use, a divide between work and home life, though Danny found it hard to keep those apart. Stable jockey Rhys affectionately called it the dog house, as the decor was like a student digs, with little more than a portable TV and kettle. But Danny reminded them of the beautiful views down the valley: one thing he knew wasn't reliant on coughing up yet more money he didn't have. Perhaps he could twist the arm of this new owner to get a refurb, though it would only improve staff morale and not necessarily results. Luxuries like that were at the foot of a long shopping list.

'Good day at the office?' Sara called from the lounge. Her words bounced off Welsh slate floor and low ceiling.

He entered and slumped on to the settee with a sigh, kicking off his black shoes.

'Never mind,' she added, balancing a ham and cheese toastie on the arm of the chair.

Danny flicked on the telly.

'Jack's already down, not long ago. Teething, bless him,' Sara said, rubbing her eyes with the back of her hand. 'Missed his afternoon nap, which meant I missed mine too. Things will turn.'

'Might not need to,' Danny said, a smile spreading like wildfire across his face. 'Came away with something way better than a winner.'

'What?'

'Some guy, says he represents this loaded businessman, reckons he's looking for a yard to invest in and ours fits the bill.'

'What do you make of it?'

'Gonna get back to him pronto, just okaying it with you first.'

Sara didn't reply.

'Well?'

'Who are they?'

'Don't know exactly,' Danny said, putting the remote down, 'but he seemed pretty genuine.'

'Just be careful,' she said. 'It's in your blood to take risks, don't want our fingers burnt again.'

'They're the ones taking the risk,' Danny said. 'If it turns out they're not good for the money, we'll just quit and run.'

Danny had successfully fought off the gambling urges that'd plagued his whole adult life. After stumbling across a long line of losing bets on a bookie's statement, Sara once asked him, 'Sure you like money?' Danny replied, 'I like gambling more.'

The need for a bet was always there, bubbling under the surface, but he'd managed to suppress it and, now with Jack to look out for, he promised he'd never go back to those old, destructive ways.

Sara bit down on her toastie. 'We'll be putting all our eggs in one basket with an owner we don't know the first thing about.'

'But right now we've got no eggs.'

'Don't you think it'll scare away the few loyal owners we *do* have on our books?'

'We don't just want this, we need it,' Danny said. 'Take results today, I'm working with low-graders, they'll never amount to anything, I'm no magician.'

'Did he tell you how they're able to flash the cash when everyone else is struggling to make ends meet, could be robbing banks for all we know.'

'Don't care where the money's coming from, like to focus on the fact they're willing to throw it our way. Buy new recruits, bloodstock. Even spruce up the yard and add staff, so this Ethan says. These people have got the financial clout to take on the big boys. Success breeds success, the more big winners we have on TV the more new owners will come flocking.'

'All seems a bit too good to be true.'

'They want results and with the right tools, reckon I can deliver. No more scrimping to pay the bills and feeling sick after a runner flops. This is the break we need. Can barely cover the interest on this place otherwise. I wanna make this work, for you and Jack.'

'Don't bring Jack into this, emotional blackmail.'

'But you're both my future.'

Sara sighed. She picked up the remote from the wooden coffee table and the screen turned black. 'Don't think I want to know but how are we off, money-wise?'

'We're fine,' Danny said, eyes remained fixed on the telly's blank screen. Voice trailing off, he added, 'all going to plan.'

'I can read you like a book, Danny. Don't say we've blown the lot,' Sara said, wrinkling her nose.

'Got some put by for a rainy day and, god knows, enough of them in the valleys. Thirty grand left in the kitty, after mortgage and the rest.'

'And after that's gone, what then?'

'We'll be fine,' Danny repeated.

'Skint, you mean.'

'The training fees are covering costs.'

'But not making a profit.'

'Not yet but what business does in the early years?'

'I'll have to go back to work,' Sara said.

'Not having that,' Danny said, 'Jack needs you.'

'I'll get childcare.'

'No way,' Danny said. 'I'm working round the clock and, if you're gone, the only face he'll see is a stranger's. Not having him raised like an orphan, don't care how tight things get. We can make cutbacks if things got really bad, that'll do it. Like holidays, Jack won't remember them any case.'

'I will,' Sara said.

'But don't you see, if we give the green light to this, we won't need to.'

'But I'm worried about you, away all hours as it is. Jack won't know you come his eighteenth.'

11

'It's him I'm doing it for, set him up in life.'

'I'm sure he'd rather have childhood memories of his dad.'

'And he will, this Ethan's promised extra staff to help out. If they were up to no good, drug runners or diamond smugglers, don't think they'd be flashing the cash so publicly.' He sighed. 'Can't believe this.'

'What's that supposed to mean?'

'I mean, wasn't expecting a fanfare, but an okay would do.'

'All right!' Sara snapped. 'But don't come running to me if you take on more than you can chew.'

'Why the crusty mood? Thought you'd be chuffed.'

'Tired, that's all.'

Danny thought Jack arriving into the world would bring them close together but the lack of sleep and time they spent with each other was driving a wedge.

'We're in this together, one hundred per cent, yeah?'

'Yep,' Sara said, though Danny wasn't convinced he'd won her over on this one. She left the room and reappeared with Jack in arms. He was subdued, not fully woken up. But his tiny blue eyes lit up seeing Danny.

'This is Daddy,' Sara sang playfully.

'All right, very funny, I know I've been putting all hours in but it's for your sakes,' Danny said, arms outstretched and taking Jack from her. 'Can't help leaving and returning from the track in the dark, when this little fella is away with the fairies.'

'You could get Kelly to take over the odd trip,' Sara said. 'She's old enough to drive the van.'

'Perhaps,' Danny said. 'Now, how's my little poop-machine been today?' He bounced the one-year-old on his lap. 'Been looking after mummy?'

Jack's giggles grew to wild laughter. Danny raised his son above at arm's length and lowered him to blow a raspberry on each cheek. Jack let out an excited cackle. Danny did it again, and again, getting the same reaction each time. 'You're going to grow up strong like Daddy, be a jockey, ride me some winners.'

'Over my dead body,' Sara said. 'Got enough to contend with worrying about you breaking your neck.'

Danny tried rescuing the situation with, 'You've got your mummy's looks and brains, can go to uni instead.'

Sara's lips formed a line, as if she'd seen through it. 'Can't this be enough, what we have right now. A lovely little yard, ticking along.'

'Gotta set goals,' Danny replied. 'You'll rot if ya stand still in this game.' He leant across to give her a reassuring hug but she ducked away from him. 'It'll work out, I'll make sure it does.'

CHAPTER 4

Danny looked up at the white clock-face, above a sparse picture gallery of race presentations and trophy ceremonies supposed to entice wavering new owners to jump on board. Although blessed with a photographic memory, he'd often conveniently forget most were taken from his riding days. He hoped they'd soon be replaced by his training exploits. He glanced over at the trophy cutting a lonely figure and gathering dust in the glass cabinet.

He sat back in his executive chair cut from real leather and dyed racing green. Massaging temples, he wondered what needed asking.

He checked the time again and leant forward. Some research can't do any harm, he thought, before any deals are struck.

He stared at Ethan's business card. Ethan Player – Racing Manager. There was a contact telephone number but oddly no address or email. He then typed 'Ethan Player' into the search engine on his home page. The results were flooded with websites and links for some archaeologist that'd apparently appeared in his eponymous TV show on an unheard of cable channel in the States and there also appeared to be a professional photographer of the same name. He carried out the same search in images but couldn't match the face he'd met on track the day before.

About to delete his temporary files before the subject arrived, he decided to narrow the search to 'Ethan Player racing' but was now flooded by sites selling Ethan James' Rally Racing PC game with four-player mode. Still no relevant results. Was that his real name or was he also using a nom de plume?

He added manager to the search but still nothing. Seemed this particular Ethan Player had no Internet presence at all. He'd now found his first question to ask.

He couldn't sit still and went over to the window. He knitted the business card between fingers as he parted the blinds slightly. He was good with his hands, talents honed from his days as a housebreaker: picking locks, cracking safes, breaking windows were all high on his CV. But that was a very dim and distant past he tried hard to forget.

He looked down on a bottle-green Range Rover pulling up on the shale drive and felt his stomach tighten. This meeting could make or break his training career. It felt more like a job interview.

Mustn't keep him waiting.

He rushed downstairs, towelling his hands on his black chinos. He opened the door. Ethan removed shades and they shook hands.

'Make yourself at home,' Danny said, as Ethan shadowed him into the office. 'Drink?'

'No,' Ethan said and removed his suede coat, draping it over the chair opposite. 'Teetotaller.'

'Tea then,' Danny said.

'I won't be staying long.'

Danny barely had time to sit behind his desk when Ethan came out with, 'I hope I haven't had a wasted journey.'

'You haven't.'

Ethan smiled. 'Thought as much.'

'Talked it over and if your offer's still on the table, it's all systems go.'

'Glad to hear.'

'Before contracts are signed and rubberstamped,' Danny said, 'Can you tell me more about you or this business partner? I find it's good to know about each other, make the relationship run more smoothly.'

Ethan's smile had gone. 'What do you want to know?'

'Anything.'

'Spent four years in the Royal Marines,' Ethan said. 'Brighton and Hove Second Battalion.'

'Thought tattoos were a no-go,' Danny said, pointing out the black ink on Ethan's forearm.

'Sharp, I like that,' Ethan said, 'There's a collar and cuff rule. Anything above the neck or below the wrist is frowned upon. How would you know that?'

15

'Looked into it as a kid,' Danny said. 'Turned out I should've eaten my greens, didn't make the minimum height. Jockey was Plan B.'

'And my boss likes to be known by the nom de plume The Jaguar,' Ethan said, as if keen to steer the subject back to business.

'Any chance of his real name?' Danny said. 'Make Sara happier about this whole thing.'

'As I said, The Jaguar is extremely private, I'm sure you understand and respect those wishes. There are other yards.'

'No need,' Danny replied swiftly, passing a sheet embossed with Samuel House Stables in red. 'This details the training fees, extra costs like vets' bills and travel needs to be added.'

Ethan gave the sheet a cursory glance. 'There are a couple of people I want you to meet.'

'Oh yeah,' Danny asked, suspecting it might be The Jaguar.

'The vet and farrier I'll be using, you'll have no bother with either. Cut some costs having the vet Sam Delaney on call and the farrier Wilf Abbot in-house.'

'Don't hang about do ya,' Danny said. 'You'll want representing at Cheltenham.'

'The December sales?' Ethan asked.

'Yeah, they start in three days' time.'

'Of course.'

'What budget we talking?'

'£120,000 will be wired into your account as soon as the ink's dry on the contracts.'

Danny thought of his Dad's funeral to fight off a smile. 'I'll get them drafted asap.'

'The money will clear in time.'

'I'll get on to ordering a sales catalogue,' Danny said. 'Any preference: French imports, ex-pointers, hurdlers, chasers?'

'Just buy well,' Ethan said and smiled. 'Who's the girl I passed out there just now?'

Danny knew Sara had taken Jack to playgroup. 'Kelly.' He got to his feet. 'And she stays.'

'Good to hear,' Ethan said.

'She's a hard worker,' Danny said, now at the rear window, overlooking the stables. 'Gives her all for the yard. She goes nowhere, whatever your plans.'

'It's still your name above the front door,' Ethan said. 'I'm not here to change the status quo, upset team morale.'

'Do you want a quick look around?'

'No need,' Ethan said, shades back on. 'I'll be back tomorrow to finalise the deal, go over the finer points.'

CHAPTER 5

Danny parked up his Golf at the home of National Hunt racing. He was early, like on the nervy first day of a new job. He'd circled six lots of interest in the presale brochure now lying on the passenger seat.

The arena was already thick and crackly with excitement and anticipation in the Centaur complex on Cheltenham racecourse; an amphitheatre for the rich and powerful among the owning elite in search of the next Gold Cup winner.

Danny registered for his buyer's number and signed forms. He then dropped onto a bench in the shadows near the back, legs twitchy. He thumbed a stray *Racing Post*, catching the headlines: Favourite for the King George gone lame, Armed raid on bookies near Newport and Former champion trainer Calvin Blake found dead. Any good news these days?

He was about to make his way to the sales ring when he felt a firm hand on the back of his black jacket. It was jockey-turned-trainer George Evans. Must be late fifties now, an old stalwart of the West Country jumping set. He'd clearly discovered food since hanging up the riding boots. 'All right Danny, heard you've got a few empty boxes need filling.'

'Here we go, if they're anything like the two duff 'uns you sent me last time, I'll take a rain check George.'

'Felt bad about that, truly I did, but can't always be right,' George said. 'Forgiven?'

'Just another two notches on the bedpost of disappointment,' Danny said and smiled.

'Listen, got one that could well make it up to you,' George said.

'Yeah?' Danny said.

'Going for a song. Would take him on myself, but things are tight down at Nine Acres, with one owner parting ways and another dying on me.'

'Go on.'

'Seven-year-old gelding, super conformation and bred to jump. Salamanca's his name but we call him 'The Tank' at home. Won a couple of point-to-points in Ireland and ran well on his British debut in a good novice chase at Newbury, before winning two races at Exeter.'

'I've heard of him, beat one of mine that day,' Danny said. 'See you're conveniently glossing over a flop at Newton Abbot on the hat-trick bid last time.'

'About to get to that, just a bad day at the office, wasn't right in his coat, didn't eat up either, blame myself.' George shrugged. 'But back in business when third behind a few leading lights at Exeter latest and needed the run that day. Now's the time to snap him up, Danny, before he shows his true class.'

'What's the price tag round his neck?'

'On arrival. Must be seen this one.'

'You tease,' Danny said and paused. 'I'm in that neck o' the woods on Monday.'

'Morning?'

'Say nine,' Danny said.

'Look forward to it.'

Danny glanced across. Circling the sales ring was Ethan, a tier below Danny, clearly here to check the money didn't go up in smoke. He nodded Danny's existence.

'Come check up?'

'Merely an interested spectator, always wanted to attend one of these,' Ethan replied. 'Carry on as you are.'

Danny felt his throat narrow. Although he'd been to this sales ring, he was merely an assistant trainer shadowing Crane then. He now held the strings to a much larger purse. Although greater purchasing power gave him a gilt-edged opportunity to boost the yard's equine talent, he also knew there was potential for farther to fall. He was bidding against the shrewdest eyes of top trainers, bloodstock agents and high-flying owners in the land and beyond, all keenly biding their time, like festival-goers awaiting the opening act at Glastonbury.

Danny caught the rich smell of coffee from his left and wondered whether there was time to get a caffeine fix too, keep himself alert. These guys won't wait for a hesitant bidder. His mind had to be sharp as a tack to come away from this place with the right buys at the right prices.

He looked over at an elderly man cupping a polystyrene beaker. His swarthy face was shaded by a grand leather cowboy hat. He wore a silver necktie and a tassel-fringed suede jacket, looking like he'd just ridden in off the prairies. Danny expected an American accent to come back, but instead a thick Edinburgh brogue said, 'You'll find it in the main stands over there.'

Reminded Danny appearances can be deceptive. No more so than in the sales ring below. He'd need to draw on all his guile to pick up a bargain for this Jaguar.

He noticed the member's badge of the coffee drinker read: Marcus Sowers; a name familiar to Danny as a leading and outspoken owner.

He expected a hollow feel in such a grand hall, with high ceilings and hard floors, but it didn't seem so cavernous now, packed with enthusiasts with the money and desire to snap up the next big thing. The chatter in the room was like humming insects.

Tense business, this buying lark, he thought as he scanned the room, all eyes wide and more swallows than an English summer, I bet.

Perhaps he'd finally found a buzz to replace that constant craving for the rush of having a hefty wager, like a nicotine fix for quitting smokers. This was effectively one big gamble, after all, except it wasn't his money at stake, which almost made it worse.

As the gavel came down, the attentions of the packed arena fell upon the auctioneer. Danny felt his sticky palm tighten around the paddle number four-two-one. With the formalities over, the ringmaster's rapid-fire chant began, sounding more like fork tongue on his first visit. He could now make out the important figures.

Biding his time for the fourth lot, Danny glanced down and couldn't help notice something. The image of a blurry cat in full stride was inked in the narrow band of skin between the leather collar of Ethan's jacket and his blonde neckline.

Was it a jaguar? Was *he* The Jaguar?

'And now we come to lot four,' the auctioneer announced.

Here we go, Danny thought, first of the six lots he'd circled. He'd also pencilled for each a ceiling bid to meet but not go beyond. He hoped his compulsive streak from his gambling days wouldn't cloud his judgement. Get swept away on a wave of adrenalin.

It was time.

Lot four was Buttercup, an unraced son of champion jumping sire The Moon Shadow. With no form in the book, this was a bit of a punt. But as the gelding strutted round the sales ring, looking about as if he owned the place, he knew this one was worth going that extra mile for. The four-year-old bay with a white star on his face was a lovely walker. Danny's alert blue eyes searched out the potential big players. At least three of the high-rollers were paying attention. The phones were also hot. It didn't look good. Danny couldn't come close to matching the financial clout of these. His pulse quickened and grip on the brochure tightened, he enjoyed the buzz of being part of it, though. The bidding started at twenty thousand pounds. No immediate takers. Danny also played the waiting game.

The digital price had dropped to ten thousand, get things moving. It did the trick as the figure had soon risen beyond that initial entry price and a bidding war ensued between Marcus Sowers to Danny's left and high-profile trainer Edward Crowther across the way. Before Danny could raise his arm as a new bidder, the price had smashed through his own thirty-five thousand roof.

'Sixty-two, sixty-two, final chance,' the auctioneer said and glanced over to Edward Crowther. 'It's against you.'

Crowther raised his camel-skin clad arm. 'Sixty-four, sixty-four, sixty-four thousand, sixty-four, any more, sixty-four, last chance.' The gavel came down.

This was an eye-opener to Danny, a sharp learning curve. These guys weren't to be messed with and he just hoped they hadn't taken a fancy for the other five lots he'd circled. He wasn't going to get lured into a bidding war and blow most of the funds on just one horse. It was a high-risk business as it was but putting your eggs in one basket made it sink or swim.

Another failed bid. Danny swallowed hard.

Ethan kept looking up at him yet said nothing. Danny felt like he was in his driving test all over again. Being watched, assessed, every move. He didn't want to come away empty handed though he certainly didn't want to bid for just anything that came up. Instead, he held his nerve and played the waiting game.

The occasional waft of manure, rose above the musty smell of straw and sawdust carried in from the stabling area, caught the back of Danny's throat.

Next on Danny's shopping list was a five-year-old mare of great potential who'd won in France, called Pepper Pot. He stuck to his guns and managed to net her for thirty thousand. With one in the bag, he felt buoyed and was also the final bidder to raise his paddle for a big, rangy Irish point-to-point winner The Watchmaker, snapped up for the princely sum of forty-five thousand. The latter went close to breaking the bank, but he was such a good-looking individual Danny simply couldn't leave the sales without him.

Completing the must-have list was Pick Nick, an unraced five-year-old son of a classy jumper, out of a mare that also won Graded races over fences. Despite some strong opposition from a phone bidder, Danny held firm and snapped up this athletic gelding for twenty-five big ones.

In total, Danny left the sales with four new recruits, while Ethan left without a word and one hundred and fifteen grand lighter. Was he annoyed or aggrieved by those choices or the way Danny bid?

Either way, Danny thought, it was now too late. The die was cast.

He went midway through proceedings to confirm his details and settle up with the auctioneer's staff at a desk on ground level. He was stood beside a 'face'; one who'd bid against him for The Watchmaker. Although it was comforting to know a

22

shrewd eye also saw something in that ex-pointer, the bidding duel pushed the price up another ten-K. Slim, clean-cut, hair suspiciously black for a man of 50-ish. A gold badge was pinned to a collar on his green wax jacket. Eyes as serious as the cash changing hands. Danny picked up an overpowering whiff of cigars as the man leant over the desk to sign a form.

The auctioneer's assistant said, 'See you in January, Michael.'

Clearly a regular at a venue widely regarded as a Harrods shop window for buying jumping stars of the future.

Danny's job was done, for now. Just the small matter of training them to fulfil their obvious potential.

CHAPTER 6

'Salamanca's out the back,' George said. 'This way.'

They turned into the stable courtyard, a square of blotchy concrete paving at the heart of Nine Acre Stables in Somerset.

And there he was, could hardly miss him. Danny's pace and breaths slowed, drinking in the magnificent specimen of a jumper, glossy chestnut coat gleaming like polished mahogany in the cold winter sun.

The seven-year-old stood proud, like a Lord surveying his estate. Shadows defined a large ribcage and rump, and a flash of white marked his face.

'He's a monster, over seventeen hands.' George slapped his charge's thick, strong neck and then ran his yellow-tanned fingers over the gelding's broad chest. 'A real brute, proper jumping stock, mind, takes after his dam who won the National decade back, so stamina no problem, will stay longer than the mother-in-law.'

'Size ain't always important,' Danny said. 'You of all should know that, George.'

George smiled. 'But a good big 'un will always beat a good little 'un and if he ever makes a mistake I feel sorry for the fence. Won't stop this one, uproot it like a bulldozer he will.'

'Take it he's sound.'

'As a pound,' George said. 'I'll dig out his full service history if ya like.'

'No need, trust you. What's the damage?'

'You'll be glad to know, we're not talking telephone numbers.'

'Hit me with it.'

'Thirty-K.'

Danny's brow creased.

'Fit as a flea and ready to go,' George added, as if picking up on Danny's reticence. 'Mind, don't need me to tell you that.'

'Enough of the sales pitch, George. Wanna know if he's strong in there.' Danny ran his hand down the sloping shoulders, checking muscle conformation. 'The heart and mind makes a champion, that and a good set o' lungs. Need to send him over a few fences, that all right, give him a test drive.'

George sucked in some of the fresh morning air. 'But you'd better be serious about making an offer. Missed two lots already, not good with the season up and away.'

Danny eye's flicked between Salamanca and George. 'What's the catch?'

'Catch?' George asked, head tilting. '*Moi?*'

'We both know he's worth more than thirty.'

'Okay, okay, cards on the table time,' George said. Those Jack Daniels eyes dipped. 'The owner only went and dropped dead on me, didn't he.'

'Blimey,' Danny said. 'Sorry.'

'Too right,' George replied, 'gonna lose four of my best inmates as a result, along with this one. Family want the cash from a quick sale, worse luck, not as keen on the gee-gees as old Donald. Bloody shame. Left me two veteran chasers, old enough to smoke they are, and the other horses, well, they're more like rocking than rolling. I'll give 'em a quick sale all right.'

'Explains the price.'

'No skin off my nose, not a penny goes to me.'

'Won't you get aggro?'

'What do they know about the price of fish, or horses for that matter? Stinking rich they are, anyhow.' With every answer, Danny's interest grew. 'Do I care? You'll find that out, when you get a bit older, Danny. Don't give a toss about things you'd waste time worrying about years back. Between you and me, reckon I'll leave the game before the season is out.'

'Got a good few years left in ya,' Danny said, slapping his back, though suspected George wasn't joking.

'We all need something to retire on, coffers will be empty if I carry on to the bitter end,' George said, mood flatlining. 'Now, you going to give 'The Tank' a spin or what?'

The young stable-lad anchoring Salamanca gave Danny a leg-up and the reins. He struggled on board.

'Out of practice are we?'

'Need a step ladder, different weather system up here. Bring on a nosebleed.'

'Turn left and there'll be four schooling fences facing you, just one round of them mind, he had a good workout yesterday.'

Danny steered 'The Tank' to the training ground. Seemed relatively placid, perhaps he was a gentle giant.

But then he pushed the button. A shake of the reins appeared to flick a switch in Salamanca's mind. He took off more like a Porsche than a tank. His big head strained at the leash. Danny felt he was no longer in charge and tried to pull him up, settle both their composures. But Salamanca had decided he wanted to gallop and continued to take a fierce hold, hind legs kicking out in protest to the messages transmitted down the reins.

'Whoa boy, bloody hell,' Danny huffed. 'Think yourself bit of a playboy, don't ya.'

A couple of sharp yanks on the rein and a calming hand down the gelding's neck did the trick. They'd slowed enough for Danny to about-turn. Survival instincts told him not to send this quirky chaser over those replica fences but he had to check if Evans' hype was justified or just hot air.

'Come on boy, let's see what ya can do,' Danny whispered in Salamanca's big ears. The back of his boots met with Salamanca's barrel to giddy him up. They once again shifted up the gears to racing pace on the approach to the first fence. Danny pushed him into it but Salamanca jinked and cranked the handbrake on. He was shunted up Salamanca's withers, mouthful of mane. Yet momentum carried them the other side in some shape or form.

Danny marvelled that, despite the wayward approach and unorthodox jumping technique, they hadn't even touched a twig. Salamanca was demonstrating raw talent like nothing he'd seen before. Danny knew if he could tame the beast, he'd be on a winner.

The next came upon them and, as if Salamanca was now resigned to completing the round of four jumps, he attacked the fence with more purpose, another fault-free leap. Danny caught sight of the distant round figure of George from the edge of the grass.

His focus returned to the upcoming fence. Another clean jump.

Give me just one more like that, Danny thought, and you're coming home with me. They met the fourth in the row of fences on a perfect stride and cleared it like a showjumper. Full marks.

Danny was fired up by the precocious talent beneath him and went to stick a thumbs up to George, but he'd retired to the stables, clearly seen enough. And so had Danny.

He noticed Salamanca was breathing heavy, making a faint whistling noise. Odd for a fit racehorse, Danny thought, perhaps needs a wind operation. Maybe that's what held him back.

Danny dismounted and led Salamanca to his master, now dishing out gallop order for the next lot to what looked like the head lad.

'Made your mind up?' George asked, stroking his second chin. 'Growing a beard here.'

'Can see why ya didn't want me to have a spin on him, bucking and kicking most of the way, total fruitcake.'

'You'll get on well.' George's smile soon dissolved. 'He's got a quirky side, I'll grant you, but the talented ones always do. Fine line between genius and madness.'

'Reckon this one's already crossed that line.'

'He'll settle with age.'

Danny was prepared to take a punt but wasn't willing to let on when there was haggling to do. The fact he could potentially blow the family kitty on this one new recruit sobered him. 'Gonna think about it, I'll drop you a line.'

'What's there to think about? Didn't have you down as the cautious type.'

'I'm not,' Danny said, 'but why the rush?'

27

'Like I said, the owner's family want it wrapped up sharpish, so we can all move on.'

Danny was about to leave when George added, 'Twenty-eight-K and daylight robbery at that.' It did indeed feel like a bargain to Danny, though he fell short of saying as much.

'Twenty-six, cash,' Danny said, 'and we can shake on it here and now.'

'Deal,' George said. 'Dear ol' Donald knew how good Salamanca was but his family are none the wiser. Shouldn't get any comeback from them.'

'Just say it went to a good home.'

As they shook hands, George held the grip and said, 'Do him justice.'

Danny smiled and said, 'Sure.'

'I mean it, this one's special, don't waste it.'

CHAPTER 7

A cold gust stole Danny's breath as he patted the mottled grey neck of mare Silver Belle, whose coat had whitened with age. Her waterproof turnout rug flapped away. She'd been forced into retirement after picking up an injury on her final start last season.

Unlike many racers, she'd quickly settled in at her new home down the lower field with the recently befriended Ronny, a Shetland pony with intelligent eyes and chestnut coat with flaxen mane. He came bouncing over on those short, sturdy legs, curious to see what all the fuss was about. Danny whispered in Silver Belle's large ear, 'What do ya think I should do old gal? Reckon I've made the right decision?'

Her head nodded as she snaffled Danny's hand. He replaced the mint that'd vanished from his palm and smiled. 'I'll take that as 'yes', same time tomorrow, gal.' Ronny stuck his muscular neck between the struts in the fence, alert ears pricked. 'And you Ronny. Gotta go earn your keep.'

He trod over muddy grass back to Samuel House, scraped his boots and settled in his leather chair.

He'd just booted up the laptop when he looked up as there came a knock at the door. Kelly appeared. The soft light streaming through the lace curtains lit up her cute face, clear skin shining like white gold. Her black hair, shaped in a nineties bob, shimmered, and her brown eyes sparkled. She said, 'They're here.'

She was tailgated by Ethan, who brushed her arm, hands briefly connecting, and two other men, presumably the new vet and farrier.

'At ease, gentlemen,' Ethan said, army ways had clearly left their mark. 'I'd like you to meet Sam Delaney and Wilfred Abbot, both came with me from Nick Mellor's yard in Devon.'

Danny offered his hand to the forty-something wearing overalls standing nearest. His wiry red hair resembled a Brillo pad and looked a nightmare to brush. By the look of it, Wilf had long since given up trying. His white skin was pocked, like some moonscape.

Danny's eye-level met his chin. He looked up at those dark brown eyes, as feral as his hair.

'W-W-Wilf,' he said.

Danny stepped forward and offered his hand. 'Look forward to working with you.'

Wilf nodded.

'Okay,' Danny said, just to fill the silence.

'You can't shut him up once he gets started,' Sam said, melting the ice. His hand rested on the shoulder of Wilf, whose face shot off to the left, a nervous tick.

'Yes, quiet as a cat this one,' Ethan said. 'But you won't find a harder worker this side of the Severn Bridge.'

'Eh!' Sam said and smiled.

'Present company excepted,' Ethan said. 'And this is Sam, I'm sure you've figured out, the equine vet I'll be using.'

Danny turned to Sam. He had closely-cropped black hair, with a bleach-white birthmark near the fringe. A week's growth covered his strong jaw-line and he wore a flannel shirt over charcoal trousers.

'You'll have no trouble with him, either,' Ethan added.

'Glad to hear it,' Danny said.

'I won't be working solely for this yard, just so you understand,' Sam said. 'Will be on call-out in the area.'

'So won't have him all to ourselves, worse luck,' Ethan said.

'Wouldn't expect it any other way, we're only a small yard,' Danny said, keen to play the easygoing boss. 'Hopefully won't have to need you that much this winter.'

'Perfect set-up you've got here,' Sam said, lifting the lace. 'Wouldn't think that green was possible.'

'Only cos it rains most of the year, you'll find that out soon enough.'

'Slopes must help for getting them sharp, I bet,' Sam said.

30

'Gives me a workout 'n all.' Danny picked up a folder from his desk. 'I've looked over your papers and I'm pleased with both your CVs and the rest,' Danny said firmly. 'I understand you're both contracted by Ethan.'

Ethan stepped forward. 'As they're new additions, I'll deal with wages and so on.'

'One less thing to worry about,' Danny smiled. 'Look forward to future success.'

'Here's to a long and fruitful partnership,' Ethan said. 'Plenty of winners.'

'Plenty of winners,' the others echoed.

'Feel a toast coming on,' Danny said. 'Tempt you to a dram of the hard stuff?'

Sam and Ethan said in unison, 'Driving.'

'Just shake on it then,' Danny said.

They exchanged handshakes and departed, leaving Danny alone in the office, picturing future successes. Now, no longer a pipedream. He went over and dusted his only trophy as a trainer; a small silver plate.

Soon give you some company. Everything was fitting into place.

He sunk two fingers of whisky in a private toast. He heard the distant clap of a car door and rushed to the window to see them leave. He looked down on the arcing shale driveway. It's as if he needed to cement in his mind this was actually happening, they weren't a mirage, some fantasy he'd concocted of how he wanted his career at Samuel House to pan out. But there they all were.

Sam and Wilf had climbed into a blue Peugeot. Sam driving.

Ethan stood by his Range Rover, smiling. Kelly came into view and, like a lovesick puppy, ran to meet him. They kissed with tongues.

'Doesn't hang around,' Danny muttered.

He looked on as Ethan's hand ran down to the small of her back and ushered her into the passenger seat of the bottle-green four by four. Before Danny had time to react, Ethan gave a parting glance up to the window. The blinds fell back into place and Danny stepped away.

9.12 AM. Tuesday. Danny's eyes were fixed on the CCTV screen, its bubble-wrap and cardboard boxes still to be shifted from the corner of the study.

It wasn't the horses lounging in their boxes that made him stare intently. Ethan's shadowy outline had lingered by the V in the metal grill of Salamanca's stable door. Ethan had paid the yard daily visits since signing on the dotted line a week ago. Regular as clockwork, he'd show up at 9.10 AM, after the new recruits had completed morning workouts.

Danny wouldn't normally mind, he liked owners to take an active interest, but he suspected there was more to the shadowy figure on that screen. Ironic Ethan was keenest to add all these security cameras as they allowed Danny to keep a close eye on him, rather than the horses. He felt Ethan's interest went beyond the call of duty as a racing manager.

He heard floorboards groan out on the landing.

'Come look at this, Sara,' Danny said.

'What?'

'State-of-the-art CCTV,' Danny said. 'Sixteen split screens covering each box, move the cursor over one and look, goes full screen, more detail that way. Can't beat it.' Sara rested her hands on his shoulders. 'Sensors on each of the cameras pick up any big movements, if one of the horses gets agitated or cast in their box. And then, via this computer, sends me a text alert.'

He looked up, she was fighting off a smile.

'What now?'

'Boys and their toys.'

'Come on, it's impressive, give me that,' Danny said, mirroring her smile. 'And it's hardly a PlayStation.'

'Only teasing.'

'Work starts on the all-weather gallop strip Monday, hopefully finished by the next cold snap. And got an email from the designers this morning saying the yard's website was going live, things are finally happening. No more talking and dreaming, Sara, we're actually gonna go places this season, you watch.'

'Hope so,' Sara said, lips touching the crown of Danny's head. 'Really I do.'

With Jack's distant wails, she was gone.

An envelope symbol popped up in one corner of the screen. Danny clicked on the desktop icon and called up the email account. He waited calmly, thinking it was a test mail from the techie guys to check his website's contact page was working. He wished it was. The sender address was blocked. There were only three words in the body of the message. But they were enough to make Danny's pulse quicken and face drop.

BEWARE OF THEM.

Must be four or five times he read those words, until they sank in.

Beware of who? Who are *they*?

Probably spam, he reckoned, shrugging it off dismissively, or some jealous trainer yet to attract a big owner. He hadn't felt this good since his wedding day or the birth of Jack, and didn't want anything to come in the way of it.

Like dismissing some worrying symptom, he'd rather brush it under the carpet than go check it out at the doctor's.

That's what you get for going public with the email address, he thought, opens the door to all the psychos and saddos out there.

Danny calmed himself by poring over the list of new acquisitions again. He didn't need to. He knew their breeding and form inside out. It did, however, gave him a source of pleasure just to see these promising types, on paper at least, now in his care. Jack had his blanket. This was Danny's comforter.

He picked up today's *Racing Post* dated 18th December. Keep up to date with the goings-on in the racing world. Headline on the inside cover read: Bookies on high alert after another armed raid.

Not another one, Danny thought, before reading on.

Bookmakers in South Wales are said to be vigilant and on high alert in the face of a series of armed raids to hit the region. The Barry branch of the Raymond Barton chain was the latest in a series of shops targeted by two armed robbers at 9.30 AM yesterday morning.

Chief Inspector Barnes, who is leading the investigation, confirmed: 'Enquiries are ongoing and we are investigating numerous possible leads, including that it may be an inside job. No further comment will be made at this stage.'

One customer, who witnessed the terrifying Barry raid first hand and wishes to remain anonymous, recalled: 'It was a nightmare. Both wore masks, the one at the counter was flashing that gun around, kept shouting, 'Be quiet as a cat, keep down or die.' There were about a dozen of us in there, mostly regulars, all still in shock. I'm still shaking.'

Below listed the bookie raids, where and when, totalling fourteen shops spread over three years. Most were Raymond Barton shops, though there were a few Wheeler's branches in recent months. At the foot was the Barry shop.

His mind was replaying the moment he was introduced to the vet and farrier. Something Ethan said struck him as odd at the time. 'Quiet as a cat,' he'd described Wilf. Danny had heard 'quiet as a church mouse', but never cat.

Was Ethan one of them? Was that how *they* funded the yard? Blood money. If so, the email took on a new sinister meaning. He tore the article out, folded and pushed it safely in his jacket pocket. Out of sight and all that.

Sara's cautionary words came back to haunt him, 'Could be robbing banks for all we know.'

He then laughed. Mind's playing tricks again, he thought, and turned to the British Horseracing Authority – BHA – race-fixture list to plot and plan the best paths to take the new recruits.

But his thoughts were nowhere near it. And he wouldn't settle until he knew for sure Ethan was legit. He knew nothing of the man, other than he's a trained killer. The jury was well and truly out.

34

CHAPTER 8

Let's see what you've got kiddo.

Danny pointed Salamanca towards a line of three practice fences, something like the real thing, only with a bit more give.

He swallowed hard. He hoped there'd be the same exhilarating buzz he'd felt prior to handing all that cash over to George.

Perhaps Salamanca only produced on home soil and wouldn't perform over these, a one trick pony.

Twenty-six grand was a lot of money, particularly as he'd yet to come clean to Sara it had come from their 'rainy day' funds. He hadn't lied. She hadn't asked. Probably not wanting to know. He wasn't proud but saw no other option. Couldn't spend the next thirty years grafting at the gaff tracks just to scrape by.

Sara had warned, 'Don't put your eggs in one basket.' Merely following her word, he reconciled, diversify. Spread the risk so there was something to fall back on if The Jaguar left them high and dry. Though he wouldn't use that as an argument, if it ever came out.

Last night, he'd even dreamt that Salamanca plundered a big prize on his rookie campaign and was geared up to tackle the Grand National but he woke up as they were going to post in the Aintree feature. He longed for that dream to become reality before awkward questions were asked.

For now, his concerns lay with the three walls of tightly packed birch in the way. Salamanca's pricked ears acted like a viewfinder as Danny homed in on the first.

Salamanca was on his toes, clearly well versed in what lay ahead.

'Here goes nothing,' he muttered, words carried down-valley by a freshening breeze. He pushed on.

Thirty yards and Salamanca had picked up into a fluent, purposeful gallop. Least George hadn't sold him another lame duck, he briefly thought.

He threaded the whip to his left hand as he felt the gelding try lugging that way. Had his quirky side resurfaced in these strange surroundings? The persuader was primed as a mere precaution, not planning or wanting to call upon it. But that soon changed as Salamanca barely lifted his lead leg over the first, they parted the birch, which now needed fixing. He hoped Salamanca hadn't suffered similar damage. Danny suspected he was more shocked than the horse. He slapped him on the shoulder as a wake-up call but it only served to fire Salamanca up, taking off on the approach to the second fence. 'The Tank' was seemingly unfazed by a jolting mistake that would've floored lesser types.

Danny considered pulling out, abort mission and cut losses, allowing him time to collect his muddied thoughts, and steady both confidence and composure.

But, since being hit, Salamanca was having none of it and already had the next fence firmly in his sights. Perhaps the added energy would see them over in more convincing fashion, he hoped.

'Go on, boy,' Danny growled in those ears. 'Don't let me down.'

Another howling mistake and even Salamanca took a few strides to find bearings, like a punch-drunk boxer. What the fuck's wrong with ya? Danny fumed.

Another slap, firmer this time. Get it together, quick. Was the bugger playing games?

The third and final fence, much to Danny's relief, was now just yards away. No backing out now. He let Salamanca tackle it in his own inimitable style, no guidance from the saddle. A change in riding tactics but the same outcome, uprooting the fence. And then, despite Salamanca's best efforts to bolt out of the schooling grounds, Danny managed to anchor him to a walk. He was still fresh as a daisy and not a mark on him, despite destroying three fences.

'They weren't wrong,' he thought aloud, dismounting. 'Proper Sherman, aren't we?'

Salamanca was nodding on the spot, he wanted more. But Danny had seen enough for one day, thank you very much. Despite being in awe of the strength and toughness of the horse, he was angered by those antics. Couldn't afford to give away ground at every fence on race day.

Danny was well aware this stubborn bugger was bred to jump. That's what he was born to do. Not even a Flat-bred could screw up that badly over those fairly kind fences. Perhaps he was right and Salamanca was taking him for a ride in more ways than one.

Was the horse blind or stupid?

Maybe it was neither, he thought. George said he was a clever sod. Perhaps he'd just grown bored by those fences. He dwarfed them and as Danny had just witnessed, he didn't turn a hair from breasting them at racing speed.

There was a way to find out.

'Come here mister. Bored with those, too easy for ya?' he said, no one else about. He boarded Salamanca, gathered up the reins and got comfy in the saddle. He'd need to be balanced for the ride ahead. 'See if ya give these more respect.'

Danny trotted Salamanca out of the schooling ground and let him stretch out, burning off some of the aggravation seemingly pent up in both of them.

Across the valley they went. Lifting his knees high, Salamanca's lengthy, rakish stride simply ate up the ground. They'd soon crested the rise.

First challenge lay ahead; a wooden fence marking the boundary of the land belonging to Samuel House. Three struts high. No bigger than the fences Salamanca had just done his best to flatten.

Danny reckoned Salamanca wouldn't be so sure about a different looking thing and instinctively give this actual fence the respect it deserved.

A big risk that could easily result in a gash or even worse if proven wrong. Or the horse may decide not to play ball, put the

37

brakes on and send Danny flying into the next field. He would prefer picking up an injury rather than his horse. Can always get a replacement rider, but Salamanca was one of a kind.

Danny treated this as an initiation of sorts, might even help bond with the horse.

The fence was stood on a slight incline and he knew they'd need to build speed and momentum to make the other side partnership intact.

He gripped the reins and pushed Salamanca's withers. The chestnut responded in kind.

Danny held his breath on the approach, calling upon all his concentration. Three-two-one. He hoped Salamanca would too. And he did. Front legs lifting high and landing gear tucked neatly, knees bent and power-packed hind quarters providing the engine for take-off.

The fence went with a blur and was gone, their landing cushioned by thickets of wild grass the other side.

The rush of cooling air brushed over his flushed cheeks. The moss-green grass breezed beneath them as they crossed the many peaks and troughs of the meadows. Danny felt it hard to contain his excitement. He was now buzzing more than Salamanca as they joined the well-trod path hunting parties had taken, before the ban. He was trespassing but didn't care. He crested the rise that marked the boundary of another farmer's land. His sights now aimed at an inviting gap between two large oaks, no more than three horse widths apart. His body compass told him they weren't far from a field sloping to the Rhymney road.

Head down, Salamanca charged on, seemingly willing to tackle with relish whatever was thrown his way, like a fearless schoolboy. Danny was carried along by that exuberance, warming to this foolhardy take on life. Blissfully reliving his own youth for an all-too-brief moment.

A star in the making, he beamed, as they flew between those thick trunks.

But his enthusiasm was cut short as a brook came into view, a tributary winding its way off to the River Rhymney, beyond a dip in the land. He'd now ventured into alien territory and he slowed the gallop, fear of the unknown.

Salamanca also gave it respect, stride shortening, as if he'd not come across one before. The fast flowing stream was no more than four feet wide. Not a problem on its own, the water jumps at Aintree were wider, but there was a sloping bank of mud and stones either side here. Still no great problem but it was the added pressure. He had to meet it right rather than merely want to.

He reckoned this was all new to his ride and would teach him a great deal. The strapping chaser took off well before the ground fell away and landed clear of the earthy bank the other side.

Danny whooped as they strode up another incline. Salamanca had clearly been blessed with his mother's stamina and jumping prowess. Danny was comforted by a familiar wooden fence up ahead, not far now to home soil.

Danny didn't know for sure how much energy Salamanca had in reserve and feared clipping a nail or splintered wood. Failing to pick up those sturdy legs in time would mean a nasty cut. He couldn't back out now, so buoyed was Danny by this life-affirming, glorious country spin, he went at the fence full-throttle.

Salamanca tackled it with similar gusto, proving Danny's fears were unfounded. They cleared the wooden struts with air to spare. This was better than he could ever have dreamt. The inexperienced steeplechaser beneath him was cleverly negotiating these tricky obstacles like an old pro.

A dip and then a rise before a low dry-stone wall came into view following the contours of the brook. Mistiming would put Salamanca out for months, if not end the gelding's career before it had truly started. He was tempted to go the long way round, via a brambly hedge at the bottom of the meadow. But if it was good enough for the hunters, a classy jumper like Salamanca should clear it in style. Or was Danny being whisked away by Salamanca's enthusiasm? He wasn't sure who needed taming the most. Perhaps this short sharp shock would help them both.

Danny pushed on. He knew it was a gamble. But life was about risk-taking. And it was too late to lose nerve now. Three-two-one. He prayed they'd meet it on a good stride.

How could he ever have doubted? The grey stone wall flashed under them, almost as soon as they'd left the ground. Danny slapped Salamanca's glistening neck. He felt like a free spirit, among nature, after years cooped up in the city.

This was what it's about, he thought. He felt heady, drunk on a cocktail of adrenalin and fresh air. He slowed to stand. King of the hill. He drank in the expanse of green, down to a snaking country road off to Rhymney.

Before embarking on the descent, he leant forward and wrapped his arms around Salamanca's neck. Bursting with pride, like a proud parent. Salamanca was seemingly having none of it and rocked his head free of the embrace as if to say, 'We'll be having none of that, soft sod.'

He set about the journey downhill before banking off left to complete the gruelling circuit back to the yard. Salamanca appeared more settled now and was actually responding to the signals Danny transmitted down the reins. The beast within had been tamed, Danny hoped. They'd bonded.

Back at the yard, Danny reckoned it would take a long time before he'd come down from this natural high, better than anything he'd popped or downed in his youth.

However, he was quickly sobered. Salamanca had yet to fully recover normal breathing patterns and was making a noise a good five minutes after the country spin. Not knowing the limits, Danny hoped he hadn't pushed Salamanca too hard.

He dismounted and phoned Sam, 'You okay to come down.'

'Nothing major?'

'Hope not, just given new boy Salamanca a proper workout and he's come back gagging, making a roaring sound. We went over the hunting course and reckon it's shone a light on a problem that regular schooling hadn't.'

'How's the chap doing now?'

'Settling down, finally. Was a bit shaky when I got off, we both were. What do ya reckon?'

'Probably a wind problem, needs checking. I'll be over in the afternoon, will know more then.'

Danny returned to the stable courtyard and boxed up Salamanca. Wilf was busying himself filing down the back hooves of Pick Nick. He looked up and shifted his weight as if surprised to see Danny, or was he trying to steady the feisty youngster.

After lunch, with no runners to send out, Danny was brushing down Salamanca, who wouldn't let Kelly or any of the other lads near him.

Those practice fences won't repair themselves, he thought, one of countless jobs to do around the yard. But Danny didn't mind dropping everything to groom his star. Investing time in his pension fund. After such a spirited display cross-country he already had eyes on tackling the Grand National in April. Ever the dreamer, he'd already entered Salamanca for the big one. Follow in the hoofprints of his dam. He turned to do the other flank and, from nowhere, there was Sam, who said, 'I'll give the patient the once-over when you're ready.'

Danny backed away to give the vet some space.

'Chances are we'll need to scope him,' Sam said, fishing for some implement in his bag. 'If he's clean, he may need to be hobdayed.'

'Bit drastic,' Danny said, 'cutting a hole in his neck.'

Sam said, 'May need it, to fill those colossal lungs of his in the heat of battle, whatever it takes. But that would be a last resort.'

'How long would it set us back?' Danny asked, always liking to know the worst case scenario. He was mindful of the shrinking window of opportunity to gain a confidence-lifting win under the patient's belt. It would also help increase Salamanca's official rating and boost chances of making the cut when the Grand National weights were published.

'Depends on the horse, but couple of months to be safe.'

41

'Let's not go there,' Danny said. 'Would ruin any dreams of National glory.'

Sam stood back and gave him a look. 'Not for me to say but – sending a novice over those fences this early in his career?'

'You're right, it's not for you to say,' Danny said defiantly.

'Just airing an opinion,' Sam said.

'Well don't,' Danny snapped. 'Stick to your job and I'll do mine.'

The icy silence was broken by Sam. 'We needn't have gone there.' He was peering into Salamanca's mouth, despite the patient trying to nut the vet. 'He's swallowed his tongue, blocking the airways. Probably why he's coming up short in his races. Surprised his former connections hadn't picked up on it.'

'They pushed a quick sale, reckon they didn't have time. So a tongue-tie might do the trick?'

'Before we do anything invasive, it's certainly worth seeing how he comes out of a gallop wearing one.'

'Will do later today, sooner we get this sorted the better, eh, Salamanca,' Danny said. Salamanca was scraping his hind foot on the concrete, seemingly annoyed by all this attention.

Danny suspected all he wanted was a day relaxing out in the paddock with Silver Belle. But he was now in full work for a Grand National prep race at Chepstow in a few weeks' time. Like a boxer in training camp for a bout, he needed to follow a set routine, build up fitness levels and sharpness in body and mind. Setting him loose in a field would only risk injury.

'Let him settle in the box before doing anymore workouts,' Sam said, hand running down the flash of white on Salamanca's face.

'How's he look to you?'

'Sharp, just a few pounds of condition, but I'm sure he'll burn that off soon enough,' Sam said, checking the gelding's ears and eyes were clear. 'We'll have you back in the winners' circle before you know it. Looks well in his skin too.'

'Hope you're right,' Danny said, buoyed by that second opinion. With no assistant trainer, it was good to hear positive vibes from another professional. 'And sorry, should've checked his mouth before calling you out.'

'No worries,' Sam replied, 'it's normally the legs that go wrong, easy to forget they support half a ton in full flight and, unlike us, they've four of them to go wrong. Done enough bandaging and splints for one week thank you.'

Danny smiled.

'I'll need to inoculate the whole string soon,' Sam added. 'Got a call-out down Rhymney way later this afternoon. I'll do it in the next week.'

'Kelly will be here, chances are I'll be off at the races,' Danny said. 'Either way, you know where they are.'

Wilf was now stood in the shade, tool-bag in hand, alongside Sam's Peugeot.

'Think you're wanted,' Danny said.

Sam looked over to the parking behind Samuel House. 'Give me a bell if he's still blowing hard.'

'Will do,' Danny said. 'See you around.'

CHAPTER 9

Danny waited in eager anticipation. He stood alongside the white plastic rails penning the newly laid gallop strip, courtesy of The Jaguar.

The winter sun was strong enough to burn off the morning haze, though the crisp air felt cool on his face.

His blue eyes pressed firmly against powerful zoom binoculars. He saw brown and black dots grow larger, slowly morphing into three athletic jumpers in full stride.

Danny had requested two local jockeys to join Rhys in working his new recruits, promising they'd have first dibs when their mounts made the racetrack. He wanted experienced riders to test them out, rather than call upon the stable lads.

First to pass was The Watchmaker, whose powerful quarters propelled him up the incline towards Samuel House, showering Danny with a mix of wood chippings and sand.

The horse was blowing hard, steam from flaring nostrils and glossy coat. It's what Danny expected. Nearly six months since signing off a career in the competitive Irish point-to-point scene. This serious workout would open up his lungs and was the first of a handful planned in the build up to his imminent debut under official National Hunt rules. Danny was eyeing a minor beginners' chase for that one, give him a penalty kick to convert before tackling stronger types deeper into winter.

Next up was Pick Nick, the unraced youngster. Smaller than the lead horse, yet a well-made bay and a good mover. Breeding to die for too.

He was the one Danny held out greatest hopes for. Even though he was untested in a competitive sense, Danny's wild card purchase oozed quality. Rhys was purposefully hugging the rail presumably preventing the green youngster from hanging off a true line. He trusted the stable jockey would treat this bright young spark with kid gloves. Danny didn't want Pick Nick upsetting before he'd even set hoof on the track.

Danny lowered his binoculars again next to a digital stop-clock as Pick Nick neared within range of the naked eye. He was certainly striding out well, plenty of zest about him, Danny reckoned, probably down to youthful exuberance. Everything was new at that age. Danny could relate. He was the same as a teenager which is effectively what this gelding was in horse years.

Danny's brow creased as he noticed the youngster was holding his head carriage slightly off to the left, suggesting he was hurting somewhere, though he might just be pulling at Rhys' reins.

The third to pass was Pepper Pot, a lovely looking mare who'd won her only start in a Flat race reserved for jumpers in France, known as an AQPS. Although on the small side, her conformation was superb, strong lines and powerful rump and shoulders. Could easily be mistaken for a colt. She certainly possessed the strength of one and he knew she'd enjoy the weight allowances, enabling her to race off lighter than her male counterparts; a big advantage once she made her eagerly anticipated British debut and that would be soon, given the way she glided effortlessly by, barely out of second gear.

A sparkle lit Danny's tired eyes. He liked what he saw. There was no need to punch the timer hung from his neck. It was all there before him. This trio were expensive purchases at the sales, costing the princely sum of £115,000 between them, but they looked the part. Worth every penny, Danny thought, and the rest.

He turned and made his way back to the stable block. Have a post-gallop chat with Rhys and the others, see if they agreed with Danny's initial favourable impression.

Rhys was already unbuckling the breast girth on Pick Nick, who was now glistening in frothy sweat.

'How'd he go for you?' Danny asked.

'Sweetly, but too keen. He's a youngster I guess, soon settle down,' Rhys said.

'Reckon he's near to making his debut,' Danny said. 'Can't wait to get a run under this one's belt, some competitive experience will bring him on a ton.'

'Don't doubt it,' Rhys said, never one to wax lyrical about the regard he held for his rides. 'Just make sure I'm the one steering.'

After similarly positive reports from the other riders on Pepper Pot and The Watchmaker, Danny's day was already made.

The constant anxiety he'd suffered since the sales spree had suddenly diminished. He'd always felt he'd made the right choices but know he knew for sure. What he'd just witnessed on the gallops went beyond his expectations. The Jaguar will be pleased.

He returned to Samuel House. Sara was sat in the lounge, playing with Jack.

He swept his son from the play mat and swung him up in the air. 'Hello you.'

Jack smiled.

'Did they go well?' Sara asked; seemingly picking up on how much this meant to their future.

'Like a dream,' he said. 'They're ready to race.'

'That's great,' she sighed, palpably relieved. 'Sorry to rain on your parade, but the faces Jack made just now, think he needs changing. Got to put the tea on.'

Danny smelt Jack and backed off, smile now gone. He wished he'd stayed out on the gallops to watch the second lot.

That afternoon, Danny was sat in his office waggling a ballpoint pen. He'd made a mug of coffee he didn't really want. He felt exactly the same whenever he needed to remember something important, but hadn't written a reminder. Mind on two things. Sara always said he was useless at multitasking.

He couldn't put his finger on why he was unable to fully embrace the recent positive happenings at the stable. And he guessed until he was sure where this money came from there was no way he would.

If it ever came out the yard was funded by illegal means, he knew the horses would be whisked away overnight, along with any prize money, and Danny's training career would be in tatters before it had truly started.

Better to find out the answer now, before things went too far down that road. But, aside from asking Ethan upfront, there was no way of proving or disproving his part in the robberies. If tackled, Ethan was sure to deny it either way and any insinuations would only serve to stir up tensions with the new owner at these delicate, fledgling stages of their relationship. That's the last thing he wanted as Ethan made it clear from the outset, 'there are other yards'.

Danny wasn't prepared to see these promising horses taken from his grasp before they'd even made it to a racetrack.

'What's wrong with me?' escaped his lips, leaping from that train of thought. Whatever happened to innocent until proven guilty? The fact he held no proof whatsoever, merely the peculiar phrasing 'quiet as a cat' and some vague email threat, should've told him enough. He'd let a fertile imagination grow wildly out of control.

Go check on the horses, he thought, see how they'd come out of the morning gallops. He was halfway along the landing when a glance into the study made him stop.

That's it, he thought.

He returned to the office and rifled through bills, invoices and newspapers cluttering the desk. He picked up the *Racing Post* dated 18th December, now stained by coffee rings.

He rushed to the study and rolled the air-cushioned office chair up to the CCTV screen. It hissed as he dropped his weight on the padded seat. The screen flashed into life as he shifted the mouse. He clicked the desktop symbol and ran the cursor over the icon named 'stored files'.

He picked out footage for Monday 17th December – the day Raymond Barton's Barry branch was raided.

The sixteen screens in one began playing monochrome footage. He dragged the scrollbar along the base of the screen until the clock in the corner neared 9.10 AM. Danny knew Ethan paid regular visits at that time of day and resumed 'play' mode.

He stared intently at the screen showing shots of the fifteen stable boxes and the shaded parking area behind Samuel House. Come on Ethan, Danny thought, where are you?

The screen clock turned 9.11 AM and still no sign.

His Golf stood alone in the parking area. Danny's mind spun back to that day. By then, he'd be on the road to Worcester with one of the yard's lesser lights Tell Tale in tow; a wasted journey as the gelding ran a stinker in a race he was entitled to win on form.

It wasn't looking good. Ethan had normally arrived by now to check the horses.

9.12 AM. Hopes of quashing any suspicions and fears had faded. Ethan was conspicuous by his absence. It suggested he had more important places to be on that particular morning. The bookie's in Barry perhaps.

9.13 AM and Danny's gaze homed in on screen sixteen – the parking area. A dark shape had entered stage right. Danny skated the cursor over the image and it blew up to fill the screen. The shape, as Danny hoped, was a Range Rover, parked up alongside his Golf. For several seconds, nothing happened, as if the footage had stuck.

9.14 AM. Danny was about to reboot the file when the driver's door flung open and Ethan appeared, stretching his legs. Danny picked up the *Racing Post* for last Monday and checked the article. The raid had taken place at 9.30 AM.

Not even Ethan can be in two places at once, he thought, panic over.

When he looked up, Ethan was gone. Danny flicked back to the split screen. He focussed on screens four, seven and twelve. They housed The Jaguar's first crop of jumpers: Pick Nick, The Watchmaker and Pepper Pot.

He eyed screen four as Ethan reassuringly came into shot, inspecting Pick Nick, who was stood face close to the grey wall.

Danny paused the footage, sat back and smiled, hands cupping the back of his head. That screen-capture alone proved

48

Ethan's innocence, without having to ruffle any feathers. He jotted a mental note not to leap to any conclusions without hard evidence in future.

CHAPTER 10

Danny felt his fingers tingle as they gripped the leather steering wheel. He hadn't felt this mix of excitement or nerves professionally since lining up Silver Belle at the tapes for the Cheltenham Festival. He left the M4 eastbound at junction 48. He glanced across at Rhys in the passenger seat, face in the *Racing Post*. Danny hoped he was working out tactics from the running styles of the opposition though, knowing Rhys, he was catching up on any gossip in the racing world, suspensions for fellow jockeys and the like.

Rhys had promised to help tack up after losing out three-two in a snooker match the other week. After an uncharacteristic no-show from Kelly, probably fawning over Ethan, he was forced to cash in on the favour.

He parked up at one end in a line of horse-boxes, all varying size and condition. Danny glanced over at the grey stand with Ffos Las lettered on its side as he released the seatbelt. Danny was grateful the racing authorities green-lit this to be the first turf track built in Britain since 1929. Saved travelling farther afield to courses like Wincanton, or Worcester, and on tolls crossing the Severn Bridge.

It was nestled in the heart of Carmarthenshire, near Llanelli, and stood upon the former site of Europe's largest open cast mine, among rolling hills. Hard to imagine it now, Danny thought, as he looked over at the emerald circuit beneath an open sky. He led The Watchmaker to the stabling complex, shadowed by Rhys with Pepper Pot in hand.

Danny feared one of these two expensive purchases would pick up a career-threatening injury before their careers had time to blossom. That in mind, he chose this West Walian venue, with its level configuration and long straights allowing the runners to stride out, along with the first-rate drainage, providing consistent and uniform ground to race on. Patchy underfoot conditions were just as dangerous on the horses' legs and soundness as the risk of falling in this game, Danny knew.

Once both of his runners were checked and settled into the stables, Danny loitered by a modern-looking bronze statue fronting the parade ring, depicting a racehorse in full flight. He eyed the line of bookies' pitches set up beside the stands, away from the main betting ring.

Some of them represented local bookie chains, one painted in blue and yellow was for Wheeler's Bookmakers, another Raymond Barton, alongside Craybourne's, all hollering out for custom, like market traders, over the many one-man outfits in competition.

'Four-to-six The Watchmaker, nine-to-two bar,' the Wheeler's rep shouted. 'Like buying money,' he added, smiling to a wavering punter clutching a wad of notes nearby.

Danny squinted and could make out they'd all priced up The Watchmaker as the hot favourite for the opener.

He was glad punters shared his belief in the Irish import, entered for a beginners' chase that had cut up to just eight runners and was now only minutes away. A small field was a big plus in Danny's eyes, less chance of getting brought down by a faller, or squeezed up by meandering rivals in a crowded pack.

No sign of Ethan. Danny felt sure he'd turn up to the unveiling of their brightest hopes. A big day for The Jaguar and, if results went bad, Ethan's job would also surely be on the line.

He was equally certain he'd notice if Ethan was in attendance. Those black shades and striking blond hair, he'd stand out in any crowd.

Just twenty minutes before The Watchmaker's date with destiny, Danny went to lead him into the pre-parade ring. He seemed remarkably calm, almost lethargic, for one about to make his first run under official rules.

Mind, he wouldn't know that, Danny thought. 'Ignorance is bliss,' he muttered as he ran his clammy hands over his black trousers.

51

The relative youngster was acting with maturity beyond his years. Danny hoped this would stand him in good stead out there on the track.

Rhys was tucking The Jaguar's yellow and red striped silks into his britches as he approached Danny, now slowly circling the parade ring with The Watchmaker, awaiting the bell to tell jockeys to mount.

'You know the drill,' Danny said, 'been over it time and again. Take things steady early, find a good jumping rhythm and go from there, make your move four out, don't want to play games and toy with this modest bunch. You're on the best horse, show them.'

'Right you are, boss,' Rhys replied, touching his yellow cap. Danny felt he'd never completely get used to ordering his good friend about. Any other setting and he'd likely get an 'F-off.'

Rhys was tapping his leg with the whip, as if starting to feel the nerves also.

'He'll eat these for breakfast, you know that,' Danny said. Eyeing the whip, he added, 'Probably won't need that.'

'Right you are.'

'If he starts racing lazily, or a rival raises its game to challenge, don't be afraid to get stuck into our boy, he can take it, broad shoulders this one. But can't see that happening, Rhys, long faces all round if this gets turned over.'

Rhys said, 'All right, got the message.'

'Sorry,' Danny said and smiled, upper lip slightly trembling. 'Rambling, always do when I'm bricking it. Get more nervous watching from the sides than in the saddle.'

'I've worked him 'n all,' Rhys added. 'Know how good he jumps and moves.'

'Then go out there and let everyone else know.'

Rhys mounted and cantered to the start.

Bunching clouds had swept in from the west off the Atlantic, darkening the setting. Danny hoped it wasn't a portent of things to come.

52

He glanced across at the bustling hospitality tent. Still no sign of Ethan though he thought he caught a glimpse of a girl that looked the spit of Kelly. She was holding a champagne flute. He couldn't be certain through the crumpled clear-plastic windows of the awning. He was about to venture over and play hell when he did an about-turn.

He'd told staff he ran a three strikes and you're out rule though secretly he wouldn't get rid of Kelly. She was part of the set-up, as much as the horses. In any case, he knew she'd never exploit her status, overstep the mark. That was the Kelly before she'd hooked up with Ethan, though. He thought it best to have words about this, but not now. Pick the right time; he had more important things on his mind.

On his way to grab a decent viewpoint in the stands, he stopped in his tracks as the speaker system blared out. 'This is a racecourse announcement, please could the driver of a green Range Rover,' the woman's voice read out a personalised registration beginning with EP12. Ethan was here. As if the stakes weren't high enough, the prospect of that trained killer on the warpath would be a double blow if The Watchmaker got beat.

Probably blocking off the car park with it, Danny thought, flash git.

And then, as if he needed confirmation, he saw Ethan emerge from the hospitality tent, with an owner's badge pinned to the lapel of his neatly-cut black suit. He chucked the remainder of his champagne on the grass and then the glass. So much for being a teetotaller.

Danny kept a safe distance and needed no encouragement to carry on his way to the stands, hoping he hadn't been spotted.

Surprised Ethan hadn't listened in on the riding instructions, probably making the most of the sponsor's hospitality.

Standing six rows back with binoculars primed, he waited. He felt an all-over tingly sensation, excitement more than nerves now, like the night before Christmas as a kid. He couldn't worry anymore; it was out of his hands. He'd done all he could, prepared the new recruit to be fighting fit and ready to go.

He just hoped Rhys didn't do something stupid, a clear round would be enough to seal victory. A stylish display and he suddenly wouldn't mind hearing what Ethan had to say.

But, just seven fences into the race, it wasn't a question of The Watchmaker winning, more one of saving face.

Danny had asked Rhys to look on from the rear of the small field and that's what he was doing. Except he wasn't hard on the steel stalking the others menacingly, as Danny had hoped, or imagined. More like a good twelve lengths off the pace with Rhys flat to the boards, throwing everything bar the kitchen sink. The excitement had quickly fermented to bitter disappointment. Where was the horse he'd witnessed quicken past lesser stablemates, and jump low and efficient at home?

Another howler at the eighth fence and The Watchmaker had stopped to little more than a walk. Danny had now dropped the binoculars and was planning the quickest route through the race-watchers to get away. He kicked the steel pole of a handrail on his way down though his foot came off worse in the argument. He felt like sinking a few numbing pints in the bar at the top of the stands but he was driving the van and if Ethan did decide to show his face in the parade ring for a post-mortem on The Watchmaker's performance, beer on the breath wouldn't smell good.

Danny met Rhys, who'd already trotted safely back to the cinder offshoot leading to the stables before the race was even over.

'What happened?' Danny asked up.

'Dunno,' Rhys said, loosening his neck strap. 'Never travelled or jumped, awful it was, embarrassing.'

'Breathing okay?' Danny said, mindful of Salamanca's previously undetected problem.

'Fine, better than I am,' Rhys said, boots smacking tarmac, 'just wouldn't go with the others.'

'Mulish?' Danny asked. The Watchmaker hadn't shown any quirks when winning a point-to-point in Ireland by all accounts or in his homework at Samuel House, but it needed asking.

54

'Not really,' Rhys said. 'Hate to say it, guv, but the boy mustn't be the hot property we thought.'

Not the words Danny ever wanted to hear. 'He's not a morning glory,' he said defensively.

'Being good in the nets is no use,' Rhys said. 'The wicket is where it counts and this boy was out for a golden duck.'

The runners had only just crossed the line when Rhys was called into the stewards' room to explain The Watchmaker's effort, or lack of. They accepted the same answers and a routine blood test was ordered.

'Shit! Shit! Shit!' was Danny's mantra on his way back to saddle Pepper Pot for the third race.

A raindrop splashed on the bridge of his nose and he held out his palm. Too late to get some juice into the ground, he thought. Shame, as most French imports loved the soft.

Still no show from Ethan as Danny was shortly to lead his next baby into battle. Probably lost in that tent again, he reckoned, getting pie-eyed while swooning over Kelly. Couldn't blame him for wanting to get drunk right now, though.

Rhys approached, same colours, not a spot on them after the last early retirement.

'Forget playing a waiting game with this one,' Danny ordered. 'Bred to stay more than this two miles, so use her stamina, get the lead and stretch the others. See how good she is.'

'Should make up for the last one,' Rhys said and looked skyward.

'Hard to be bullish now but we gotta keep the faith, eh, Rhys. We know she's a little terrier and she's gonna prove hard to catch in today's class, receiving weight from the others.'

Back in the stands, he shifted his weight on shiny new shoes. Having never had a 'proper job' - as his mum called it – he'd yet to wear in these leather slip-ons. 'Important to dress smart on track,' Crane always used to say. 'Never know who you'll meet.'

As Pepper Pot circled at the start, Danny sucked in the cooling air and adjusted the zoom on his binoculars, take his mind briefly off what fate held in the next four and a half minutes or so.

Being sick in the public stand wouldn't give a good impression, particularly as prospective owners wined and dined in the glass-fronted bar behind.

One last check of the electronic bookie boards glowing orange below, he could make out Pepper Pot's odds had drifted like a barge, doubling from two-to-one out to four-to-one. Fresh doubts surrounding Danny's ability to train had clearly been factored into the mare's price. Fickle bunch, these punters.

As the tapes rose, Danny found it harder to keep the binoculars still and wished he'd asked Sara for those army-style anti-shake ones he'd seen in town as a Christmas treat, instead of the usual socks and smellies instead. Perhaps Ethan had a pair left over from his army days, though he wouldn't expect any presents if Pepper Pot didn't win.

He looked on as Rhys followed orders and pushed the diminutive mare to claim the box seat and had built up a healthy six-length lead going into the home-straight for the first time. Everything to plan, Danny thought, shaking now gone.

Danny's eyebrows arched as he saw Rhys' give his ride a few love taps with his whip, presumably to keep her mind on the job. But they soon increased in strength and frequency. Yet, despite this, the nine-strong pack were closing, bearing down on her. She looked like a mere pony, trying valiantly to stave off the larger opposition.

Danny felt his cheeks burn, but the sun was hidden and the stands were sheltered from any wind. He loved to go racing, mingling with racegoers, the smell of burgers on hotplates and the thrill of the race. However, he'd rather be anywhere else but here right now. Another bad jump and he could no longer look. He preferred the more pleasant view down the Gwendreath Valley towards Carmarthen Bay though it didn't prevent the car crash unfolding on track. He looked back, fearing the worst and that's what he got. Pepper Pot was headed, now a spent force.

He was only thankful he wasn't a 'face' yet, having only taken out a license last year, as the jeering punters below listened to the commentator call, 'Paper favourite Pepper Pot has already surrendered the lead by the halfway point and is now being swallowed by the main bunch of runners, beating a hasty retreat, something seemingly not right there.'

You're telling me, Danny thought, and rushed to the stables.

Pepper Pot had already run her race and it was time to collect her for the trip east down the M4.

On his way past the betting ring he crossed paths with Sam.

'All right, fancy seeing you here,' Danny called after the vet, putting on a brave front.

Sam turned and said, 'Gave me a fright there.'

'Hope you didn't put too much on my two.'

'No,' Sam said.

'Guest of Ethan?' Danny asked.

'Doing a bit of networking, surprising how many farmers and livery owners you meet on track. More of a busman's holiday, afraid to say.' Danny suspected he was more likely lured by the free drinks in that tent. Sam appeared restless and Danny wasn't in any mood for small talk.

Sam relieved the situation with, 'Best be off.'

'Be in touch,' Danny said.

Sam went on his way towards where the tent and stabling area were situated.

Reckoned as much, Danny thought, soaking up the hospitality more like.

He went to get the post-mortem from Rhys on the disgraced mare as he walked back up the offshoot.

'Feel like a broken record, guv,' Rhys said. 'There was just nothing there when I asked her, hearing the pack close.'

'No matter,' Danny said, though he couldn't bring himself to mean it, not yet. He needed time to get to grips with what had happened in the last hour or so. 'We're all in one piece to fight another day, just have to forget about this one.'

He turned and patted Pepper Pot's bay neck, 'Back to the drawing board with you, madam.'

'Don't need hosing down,' Rhys added, 'barely broke a sweat out there. Back at the van in twenty, yeah?'

He left for the weighing room, leaving Danny to tend his fallen heroin. She flashed her tail, blissfully unaware of the anguish she'd inflicted on her new master, now leading her back to the stables for some water.

'Bloody hell,' Danny said to her. 'Many more of those and I'll have my licence revoked, for being shite.'

In all his years in the saddle, he'd never felt so ashamed to be a professional in racing, the sport he lived for.

The roar of the engine was all that could be heard as they returned home on the M4.

CHAPTER 11

Tuesday 2.14 PM. Pick Nick's time of reckoning had arrived. The well-bred newcomer was bidding to land a seven-runner hurdle race. With Christmas a memory, Danny hoped this would provide a belated present.

Sitting at his desk, he eyed the wall-mounted screen showing the next at Wincanton. He warmed his feet on a whirring fan-heater, rumbling away on the old wooden floorboards. They hadn't yet got the funds to double-glaze Samuel House.

He would've been on track in person but, after the recent woeful displays at Ffos Las, he felt it best to lie low and let Kelly take his sole runner to the Somerset track, make up for taking a sickie and spending it in that hospitality tent. He trusted she'd cope. Good experience for her to be let loose and take charge, not to mention help free up some family time for Danny.

He didn't believe his presence on track was bringing bad luck to the horses; he wasn't particularly superstitious. Not one for good luck charms or cursed tracks. Some of his fellow jockeys used to ritually put on the left boot before the right, or vice versa, or look heavenward for divine inspiration before going out to battle.

He knew from experience, like it or not, hard graft and a shrewd eye sorted out the winners from the losers in this game; that, and a spell of good health for the horses. The real reason for him holding back: he wasn't keen on bumping into Ethan again. He reckoned it was odds-on the owner's rep would be on track, expecting to see the third of the most promising new recruits make up for the debacle of the first two. While Danny felt a pleasant, buzzing sense of nervous energy saddling up both runners at Ffos Las, his palms were now glistening from a different kind of nerves, one that turned the pit of his stomach, a sickly anxious feeling, fear taking over eager anticipation.

Soon be over, Danny thought, weaving a pen between fingers. To his horror, he was more right than he'd hoped.

Having set off on the two miles with seven flights of hurdles to jump, he bit his lower lip as he saw Rhys begin to urge along the hot favourite Pick Nick. It wouldn't normally have been too concerning, most horses needed assistance from the saddle and a lack of experience could result in hitting mid-race flat spot, but this was nearly a circuit out.

The phone on his desk began to ring. Typical! Who the fuck is that? Though he had a good idea as he knew Ethan would be watching the same race and that same dismal display elsewhere, most likely from the stands. Probably wants to know why all three big hopes Danny had been talking up so much after sparkling homework had struggled to complete their races let along compete and why he wasn't there to face the music like a man.

He let it go to answering machine. Five rings and then a beep. There was a silence before a faint voice said, 'Meet me, please.'

Danny's eyes left the screen, any excuse. The voice was muffled and breathy, and there was crackling static noise, like blowing into a microphone.

'Meet me tonight, 10PM. By the Riverbank, beside the Millennium Stadium. You need to know this. Don't-' A tremor shook his voice. Another beep, before a soft woman's voice cut in with 'end of message'.

Pick Nick was now tailed off in company with the stragglers. Danny picked up the remote and killed the screen.

'This?' A tremor now filled Danny's voice. 'What was 'this'?'

The message stopped abruptly, with the caller mid-flow, as if cut off. Was he about to explain why they should meet, or what Danny should know?

He felt a pulse throb his temples and face burn. He yanked the answer machine from its socket and threw it against the wall. He then sat, suddenly sobered by what he'd done. He heard footsteps grow louder and the door swing open. Sara looked in.

Danny was now cradling his head in hands. There was a pause as Sara clapped eyes on what was left of the answer machine near the wall. She said, 'Another loser?'

'Doesn't make sense.'

'Things like that cost money, Danny, money we don't have.'

'Not now,' Danny said.

'If you can't hack it, either we give up or you find a way of coping. Because I'm not having Jack scared.'

Danny looked up. 'It's a bloody answer machine, clapped out one at that.'

'Go for a run or get a punchbag to cool off.'

'It won't happen again.'

'But what if the next one loses?'

'It's not just about the losers!'

'Then what?'

'Nothing,' Danny said. Sara made no secret of her doubts about the new investors coming in before anything was signed.

Whether it was pride or fear, he simply couldn't reveal those same doubts had suddenly resurfaced within him. 'Love, I only boil over cos it means everything to me. Why? Cos I want you and Jack to reap the rewards. If it means something, it's gonna hurt.'

First the email and now this. He had to meet the guy trying to put the frighteners on him.

While it was too early to write off Pick Nick, the bubble surrounding the well-touted newcomer had certainly deflated, if not burst. He couldn't fathom why these promising new recruits were flopping. They were performing too badly for it to be true.

He hoped Sam was right about a low-level airborne virus in the area. Any excuse would do, other than the fact he couldn't train for toffee. Crane had always said, 'harder game than you think lad, this training lark.'

He then inwardly winced at how the result would go down with the new owners, he'd forgotten about The Jaguar. One hundred and fifteen grand of stock had plummeted to less than half that value in the space of a week. Danny was left in no doubt the investors would be edgy.

Yet despite early campaign targets being set, Ethan had remained remarkably quiet about the yard's recent poor form. He briefly contemplated they were behind the horses getting beaten. They had all drifted markedly on the betting exchanges. Perhaps this is why he was chosen above the big yards, because a string of bad results from an unfashionable yard wouldn't raise as many eyebrows with the powers that be.

Or perhaps this was again paranoia taking over. After all, every trainer had quiet spells and this was his rookie season. Allowances can be made, he reckoned, though it didn't ease the tightness between his shoulder blades and the dull aching somewhere behind his eyes.

CHAPTER 12

Danny stood beside the River Taff slowly meandering through the heart of the capital. Its black waters shimmered in the half-moonlight and gently lapped against the sloping banks below. The watery sound made Danny want a piss even more.

His elbows rested on the white railings as he looked over at the large 'Now Showing' movie posters on the side of the multiplex, an extension on the Millennium Stadium. He idly checked if there was anything he could take Sara to see that they would both enjoy, though it was more to take his mind off the imminent clandestine meeting. Can't remember the last decent film I'd seen, he thought, then he recalled his dad saying much the same thing. 'They'll never beat the Ealing classics,' he'd say. Perhaps just getting old, Danny reckoned.

Emerging from the shadows like a ghostly apparition came a man wearing a black jacket and blue denims. An island of defiant mousy hair on an otherwise gleaming sea of scalp that belied his youthful attire and fresh, round face. He had a relaxed approach to shaving and his white skin was a canvas, painted yellow by the light thrown off a nearby streetlamp. He could see his breath. Their serious eyes met on level terms.

'Daniel?' the stranger said.

'What's this about?' Danny said, cutting to the chase. 'Why the message scaring me half to death?'

'It was meant to. You wouldn't here otherwise.'

'Used the more direct approach when I didn't reply to your email?' Danny said.

'What email?'

'Not important,' Danny said, inwardly surprised. Were there two whistleblowers? Neither, though, willingly giving up their secret as if it would worsen their plight. 'Your name?'

'Call me Tyler.'

'Tyler who?'

'Not important, either,' the man said. He was the one now resting his weight on the railings, facing the water and stadium. 'What is, however, is you're aware what you're letting yourself in for.'

Danny could only think of one recent arrival in his life. 'Ethan Player.'

The man turned and was now facing Danny. He looked both ways, weight shifting between Nike trainers. 'Whatever you've agreed to, walk away. It's not worth it.'

Danny felt like going on the defensive, saying it was none of his business. Who the hell does he think he is? But his concern grew. What forces at work would be powerful enough for this stranger to venture out on this cold night?

'I've witnessed first-hand what he's capable of.'

'I can handle myself,' Danny said, 'and Ethan will settle once the winners start flowing.'

'No!' the man snapped. 'You don't understand, you're in grave danger. Even if you train them winners, you'll lose out in the end.'

'Why?'

'They're not what they seem.'

'Tell me who, what I'm dealing with, I've already signed on the dotted line.'

'And I've already said too much,' the man said. 'You've come alone.'

'What do you think?' Danny said, looking around.

'It's never too late to back away from this, you've been warned, I can do no more.'

'Give me something to work with, you could be anyone for Christ sake, jealous trainer, owner.'

The man said, 'If he knew I'd been to see you, well –' The man stopped and ran his finger in a slitting motion across his neck.

Danny noticed dark rings under the man's glassy eyes, as if he was a stranger to sleep.

'I knew I shouldn't have come,' Danny replied, getting cold feet in more ways than one.

64

'I need you to keep something for me,' he said. 'If I die, pass it on to police. Promise?'

'Hand it them now, if it's that bloody important.'

'I'd be signing my own death warrant,' the man said, coolly, as if he'd had time to come to terms with this. He handed over a Yale key cut from brass, all shiny like a new penny.

'Where's the lock?' Danny asked. 'It's the first thing the police will ask.'

'It's for the lock up in Flat 132 Bevan House, on the Newtown Estate.'

'Who lives there? Ethan?'

The man forced a smile and said, 'Just tell them 132 Bevan House. They'll take it from there.'

'What about you?' Danny asked.

'I'll be okay, this is just a last resort, an insurance.' The smile the man gave came over as fake but from a good place.

They were both stolen from the moment by a twitching first-floor curtain in one of the terraced houses opposite. The man said, 'I've got to go.'

'Wait,' Danny called after. His sigh came in a cloud that disappeared into the night as quickly as the stranger. Beyond, he saw the shape of a bottle-green four by four slow to a standstill on the well-lit Riverside Bridge. Its indicator lights began flashing. Tyler was heading that way. Was he about to be picked up by Ethan? Was Tyler The Jaguar? But why would he warn Danny away? Was it mind games? Keep Danny on his toes?

Danny screwed up his eyes but he still couldn't make out the driver, only shadows. 'Oh fuck.'

He was caught off guard by a shiver, despite being warmed by three layers. That was a main road. Why would the driver stop there? Only for an emergency, unless he saw something. It had to be Ethan. Danny didn't want to hang around to find out. He turned and made for the safety provided by the bright lights and milling drinkers on St Mary Street.

65

As the season unfolded and nights grew frostier, so did results. When the cold bit, the racing menu was decimated. So too, he hoped, any virus gripping the yard. Perhaps it would allow them to make a fresh start once the thaw came.

As a failed gambler, he knew it can prove the hardest thing in the world to snap a losing streak and it was a similar story as a trainer. With every below-par performance, confidence and morale at the yard was hit and, as a consequence, results continued in free fall. A vicious circle hard to break.

Danny was sat at his messy office desk when Ethan entered.

'You can knock,' Danny said.

'I need to do a spot check on our horses,' Ethan said.

'They're all fine, but be my guest.'

'After all those pitiful displays, my boss is asking questions, you understand.'

'We're just going through a quiet spell, that's all. It'll turn,' Danny said. 'Bad results are part and parcel, that's racing. I'm no miracle worker, only human, you cut me I bleed.'

'Don't tempt me,' Ethan murmured.

'Eh?!'

'You heard.'

'Look, patience is the watchword,' Danny said. 'Got green fingers?'

'What?' Ethan asked and gave him a look.

'It's like gardening, all about the future, plotting ahead for future seasons.'

'There won't be a future unless we start seeing a return on our investment.'

Danny stood, not liking what he was hearing. Big owners getting cold feet on the back of a losing run was a trainer's darkest fear. How on earth could he expect to emerge from the doldrums when the best horses were leaving the yard.

'I'll give you updates on them,' Danny said through gritted teeth. He led Ethan to the stables and guided him horse by horse.

66

He stopped outside a box with the embossed nameplate The Watchmaker – 6yo gelding. 'Now this has the makings of a proper chaser, won those point-to-points in Ireland last winter. He disappointed at Ffos Las-'

'Disappointed?! I was there that day,' Ethan said.

'Turned out he needed the run more than I thought and wasn't happy on the ground.'

'Don't give me that, I'm no idiot,' Ethan said. 'The horse could barely raise a gallop.'

'But he's strengthened up super since and he's bouncing again in training. Out again soon.'

'Another performance like that and we'll seriously reconsider our position.'

'Got him entered up for a small prize in a few weeks. Won't be any excuses then, sharp as a tack and the winter ground ought to help,' Danny said, putting his neck on the line.

'Pick Nick up next,' Danny said.

'What happened at Wincanton?' Ethan asked. 'Or should I say what didn't happen?'

'He lacked the experience but will improve, certainly bred to.'

Ethan was now tapping away at his handheld organiser, making notes to report back to The Jaguar no doubt.

'And last but not least,' Danny said, 'is the smashing mare Pepper Pot. They reckoned she had a splint problem, set her back for her last trainer in France but she's over that and shone in her last gallop, quickened past her lead horse as if it's a tree and that one's no mug. She's another expected to do the business for us in the near future.'

'You were at Ffos Las?' Ethan asked though Danny knew it was rhetorical. 'Photographic memory? More like selective.'

'Bad day at the office,' Danny said. 'Another that's gonna improve as the season unfolds. Stake my career on it.'

'Closer to the truth than you may realise.'

Ethan's poker face revealed disappointingly little. Perhaps he wasn't buying Danny's upbeat progress reports, suspecting they were merely a smokescreen to buy more time while poor results continued.

'Sam will check each and every one,' Ethan said, 'give them a full service, blood tests, the lot.'

'There's no need for that,' Danny replied. 'They're waiting for conditions to fall right, this losing streak will soon be a distant memory, you'll see.'

Ethan said, 'Enough excuses, Sam *will* be checking them over. That's an order.'

'And I have no say in the matter,' Danny muttered. But Ethan had already slipped the gadget in his jacket and left the scene.

'What's that nasty man doing to us, Pepper?' Danny said, hand running down her face.

He'd just tightened a bolt that had come loose from her stable door and was about to phone his mum when he spotted a shadow flick across the study window on the first floor. Couldn't be Sara, Danny thought, she was off at playgroup with Jack.

Thinking it was Ethan now snooping, Danny sprinted back to the house and barged into the study. Wilf was hunched over the desk in the corner, face pressed close to the security monitor. His pale skin shimmered like silver against the lit screen displaying pictures, silent and grey.

Wilf grunted as if startled. His brow turned wrinkly as he ran a hand through that wiry red hair of his, eyes wide with surprise. The facial tick had suddenly found a new lease of life. Caught red-handed.

'What the hell do ya think you're doing?' Danny snapped, sour mood having curdled.

'It's … it's not w-w-what it looks like, boss.'

'This place is out of bounds, you knew that,' Danny said firmly, 'you're paid to reshoe horses and repair tack, not to snoop around my bloody office.'

'S-sorry,' Wilf said. He pushed himself away from the desk, as if to distance himself from any evidence, and then stood sharply. His six-foot-two frame towered above Danny, who remained stood near the doorway. 'I th-thought you'd left.'

'You're digging a deeper hole.'

'It's n-n-not what it looks like, h-honest.'

'Then why were you looking through the tapes?' Wilf shook his head. 'How can I ignore this when you've got no answers?'

'Can't,' Wilf piped up. 'N-not yet.'

'Give me something to work with, or you'll leave me no choice, gotta report this to Ethan.'

'No! Don't, please,' Wilf said, facial muscles shooting off sideways again. 'P-p-promise, you won't.'

But Danny couldn't make that promise. He couldn't afford to feel sorry for this loner if he was up to no good.

'Ethan put you up to this, didn't he,' Danny said. 'I need to know.'

As if fight or flight kicked in, Wilf was off, brushing past, an unstoppable force trailed by a biting cloud of stale sweat.

'Wilf?' Danny called after. 'Wilf!'

As the front door slammed shut, Danny didn't chase after. His attention lay in the corner. What had made Wilf risk all by logging into the security CCTV system? The look of terror on his face, lack of answers and edginess smacked of guilt.

He examined the screen. The milky grey image was of Tell Tale standing quietly in box nine, beside the breezeblock wall.

Nothing out of the ordinary, having run the cursor over the file open, it dated the footage as 17th December.

It was one of many dates Danny wished to forget as the horse filling that screen had run like a drain, tailing off in last place before waving the white flag.

Why was Wilf looking at footage of Tell Tale taken months previously? Why now?

The reason had to be important enough for Wilf to risk getting caught and fired. Was he tampering with the horses and making sure he hadn't been caught on tape doing the dirty?

And why did he fear it getting back to Ethan? Perhaps Wilf was following orders from his boss and feared the repercussions for getting caught in the act. Ethan could be masterminding a betting ring. Danny was only too aware all his runners had weakened in the betting and in the race since Ethan and co. had arrived on the scene. The ex-marine had insisted on dealing with wages for the new recruits. Perhaps the farrier's hand was forced. Do it, or hop it.

There was still no sign of Wilf on the screen. How was he doping the horses without it showing up on the CCTV? Danny closed the file and switched to live footage. Wilf always relied on Sam for a lift and Danny suspected he'd loiter around the yard until the vet was finished up.

The yard was quiet, no life, human that is, on any of the sixteen screens. He was restless and thought he'd go check the stable block anyway.

No sign of Wilf but he was met by Sam, weighed down by a leather bag.

'What's wrong with Wilf?' Sam said. 'Saw him on the way out.'

'Did he have a fuck-off face on him?' Danny said, fuming.

'Hard to say,' Sam said. 'Moving so fast it was more of a blur, didn't say a word.'

'Par for the course then,' Danny said, trying not to arouse suspicions with Wilf's colleague and friend until he found out more.

'Normally get a 'hello',' Sam said. 'Called after him, see if he wanted a lift home. Didn't even look back, no fathoming sometimes.'

'Guess not.'

'You don't look yourself, either,' Sam remarked. 'If you don't mind me saying.'

'Nah, got a lot on my mind at the mo,' Danny said, keeping it vague.

'Anything you want to share? Work related that is, no good on marriage guidance, as my ex will testify,' Sam said, rolling his eyes.

'It's kind of work related,' Danny said.

'You had an argument with Wilf?'

'Not so much an argument,' Danny said, 'more one-way traffic.'

'It's not about,' Sam said and then looked both ways, as if to check the coast was clear. Voice lowered, he continued, 'the yard's results.'

Danny gave him a look, not sure whether to reveal recent revelations. But it turned out there was no need to as Sam said, 'Wilf told me everything as well. Last night, over a beer at The Speckled Hen.'

'What?' Danny asked. Was this going to be the proof he needed to nail Wilf down?

'Well, I'm guessing you already know,' Sam said.

'Go on, need to see if what I know ties with what he told you.'

'I wouldn't normally grass on a confession told in confidence,' Sam said and swallowed loudly, 'not least by a close friend. But I guess it needs to be aired, now you know too.'

Danny was hooked. 'We need to get this sorted, swifter the better.'

'Wilf opened up, rare for him, perhaps guilt was weighing on his mind, or couldn't resist boasting to someone about what he was getting away with.'

'What?' Danny asked.

'How he'd come into money.'

'From?'

'You know as well as me - gambling.'

Danny felt like filling in the missing lines but knew he had to hear it, not put words in Sam's mouth.

'Couldn't believe my ears. Told me he was plating the runners with ill-fitting shoes on race-day. Only the ones on soft ground where the horse's action would be cushioned in the slower paces on the way to post, so as not to arouse suspicions prior to the 'off'. But in the races, they were all coming up woefully short, as if hurting.'

Danny rested his weight against the stable door.

'What made it worse, Wilf was grinning as he told me this. I mean, it's my livelihood he's putting on the line as well as this place.'

'What a fucking disgrace.'

'But you knew all this, right?'

'Had my suspicions.'

'Good to hear,' Sam said, 'thought I'd imagined it, or was going mad.'

'Nah,' Danny said. He now had the proof he needed.

'He gave me names, dates. Can recall some if you need to compare notes. Wasn't that far gone on the night.'

'Hit me with a few.'

'Let's see,' Sam said, 'I know there was Tell Tale on 17th December, The Watchmaker and Pepper Pot on 12th January, Jocular on the 19th …'

'And Pick Nick.'

'Yes,' Sam said. 'He told you as well.'

'Between the lines,' Danny said. 'Looks like we've found the fly in the ointment.'

'You think you know someone, then this happens.'

'Why not come to me straight off?' Danny asked.

'Like I said, first I heard was last night. Waiting to have proper words, take him aside when he'd sobered up, see if it was the beer talking, bravado from a barstool bore.'

'Guess it was a confessional, seeing as he's spilt the beans to you as well. What else did you talk about?'

'The usual blokey stuff: footie, films, women. Not always easy to hear, over the others. Everyone gets louder after a few drinks, apart from Wilf.'

'Cos he's got something to hide?'

'Only his stammer. He opened up about it once, bullied something rotten as a teen. Acne and red hair not a winning combo when all you want is to fit in. Got so bad he had to change schools twice. It's as if kids have a radar to pick out the weak and vulnerable, even some of the teachers had a few digs, so Wilf reckoned. Some react by becoming the class clown, or putting on a hard-man act, Wilf went into his shell and I guess he's yet to

72

come out. So best not be hard on him, eh, don't think he could take being moved on again.'

'Feel for the guy, really do,' Danny said. 'My school days were no picnic, either. But the yard's a business not a charity and, if he's damaging stock and taking from the till, he's out the door.'

Sam said, 'Just don't go to Ethan with this.'

'It's his horses and I've been getting the flack for their flops. No more.'

'Not Ethan, though.'

'Well, the police then.'

'This'll soon get out and reports will be passed on to the BHA. You'll find Samuel House hitting the headlines, but for all the wrong reasons.'

Danny knew Sam had a point but he couldn't just sit back and let it go on.

Sam said, 'I'll have a word with him. Say it's got to stop.'

'No, I will,' Danny said. 'Did you ever reveal your log-in details for the CCTV to anyone?'

'No,' Sam replied. 'But, thinking back, they were in my jacket when I left it at the pub one night. Wilf kept it until I picked it up the following day.'

'When was this?'

'Oh, I don't know, months back.'

'Before the first of those horses on your list was got at.'

'Yeah, it was before Christmas, I took a rest from the ale in January. Another New Year's Resolution down the pan.'

'Can't believe this,' Danny said. 'What sort of a vetting system does Ethan use?'

'To be fair, Wilf was a reliable farrier at the previous yards where Ethan had sent horses.'

'What's changed then?'

'He was freelance back then, like I am now, but he's only managed to get work with you and one other yard since moving to the area. Times are hard.'

'So he thought he'd supplement his income by doing a bit of moonlighting on the side.'

'Look, perhaps I shouldn't have said anything.'

'Glad you did,' Danny said, patting Sam's shoulder. 'Let's nip it in the bud before we get too far up a certain creek.'

'What will you do? If you sack him, he's got nothing, no family. And he's easily depressed.'

'I'm not exactly over the moon about it myself.'

'Just go easy on him, give him a second chance to make up for it.'

'There are no second chances as far as I'm concerned. Lucky he's not going to prison.'

'Like I say, just don't go to Ethan,' Sam said. 'Deal with this in-house.'

'I'll take over now.' Danny ran a hand over his hair. 'And thanks again.'

Sam seemed genuinely concerned for his friend and what this could do to him. Danny was less so.

The following morning, Danny flicked to live feed on the security system. He checked the stabling quarters and could clearly make out Wilf go into The Watchmaker's box. Before he confronted Ethan, he wanted to give the farrier an opportunity to explain himself. He was surprised he'd even turned up for work after what happened yesterday.

He slipped on his jacket and casually strolled up to The Watchmaker's box. He thought playing the good cop was the best approach. Wilf would only run off again otherwise.

The door was open and Wilf was struggling to pin the gelding's front leg between his thighs. 'Good patient?'

The look Wilf gave Danny enough.

'Can I see you in my office?'

Wilf said, 'Got to shoe this b-b-bugger.'

'Finish up here, I'll be inside, okay?'

'Aye, boss,' Wilf mumbled, trying to anchor the hoof in a vice-like grip, as The Watchmaker did his best to free himself.

Danny thought it best to leave him finish the job and return to Samuel House. He waited. With no immediate sign of

Wilf, he began filing owners' invoices. But his progress was slowed as he kept checking the wall clock and the door.

Wilf's confession to Sam kept running over in his mind like a broken record and he wanted to hear it from the horse's mouth. Wilf held the answers he wanted. Yet it was now a good hour since he'd asked to meet and Danny knew, as the minutes ticked by, the likelihood of a no-show from the farrier grew.

Either The Watchmaker had continued to be a 'bugger' or Wilf had smelt danger and done a runner. In Danny's gambling days, he'd happily put money on the latter.

Although he'd have to wait, the fact Wilf hadn't stayed on to answer awkward questions told its own story in Danny's mind.

CHAPTER 13

Danny studied Ethan's face in the reflection of the glass trophy cabinet. 'It occurred to me, the other day, I don't know the first thing about you. Only you're a former marine. And got my doubts about that.'

'Why the sudden need to know anything about me?'

'I've just a bad feeling, where all this money is coming from.'

'I think we deserve a degree of trust on this,' Ethan said. 'We've been good for the money. And I'm not one for all that bonding and making friends crap, this is purely business.'

'That's just the problem. I don't know even who this 'Jaguar' is. Why he's even called that? I mean, does he keep one or drive one?'

Ethan dropped on to the leather seat opposite. He picked at imaginary fingernail dirt. 'The Jaguar is the only big cat capable of killing for the sake of killing, not for food or to protect its cubs, merely because it can.'

Danny said, 'Remind me to take him off the Christmas party list. Do ya return the same flattery about me?'

But not even the flicker of a smile. Ethan clearly wasn't joking. 'The Jaguar knows all there is to know about you.'

'It's funny, the other day, I even feared the yard was being bankrolled with the loot from those bookie raids going on.' Danny looked down at the front-page of the local rag. Ethan laughed. 'But put that crazy idea to bed as bookies don't hold no more than a grand on the premises. I mean, your hair would be white by the time you'd got enough to fund this place.'

'Take your mind off these fantasies of yours, and they are merely fantasies, and put it on training our first bloody winner. The Jaguar has become restless.'

Ethan stood and hand fished in his jacket.

Danny could hear his heart thud and felt his grip on the chair's leather arms tighten, as if at the dentist. Was it a gun?

Ethan removed what looked like a security pass, or membership card, and placed his wallet down on the corner of the polished wood. He handed the card over, laminated and warm. He turned and walked over to the gallery of glassed photos, colouring the wall opposite. Danny briefly glanced at the pass, no bigger than a business card, embossed with the emblem of a Royal regiment. But this didn't interest Danny. He made for the wallet richly smelling of real leather.

His furtive eyes and hands sifted the pockets and compartments within; skills honed on a stretch inside under tutelage of a pickpocket. Alert eyes flitting between Ethan, still facing away, and the contents of the wallet. In one of the pockets was a small piece of paper with a name Tyler Shaw followed by a string of digits.

Too long for a phone number, Danny reckoned, but he couldn't memorize the sequence. He felt he'd already pushed his luck. Ethan could turn at any moment. Danny's heart was now racing. The last time he felt this heightened state was on a big job as a housebreaker. Being caught now would surely be a fatal betrayal of trust. He was about to return the wallet to the corner of the desk when Ethan, still facing away, made him stall with, 'Find anything else of interest?'

He looked over and saw Ethan's intense eyes reflected in the glass of a large photo.

'Bit late to do that don't you think,' Ethan barked, seeing Danny drop the wallet. 'I thought I'd test your loyalty and, as soon as my back's turned, you fail me.'

'Just replacing your army pass where it came from,' Danny said, grimacing inside.

'Capable of lying to my face as well,' Ethan said and returned to the desk.

'Didn't see a thing.'

'Lost your touch more like,' Ethan said. 'Not as sharp as you once were.'

'What do you mean by that?'

77

'Like I said, I know everything about you,' Ethan said, 'you've more worthwhile form than most of your horses.'

'That's history,' Danny said. 'We all have one, you of all should appreciate that.'

'It stays with you.'

'I'm a family man now, found my vocation in life too.'

'Training winners?' Ethan asked, wide-eyed. 'Wouldn't be so sure.'

Danny was keen to change tack and said, 'What's E-Holdings? Your company.'

'It's where the money for this is saved.'

'Did a search and couldn't find anything.'

'That's because it isn't a company, merely a bank account transferring money to yours, clear? No offence but –'

Danny sighed. Brace for it, he thought. He hated the phrase 'no offence' as it was normally followed by something highly offensive. It's as if those words allowed a pass to open season on insults.

Ethan let the sigh go. 'But you're not in any position to ask probing questions, given your fuck-awful record as a trainer.'

'I want you to leave,' Danny said. 'Now.'

'Shouldn't it be me saying that, given results,' Ethan said.

'You don't own a brick of this place.'

'But I'm connected to your best horses and they are at the heart of any yard, its lifeblood. The Jaguar holds the majority vote now. Remove the horses, this place crumbles.'

'I'd get new owners no problem,' Danny said.

'In the form you're in, no one in their right mind would fork out fourteen grand a year of hard-earned to put their precious horses with a loser like you.'

'You did.'

Ethan lunged forward and gripped Danny by the collar, lifting him on tiptoes. 'Another smart-arsed reply and I'll –'

'What?' Danny asked, Adam's apple dipping.

Danny was bulldozered to the wall behind his desk. Now pinned there like a nail-gun by Ethan's forearm, Danny felt warm coffee-tainted breath on his face and the cool of a blade press against his stubbly neck. All he could do was act as if unruffled by the jolting push, no mean feat.

'I know everything about you,' Ethan snarled, 'down to your shoe size.'

'Creep.'

'Investing big money in an unknown quantity, a loose cannon, can you blame us,' Ethan snarled. 'The dream ticket that's turned into a nightmare for both of us.'

Danny couldn't recall Ethan withdraw a knife and glanced over. The letter opener was missing from the pot on his desk. Danny's breath stuttered and eyes widened, skin pink.

Ethan added, 'Another stunt like that and I'll snap your neck, rip your face off and bite your teeth out one by one. Clear?'

Danny gagged for air through flaring nostrils.

'Clear!'

Staccato nods were all he could manage.

Ethan backed off, leaving Danny fighting for air, doubled up.

Ethan said, 'And if this is about me and Kelly. I'd look closer to home when you start judging the morals of sleeping around.'

'I've been faithful,' Danny said. 'Kelly kissed me.'

'I'm not talking about you.'

'Sara?'

Ethan smiled.

'Get out!'

Ethan remained rooted, as if relishing this.

'She's rarely got time to leave the yard,' Danny said defensively. 'This is so fucking out of line.'

'Perhaps he's already at the yard.' Ethan neared. 'Bored housewife, young stable jockey. Bound to happen sometime.'

'You're such a shit-stirrer.'

'Hurt by the truth,' Ethan said.

'Make a habit of this?' Danny said. 'Violence sorts everything.'

The look of rage returned to Ethan's eyes and the tightening grip returned.

'Trying to find the real Ethan,' Danny said. 'And think we've struck oil.'

Ethan let go and the wall saved Danny from dropping like a stone, as if realising he'd risen to the bait.

'You're treading on thin ice,' Ethan said, 'particularly as you're not producing the goods, winners.'

'But that's not my fault,' Danny said. He wasn't going to say anything, but right now he feared for his life.

'Then who's to blame?'

'Wilf.'

Ethan laughed. 'What's he supposed to have done?'

'Surprised you need to ask,' Danny said, mindful Ethan was probably masterminding the whole scam. 'He's been shoeing them with ill-fitting racing plates.'

'Now I've heard it all. Be a man, admit your failings, don't blame others.'

'It's true.'

'He admitted this to you?'

'No, but he did to Sam. Don't tell me you didn't know.'

Ethan turned to look away. 'This is news to me,'

'Come off it, Wilf's your recruit.'

'If it's true and, for your sake, it better be,' Ethan said. 'It'll stop.'

'By sacking.'

'He'll be off the scene sooner than you can say traitor,' Ethan said, not a bit flustered, as if his assault on Danny was everyday behaviour. 'Hope that's cleared the air, we now know where we stand.'

And then he was gone.

CHAPTER 14

'Can I have a word in my office, say in five?' Danny called to Kelly, who was hosing down the sun-kissed courtyard. He glanced over at Salamanca, whose bold head lolled over the metal V of the stable door, gnawing at a metal bolt near a hinge. He'd become restless in recent days, a sure sign he was ready to race.

Should peak just in time for the National prep run in a week, Danny reckoned.

He settled in his leather chair and flicked on the DAB radio on his desk, hoping to change his mood. Robbie Williams' 'Angels' blared from the surround speakers mounted on the wood-panelled walls. Instinct led him to return the switch to 'off'. He simply couldn't listen. He liked the song but it was on the airwaves, almost blanket coverage, in the weeks and months after his father's death in a car crash. It was the day his life, and his outlook on it, changed forever. His stomach turned over and he felt his skin crawl. Raw emotions he'd successfully locked away were now set free, whenever he heard merely the opening bars of piano. He doubted that association would ever fade, such was its power.

His dad's sudden death strengthened his need to see those big moments of fatherhood: hear Jack speak his first words, take his first steps unaided, succeed at school, perhaps graduate, get married. Be happy, above all. Danny once asked his dad what was his greatest regret? He expected the answer to be Liverpool losing the UEFA Cup and was silenced when told it was in fact missing Danny's first birthday because he was simply too hung over to drag himself from bed. He appeared choked even saying it.

His dad found it hard to stave off the need for a drink, an addictive gene inherited by Danny, except his weakness was gambling.

Even when Danny was young, maybe four or five, he recalled thinking dad and drink didn't mix. He'd often rush home

81

with a picture he'd painted or story he'd written and his dad, who, face glowing and glassy-eyed, would slur, 'That's great, son.'

At the time, he felt something wasn't right. Looking back, he wasn't sure whether it was his dad or the drink speaking. What was real and what was fake?

Like Danny, his dad was a happy drunk, not an angry one. Perhaps that was the fault, Danny often wondered, enjoying the sensation of a heavy session down the social after a heavy session down the pit. Work hard, play hard. Live fast, die young.

Yet his dad's early death wasn't down to liver disease or a mining accident, but a head-on collision cornering a blind bend. 'Had no chance,' said the officers comforting his mum, 'didn't suffer.' Wouldn't have known anything was wrong, before lights went out. Game over.

That provided some source of comfort though it didn't stop an aching in the pit of his stomach and his limbs. Some days were better than others. Even now, on the bad ones, he would wake and there was a moment of peace before realisation struck home, that his dad wasn't there to call and chat about the races, tell him how he should've ridden it. 'Here we go,' Danny would say, 'best armchair jockey in Wales.' Or how Liverpool had got on against Man U at the weekend.

His mum never talked to him about her feelings that much. She didn't really need to. Well over a decade after *that* day, he picked up on the blank looks and pink eyes. She often stared off in to the distance, perhaps wishing she was someplace different. Another world, another dimension. One where his dad hadn't decided on a whim to overtake on that corner, or the oncoming HGV driver had stayed in the service station for that extra coffee. Life was about chance and fate, Danny had come to realise. Most involved in racing were only too aware of that. And he hoped these newcomers in the yard would be his lucky break.

He knew his dad would be right behind the venture. Could picture him saying, 'Go on son, go for it!' and then give that cheeky grin of his.

Bet he'd be on track watching his horses more than me, he thought.

With his brother no longer around, Danny had so much love to give Sara and Jack. Make them his sole focus in life, provide for them and keep them from danger. With results gone bad and threatening texts, he didn't feel he was fulfilling either of those roles.

A knock at the door broke his reverie. Before he had time to say 'yes', Kelly had entered, towelling her hands on waterproofs.

'What's up?' Kelly said. 'I've mucked out and done the feeds and watering.'

Danny's eyes flicked to the empty chair. Kelly filled it.

'Ethan,' he said.

'What about him?'

'Thought you could tell me.'

'Tell you what?' Kelly said and stood. 'Look, whatever you've seen or heard, stuff I do in my private life is exactly that, private!'

'Just be careful,' Danny said.

'Careful! I'm twenty, old enough to look after myself,' she said, cheeks flushed. 'I already have a mother! And what's Ethan ever done to you?'

'It's what he might do that worries me, this blonde, blue-eyed pretty boy,' Danny said, 'Hitler's wet dream.'

'Is that what this is really about? Can't bear seeing me happy with someone else, someone handsome? You had your chance.'

'No,' Danny said, on the back foot, 'just a thirty-something looker with all the lines, probably got more baggage than Terminal Five. Don't wanna see ya hurt, that's all.'

'Get over yourself.'

'Don't say I didn't warn you. I don't trust him but he's clearly got you under his spell, good and proper.'

'Piss off, Danny,' Kelly cried. 'You don't know the first thing about him.'

'But I plan to. He's either funding the yard or knows who is,' Danny said, 'And less of the 'piss offs' if ya don't mind, I'm your boss. This is strictly professional.'

83

'Are you sure about that?'

'Yes! You can see who the hell ya want.'

'That's big of you.'

'The Kelly I know wouldn't be acting like this.'

'Like what?'

'Some school kid. Can't you see, he's changing you.'

'Could say the same,' she said and stormed from the room.

He shook his head and dropped on to the chair. 'That went well.'

He pinched the bridge of his nose and then rubbed his eyes with the heels of his callused hands.

Although in no mood, he set about poring over the expenses account for the last month, check if outgoings were as high as he feared. Twenty minutes staring blankly at figures, foggy mind elsewhere, he closed the ledger book and chose to check on the horses instead. He turned from locking his office. Stood kissing in the corridor were Kelly and Ethan, all over each other.

'Don't mind me,' Danny said, pushing past the embracing pair.

'We won't,' Ethan replied, smirking like the cat that got the cream.

Danny knew there was only one way to discover the real Ethan. But was he prepared to stoop that low?

CHAPTER 15

Danny had finished looking over the handful stretching out on the gallops and returned to the house for a caffeine fix. He heard wild laughter from the kitchen. As he entered, it stopped. 'Don't let me stop the party,' he said.

Sara was sat at the table, hands cupping a coffee, with Rhys suspiciously close and sipping a sparkling water. Danny gave her a look as he opened the fridge.

'What party?' Sara quizzed.

'I'll go,' Rhys said, as if picking up on the cooling atmosphere.

'No need,' Sara said.

'She's right,' Danny said. 'I'm off into town, leave you to it.'

'Who's she?' Sara snapped. 'What the cat dragged in?'

Danny left without saying another word, skipping coffee. He was now fully awake. Ethan's insinuations came flooding back: 'bored housewife, young stable jockey.'

Rhys and Sara? Was there some truth behind it?

He wouldn't put it past Rhys, who, after a few beers, often confessed to conquests with girlfriends of mates.

Danny recalled the one where Rhys had to shimmy down a drainpipe from a first-floor window after being caught in bed with a woman as her husband, rugby player no less, slammed the front door. Danny had laughed as Rhys recounted the tale. He wasn't laughing now.

Instead, he wanted to be get far away, clear his head. He had no runners that afternoon and left for Cardiff centre. He parked up in the NCP and walked to his regular bookies.

He pushed the steel bar on the glass front door and swept into the Greyfriars Road branch of Raymond Barton's Bookmakers.

He was hit by Ferrari-red furnishing with plush chrome stools and a row of leather armchairs. A new decor but same old faces.

Stony was there at his usual place not far from the counter where Harry was serving Basil, an odd-job man given the nickname as he was handy with a brush. 'No job too small,' he'd often say to the regulars, though he only had one eye so had to pass up on jobs involving depth perception. He'd always park his bike alongside the fruit machines and shout out, 'What's it all about, Alfie!' and then whistle. Danny had never found the time to ask him why.

Old pal Stony was propping up a ledge, formulating his next bet. He stood at a jaunty angle, clearly still breaking in the new hip.

'Blimey,' Danny shouted across to Harry checking odds behind the counter. 'Forgot my sunglasses.'

'You'll get used to it,' Harry replied. 'Eventually.'

Danny made a beeline for Stony. 'It's all a bit flash this.'

'Says above the door it first opened in 1983,' Stony said. 'I swear it's the first time they've ever done this place up.' Danny smiled. 'And I reckon it's from taking my bets alone.'

'Lady luck giving you the cold shoulder?' Danny asked.

'I want words with her, got within a gnat's scrotum of getting a treble up yesterday,' Stony said. 'Final leg, got beaten in a photo, that bloody Ross Gleadle was riding, let me down before he has, clown school's too good for him. I'll never learn.'

Danny said, 'You said it.'

'What's the goods then Danny? Spill 'em for your old pal.'

'Salamanca in the National?'

'Who else do I lump on?'

Danny sucked in air, between pursed lips. 'Keep your powder dry in that race, more turn-ups than a Seventies' disco. But Salamanca is buzzing in workouts and got a chance if he passes the trial in style.'

Stony sighed. 'Got splinters?'

'Eh?'

'Sitting on that fence of yours.'

'Come on, forty-odd runners anything can happen, get brought down, cut up, hampered, skid on landing – the drop-side of those Aintree fences are a nightmare and there's thirty of 'em over four and a half miles, lucky to get round in one piece. Like I said, get this trial over with first. Hope the tongue-tie will do its job. Got a feeling results will change now.'

'Why?' Stony asked.

'Just a feeling in my water,' Danny said, aware that if he revealed Wilf's wrongdoings, it would be talk of the bookies before the afternoon was out.

Stony tapped the small red bookie's pen against the matching ledge. 'Wouldn't risk it, not on a novice chaser,' he said. 'Look what happened to me.' He looked up at Danny earnestly and added, 'Every man should know his limitations.'

Bit profound for Stony, he thought and asked, 'Who said that, Confucius?'

'Dirty Harry.'

Danny laughed and said, 'That reminds me.'

He returned to the 'Bet' counter. 'Can I run something by you Harry when you've got a mo?'

'Sure,' Harry said, and followed Danny to a quiet end of the counter, next to the coffee machine.

'Off the record, like, you know if someone wins big, we're talking thousands, how long does it take for you to get the money in the shop, how much do ya keep in the safe.'

'A grand max, bloody good job too, we're working in fear that it's us next.'

'The bookie raids?'

'They're targeting our shops,' Harry said. 'Unlike banks, we don't get the luxury of metal shutters coming down and automatic lock-in doors, don't even have glass as a barrier. All we get is some poxy alarm and a promise the police will be here in ten, fat lot of good if you've got a shooter between the eyes,' Harry replied, eyebrows arched. 'Why you asking?'

'Oh, got lucky with a treble I placed at Wheeler's yesterday,' Danny said, looked down at the red counter. His poker pals always reckoned he was a terrible bluffer. 'Wondering when to go collect.'

'All bets are scanned through to central office these days. If there's a big 'un come in, we phone them to order the cash through, they hold the purse strings and it needs to be okayed by their settlers before clearance. Next day, money is dropped off.'

'By security van?'

'Can't go traipsing cross town carrying that kind of money, have my hand chopped off. It's kept in there until the winner collects.' Harry's eyes flicked to the safe. 'Go call in on them.'

'Who?'

'Wheeler's,' Harry said. 'Wake up.' His tone suddenly lightened. 'Going to watch City on Saturday?'

Danny glanced over his shoulder and saw why. The bookie's manageress had appeared on the scene. She sidestepped a punter chanting 'ride it out, ride the bloody thing out' as he paced up and down the floor, barely able to look at the screen as his runner approached the final fence holding a clear lead. The manageress was cradling sandwiches from the local baguette shop and cans of diet cola.

'Nah,' Danny said. 'Got too much on. Last time I went it was a goalless draw, dull as dishwater. See ya around.'

But Harry's attentions had already turned to a customer, now under the watchful eye of his boss.

Danny called over to say goodbye to Stony, who was scribbling something on a betting slip.

CHAPTER 16

After watching Rhys finish a distant eighth at Huntingdon on another fancied runner for the yard called Talk To The Hand, Danny felt the need of some fresh air.

On a lap of the stable courtyard, he crossed paths with Sam, who held a leather tool-bag and on his way to meet Wilf loitering by the Peugeot. He said, 'I've done their biannual inoculations. Batten down the hatches, there's a storm on the way.'

Danny felt a breeze cool his cheeks. The closed sky was darkened by heavy clouds, bruised the colour of slate. A musty smell of ozone clung to the still air.

Danny felt a few drops on his shoulders as he looked returned to the house. He struggled to get the log-burner going in the lounge. Sara had left Jack on the rug, chattering gibberish.

He looked over to see her return with a tray balanced on both forearms. She used to be a waitress one summer to help pay her way through college.

He forced a smile at seeing it was a salad. Tasty enough, but he was low on energy and craved something more filling. He didn't dare say a word as she'd only reply, 'The kitchen's that way.'

They'd yet to even unwrap the place mats, bought as a wedding present by Stony and still waiting to be set on the mahogany table in the dining room. Meals were normally taken on lap trays in front of the TV. That provided the bedrock for Danny's argument to transform the dining room into a snooker room but Sara said that would be an even bigger waste of money and a room. Since moving in, they'd simply no time for dinner parties, or entertaining friends, with Jack arriving on the scene and Danny working all hours to get the yard back among the winners.

With nothing but repeats on the telly, Sara retired early. Danny finally got round to uploading photos of the horses to his *Facebook* page. He glanced at the side of the screen. It wasn't the thumbnails of the added photos that caught his eye, or the friend request from old colleague Gash, that caught his eye. It was the message: Page last updated 10.12PM 16th February.

Something came to him. The files on the security system: could they be changed, or updated by those with log-in details? The farrier had ample opportunity to note down the username and password when Sam had left his wallet at the pub.

Danny rushed to the study and flicked on the security screen. He opened the file showing Tell Tale on the morning of supposedly 17th December.

Treating the footage with a more sceptical eye, Danny spun the film on to later that morning, something he hadn't thought to do before.

By 10.40AM, Tell Tale was still lounging in his box. He couldn't quite believe what he was seeing. Danny double checked his diary. Yep, there it was, he wasn't going mad. Tell Tale was inked in to contest the opener at Wincanton, a good four hours by van. The screen should've shown an empty box by this time. This footage didn't tie up with the name of the file: 17th December.

Wilf wasn't checking whether he'd been caught on camera but making certain he hadn't by covering his tracks. Switching files.

With that in mind, he called up the details of the file. Last modified: 12.43 PM 17th December.

It appeared to have been switched on the day of Tell Tale's flop. Whoever it was knew Danny was on the road to the races by then and had access to this system and the stables. It all pointed to Wilf.

Was this a one-off? What about all the others?

Danny went to the file for 12th January. That fateful day Pepper Pot and The Watchmaker both stopped as if shot at Ffos Las.

He once again pushed the scrollbar on to late morning. The screen clearly showed both horses were still cooped up in boxes seven and twelve. They'd be on track by then, Danny recalled. Again, the file details were amended on the day of the races. It was the same for Pick Nick, also.

Crafty bastard, Danny thought. Wilf must've known Danny was unlikely to look over the afternoon CCTV footage returning from a long day on track when everything was exactly the same at the yard as he'd left it.

It was the watertight evidence he needed to prove Wilf's guilt.

He'd barely the time to soak up what he'd uncovered when an even greater implication struck him. 17th December wasn't only the date Tell Tale ran poorly but also the day of the bookies raid at Barry. This file was all Danny had to clear Ethan of the robbery, and now he knew the evidence had been tampered and was useless.

Not only had Wilf apparently been switching files, it freed up the possibility the yard was being funded by blood money.

Perhaps Ethan was the mastermind, using the yard as a way of laundering the stolen funds from laying the runners on the exchanges, betting on the horses to lose.

But, if that were true, why would Ethan insist on a new CCTV system if they were up to no good?

Perhaps the answer was hidden within that footage, Danny thought. Ethan may have ordered Wilf to switch the real file with one that clearly showed Ethan at the yard while the raid was unfolding miles away, the perfect alibi. It would cover both their backs, killing two birds with one stone.

He felt a peculiar mix of anger and relief.

Anger that someone he had trusted implicitly was destroying the yard's prospects from within, like a cancer, yet relief it was a possible excuse for the inexplicable run of bad results. Perhaps he could train winners after all and outside influences were controlling the fate of Samuel House. He felt a newfound sense of belief in his abilities. He looked up at his full licence issued by the BHA and framed on the wall.

He heard the crackle of rain on roof slate and the rustle of evergreen bushes below the study window.

91

Danny blinked his stinging eyes and stretched. He went over to the window. Through the downpour, he caught a glimpse of Sam and Wilf near a night-light by the stables.

God they're finishing up late, he thought, glad he wasn't paying their overtime. He'd seen enough for one night and switched everything off. He tugged off his t-shirt and stomped out of his jeans. He'd promised himself to do fifty lifts a night of the eight-kilo barbells Sara had bought him for his thirtieth but thought skipping one night wouldn't harm. Probably tweak a muscle in any case, given the pressure he was under.

He joined Sara in bed. They both lay there in the soft glow of the reading light above. Sara was upright, supported by two pillows, near the end of the latest Harlan Coben.

The wind now rattled the lead-light windows and the swishing skeletal branches of an elm wouldn't stop scratching the brickwork.

'Penny for them,' she said, looking down on him.

'Wouldn't waste your money,' Danny said.

'Try me,' she said and closed the book.

'It's this place,' Danny said. 'When I shadowed Crane, turned my nose up at those old-school ways of his, thought I can do better, I knew I could. Perhaps I was naïve; he always said I was wet behind the ears, trying to run before I could walk.'

'What's brought this on?' Sara asked.

'An odds-on shot got stuffed at Huntingdon this afternoon, one of a long line. Left staring at the screen I was, stunned, still can't explain it. The more this goes on, it feels like the tide will never turn. Don't know what it'll take.'

'But you keep saying they're not machines.'

'Every time though?' Danny said. 'They've given me a handful of talented jumpers and I thought I was messing up big time. Runners all collapsing like cheap tents, despite working super on the gallops. Blood tests didn't uncover anything, but reckon I have.'

He bolted upright, hand instinctively clasping Sara's forearm. She fell silent.

The pair remained perfectly still until Sara whispered, 'What is it?'

'Shush,' Danny said. 'Thought I heard somethin', a thud.'

'Probably just the wind, blowing a gale out there, knocked something over most likely. Hope the shrubs I planted make it through the night. Get some rest, please Danny.'

'Better go check, might be Jack.'

'Jack will let us know if he needs us on this thing,' Sara said, picking up the baby monitor. It was Sara's turn to grab Danny's arm, anchor him to the bed. 'Leave it till the morning, seriously, you're living on your nerves lately, you would tell me if there's anything wrong.'

Danny dropped his head back on the cool of the pillow.

'Like I always say, it *will* get better,' she said.

'Once I've given Wilf the marching orders.'

'Wilf?' Sara asked. 'He's a hard worker, from what I've seen.'

'Sam came to me yesterday. He'd thought a virus was the reason for the slump in form. That was until Wilf fesses up to nobbling the horses and laying them off, nice little second earner, while our yard goes under. It's the quiet ones ya should watch out for.'

'Still, it's just one man's word.'

'That's only half of it, caught Wilf searching through CCTV files the other day,' Danny said. 'Guilt written all over his face when he knew he'd been rumbled. Covering up footage showing the dirty deed with film where nothing happens. Acting all simple, he was.'

'What did he say?' Sara asked.

'Nothing, just did a runner,' Danny said. 'So went to Ethan, it's his problem, he pays the wages. He says he knows nothing about it, but reckon that's bollocks too. Thick as thieves the lot of them.'

'How did you leave it?'

'Ethan said he'd sort it, but can't see it happening. Only hope Wilf quits, now he knows I've got his number.'

'I'm worried all this will make you ill,' Sara said. 'Perhaps you should go see my GP. I know you hate those places, but he's very friendly and might give you something.'

'Don't need no pills,' Danny said. Mindful of his highly addictive personality, he knew that was a slippery slope best swerved. And like his dad, it'd take a leg hanging off to go see the doctor. 'Anyhow, no doubt pick up some bug in the waiting room.'

'Well come to one of my yoga classes, they'll love having another man on board, only one other there.' Danny gave her a look. 'Okay, perhaps that's not your scene. But –'

'Forget it,' Danny said. 'Can think of better ways to relax.' He wrapped his arm around her and moved in closer, but she spurned the kiss, saying, 'Not tonight, Danny. Jack will be awake by six and that means I'll be too.'

'Won't take long,' Danny whined.

'Who said romance is dead?' she replied. 'No, I'm tired.'

'What's wrong?' Danny asked.

'Nothing.'

'You've put up with me yakking on about my problems,' Danny said, 'now it's your turn.'

'Doctor warned us the sex life might go AWOL after the birth,' she said. 'That's all.'

'But Jack's a year old,' Danny said.

'He'll need a younger brother or sister,' Sara said. 'We can start trying again soon.'

'It's not just about making babies,' Danny said. 'Can be fun too.'

'Not when we're both up in a few hours.'

She flicked off the reading light and let the book drop softly on carpet. Danny plumped up the cool pillow with fists, more from frustration, and then flopped back.

'What have I done?'

'What you haven't done is more like.'

'Eh?'

'You never say you love me,' she said.

94

'I do, and I'm always thinking it, that's the most important thing.'

'Saying it is the most important thing, don't you understand?' Danny heard Sara shift to lie on her side. 'Imagine you're in a plane hurtling to the ground.'

'Don't like flying.'

'Just imagine, facing certain death and you've just time to leave a message for us. What's the very first thing you'd say?'

Danny paused. 'Alright, point taken. But why get upset about it now.'

'We're just acting like an old married couple, rarely having a proper conversation,' she said, 'and it's just been two years to the day.'

To the day! Danny swallowed. 'Shit! I'm so sorry Sara. It was top of my mind, honest. Other things swamped it.'

'More important things?'

'No! I'll make it up to you. Take you out.'

'Don't want to put you out.'

'I forgot. Didn't mean to, but I did.'

He lay there perfectly still under rumpled sheets, wide eyes staring bleakly up at the shadow puppets made by those dancing branches.

The wind battered the brickwork and wrestled with the old guttering. Rain lashed the windows. Danny curled up, fighting off the cold.

'We're still strong, love,' he said. 'No matter how bad things get with the yard, always got each other, and Jack. Us against the world, remember?'

'What's sparked all this off?' she said. Her thoughts clearly hadn't moved on.

'Sara,' he said, bracing to push the words out. Another gust thumped the wall like thunder. 'Just had a crazy thought –'

'Yes?'

'That you might be seeing someone, behind my back.'

Sara let out a laugh, above the wind and rain. 'Chance would be a fine thing.'

Danny remained still, winded emotionally by the reply.

'Haven't got time for a fancy man,' she said. 'You'll have to do.'

When there was another silence, she added, 'I'm joking, Danny.' Still no reply and Sara wasn't laughing anymore. 'You know I wouldn't. You're right, you are being crazy. Stop being a silly bugger and let's both get some sleep.'

They both lay there. Danny wasn't even close to dropping off and he suspected neither was Sara, now.

'Why on earth would it even cross –' she said and blew her nose. 'I mean, where's the trust?'

'It's just something someone said and you seem pissed off, thought it might be me. Forget I ever said it.'

'No, I can't. Who said what?'

Danny winced in the dark. Last thing he wanted was Sara on the warpath to Ethan, the one and only link to the yard's main investor. 'Who Danny? I need to know.'

'Just crossed wires, that's all. Forget it.'

He didn't mean to upset her. Airing his fears shone a light on just how much more outlandish they seemed than when left to stew in his mind.

He wanted words with Ethan. The man had only arrived on the scene a matter of months and had already as good as threatened to kill him and wreck his marriage.

'Don't know what I'm saying, sorry,' Danny said. 'Mind's gone to mush-mode at the mo.'

She pulled herself from the bedding and croaked, 'I'll be in the spare room, stay here.'

Danny did so, for a good hour though seemed like more.

What could've made that thud above the howling wind?

His imagination ran wild. He feared it could be something hitting his Golf. He was now as awake as he suspected Sara was.

He could no longer stew among tangled sheets and put on his jeans and a fleece. He picked up a torch from the dresser in the hallway and clicked the front door shut. A gust took his breath and rain stung his face. His fleece soon felt heavier. He flashed light over his Golf on the shale driveway. Looked fine. He stepped out, bracing himself. A shock of cold air nearly blew him sideways and a wall of water smacked his face, as though a bucketful had been chucked his way. Biblical stuff, he thought, sucking in sharply. If he wasn't fully awake before, he was now.

The beam swept the arcing driveway, lighting up rain like glitter. He caught a glimpse of a small dark patch, like a slick of oil on shale. Danny went over, wiping the rain from his eyes and face. He knelt feelingly on the shale. He ran his hand over the dark patch and shone light on his fingers, now glistening red and not as cold as the rest of his hand. He put his fingers to his nose but it didn't smell of anything.

Must be fox kill, he thought, carcass now carried away to the shelter of a den somewhere.

He held his hand out and let the rain wash his fingers. He shivered and, keen to strip off, rushed back inside. He towelled himself down and returned to bed. He carefully sidestepped the loose floorboard near the shut door of the spare room and slumped into bed, alone.

After what seemed a few hours, his body finally surrendered to exhaustion. Caring for a young baby and fifteen horses were taking its toll.

CHAPTER 17

One look at Sam's face told Danny something was very wrong.

'You haven't heard,' Sam said, hand brushing over his cropped hair. 'Wilf's body was found by a local farmer, on a country lane,' he added, 'hit and run, they reckon.'

'Dead?!' Danny said, little more than a squeak. 'Shit.' He wanted to Ctrl-Alt-Delete his brain.

'Had no chance. Knocked me for six as well,' Sam said. 'Such an unassuming bloke, once you got to know him.'

Danny's thoughts sped back to last night and the blood on his fingers. Was it Wilf's blood he'd touched?

But that didn't add up. 'Country lane you say.'

'Yes.'

'And this straight from the police.'

'My word not good enough.'

'Need to be certain, that's all.'

'Why?' Sam asked.

'Nothing, just trying to make sense of it.'

'Given up doing that hours ago.'

'Bloody hell,' Danny said and dropped on to his seat, looking to someplace distant, struggling to process the death of one well before his time. 'Have they got him? The driver.'

Danny clocked Sam could no longer hold eye-contact. 'Slim chance, any skid marks were washed away by the storm, so I've heard.'

'What the hell was he doing walking out there at that time? Pissed was he?'

'Dunno,' Sam said. 'Still can't believe it. One minute he's there, alive and well, the next … '

'Does Ethan know?'

'He told me. Will get a replacement farrier in no time.'

'Not why I was asking,' Danny said. 'Puts it all into perspective. Didn't hear a peep from him most days. Been here three months or so but barely knew the guy except took three sugars and was willing to betray the yard. Still, mustn't speak ill of the dead.'

'Doesn't excuse what he did, though,' Sam said, eyes seeking the floor. 'Is that all?'

'Take the day off,' Danny said. 'He was your mate.'

'Thanks,' Sam said and left.

The news had still to fully sink in with Danny. Rational thoughts could never make sense of someone dying well before their time.

Perhaps he decided to take his own life? A cocktail of guilt and drink may've pushed him under the oncoming car. He certainly chose a good night. Rain lashing down in great sheets on a snaking country lane. Visibility would drop to yards.

But why would the driver flee the scene?

Unless they simply didn't see it, though the thud on the bonnet would tell them enough, Danny reckoned. Whatever the reason, with no witnesses, little chance of tracking them down.

CHAPTER 18

Danny felt dull pain in his gut as he witnessed another one of his brightest hopes fade in a matter of strides.

He leant against the desk, restless left leg living every painful moment. Like watching a car crash unfold slowly before his blue eyes. He wanted to reach into the screen to help The Watchmaker, but that fate was in Rhys' hands and they were being called upon to push hard, yet there was no response. They were treading water in fifth with a full circuit to go.

Danny pulled the phone from its socket. He couldn't deal with an ear-bashing from Ethan, not right now.

As Rhys finally accepted the inevitable and eased The Watchmaker to a walk, Danny flicked off the screen.

'Fork out forty thou and he runs like a fucking carthorse, again,' Danny growled and then kicked the fan heater.

That chaser possessed more quality in one hoof than the rest of the field put together, he thought.

Danny's blank face was now staring back at him in the blank screen. He was numbed by what he'd just witnessed. There was performing below par and there was that. He'd been in the game long enough to know every horse, whatever the grade, could have a bad day at the office but this was too bad to be true. He'd stake his career as a trainer on it, though he suspected that was already on the line.

He simply couldn't sit back and let this one go.

Danny checked the Ludlow card. Turned out that was Rhys' final ride of the day. He gave it twenty for Rhys to change from his silks and calm down then punched the memory dial.

'All right Danny,' Rhys said, crackly.

'Not really,' Danny said, 'what happened out there?'

'You'll have to speak up,' Rhys said. 'Crappy line, breaking up, just joined the M4.'

'The Watchmaker,' Danny said, louder this time.

'Gutted,' Rhys replied. 'Can forget Cheltenham Festival with this one now.'

'How'd he go for you?'

'Same as it looked on the box.'

'This is really important Rhys,' Danny said. 'How'd he feel?'

'Flat as a witch's tits, didn't do a tap for me. Couldn't go the pace from flag fall and felt like I had a slow puncture when I asked him to quicken, same story as Ffos Las.'

'Any lameness?'

'That's the weird thing, wasn't blowing after and walking sound, real head-scratcher. Expect a call from the BHA 'n all, didn't look pretty out there. That all?'

'More than enough,' Danny said.

'Good,' Rhys said, 'felt a right bollocking on its way.'

'Nah, nothing you could do.'

Danny signed off and returned to the study. If The Watchmaker was sound, it smacked of another doping. But Wilf was now out of the picture. Something then occurred to him.

CHAPTER 19

'Why am I here?' Sam asked and then swallowed loudly.

Danny held the look and said, 'My latest runner drifted from even money to nine-to-four in the betting.'

'So?' Sam said, eyes narrowing.

'He then ran like a hundred-to-one rag.'

'Thought you'd be used to it by now,' Sam said, arms now crossed. 'What's changed?'

'This was yesterday, two days *after* Wilf died.'

Sam shook his head. 'And you're going to do this whenever there's a result you don't like.'

'This was The Watchmaker, burning up the gallops and more quality than the rest put together, a man among boys, yet he was scrubbed along and treading water before the race had yet to take shape.'

'So the finger turns to me,' Sam said.

'You said it.'

'Only because you've dragged me here, face like thunder and looking daggers. I fix horses not races.'

'Don't give me that.'

'It's racing Danny, shit happens,' Sam said. 'And where's your proof?'

'Got all the proof I need.'

'You lie.'

'But the facts don't,' Danny said. 'Since you arrived on the scene, all my runners have gone to ruin.' Danny looked Sam straight in the eye and said, 'You killed Wilf.'

Sam gave a laugh that stopped as abruptly as it began. 'I'll take it that was some kind of joke. Because if it wasn't, you'd better explain yourself sharpish, before I call my solicitor.'

But Danny held his ground, sensing Sam was bluffing. 'He wasn't in my study to switch tapes, but to prove your guilt.

Searching out footage of you injecting the horses. And he needed stopping, didn't he?'

'No!' Sam snapped.

'He never told you a thing in the pub that night,' Danny said. 'And when I went to Ethan you feared your secret would be out. Kill Wilf and perhaps it would go to the grave with him, you hoped.'

'I'm not listening to this shit,' Sam said and made for the door.

'That's it, run away,' Danny said. 'Thinking time to change your story.'

Sam stopped and said, 'Sack me if you like or go to the police but don't you dare shop me to Ethan. I never killed Wilf. He was a good friend.'

'You were the last to see him alive,' Danny said. 'Clocked you chatting at the side of the stable block that night of the storm.'

'I was there, all right! Happy?' Sam said, shoulders dropping slightly, as if unburdening a weighty secret. 'I was there,' he repeated, softer this time. 'But I didn't touch him. I wish I had.'

'What do you mean?'

'We were off to sink a few jars at The Speckled Hen, it'd been a long day. But we never got there.'

'Why go the country lanes?' Danny asked, recalling where they'd found the body.

'We didn't,' Sam said, eyes watery. 'Hadn't even reached the end of your driveway when we heard a roar from nowhere, lights off. Wilf had no chance, didn't even have chance to shout. Hit the grille, the windscreen, thrown into the air. He just lay there, rain beating down on his body, a bloody mess like road kill. Then silence. It was like some horror movie. Didn't know whether to run, hide, I mean, was it me next?'

'Thought I heard something that night, a thud,' Danny said, voice distant, as if wrapped up in his own thoughts.

'Going over and over that moment, made me sick. How I could've made it different somehow. Would've checked Wilf, but he was dead.'

'Why so sure?'

'Didn't need to be a doctor to see, no one would survive a crack on the head like that.'

'What then?' Danny asked, still not buying this. Sam had, after all, lied before.

'He got out and pulled some plastic sheeting from the boot. Ordered me to help wrap Wilf's body and put him in the back.'

'Who?'

'Ethan.'

Danny's mind flashed back to Ethan saying, 'He'll be off the scene sooner than you can say traitor.'

At the time, Danny didn't think he meant literally. 'And did you help?'

'Had no choice, he was waving that gun of his in my face.'

'You went with him?'

'No,' Sam said, 'He sped off. I was shaking, couldn't keep my hands still. Thought it was the cold and wet but looking back, I was in shock.'

'Avoid skid marks on the shale,' Danny said, allowing thoughts to escape his lips. 'But didn't the police ask why there were no tyre burns on the lane, where the body was dumped?'

'Guess they thought the tread marks had been washed away during the night, before the farmer came across him.'

'Why didn't you put them straight?' Danny asked. 'Do the right thing by your friend.'

'Same reason I'd rather you shop me to the police than face Ethan.'

'And that is?'

'I value my life,' Sam said. 'And if you'd only not told Ethan about Wilf, he might still be alive.'

'Don't fucking shift your guilt on me,' Danny snapped, 'I only passed on what you told me, lies.'

'But I warned you not to,' Sam said. 'Between the two of us, I said, remember? When you came over that day in the yard, I feared you'd rumbled me. When I saw Wilf rush by, it was only too easy to point the finger that way too, get my own scapegoat.'

'Explains why I saw you there at Ffos Las,' Danny said. 'Leaving the betting ring. How much did you wager?'

'Nothing.'

'Don't give me that!' Danny said. 'First you wreck my horses and my career, now you treat me like a fucking idiot.'

'Had a token bet on your two horses,' Sam said.

'Enough of the bullshit.'

'It's true, I thought it might help my case if I was ever found out, cover my tracks. Kept the tickets to prove it. Why would I back horses I'd doped? The big money was laid on the exchanges.'

'How?' Danny asked. 'How did you nobble them? Drugs?'

'Created a saline solution,' Sam said, eyes lit. 'One that didn't show up in dope tests. My vet's badge was an access-all-areas pass on track. I waited until you'd left for the stands and administered the saline to both runners in the stables.'

'They were subdued in the prelims,' Danny said, thinking back. 'How much?'

'To keep this quiet?'

'How much did you make?!'

'Enough,' Sam said.

'Give me figures.'

'About 20K,' Sam said, 'anymore and the exchanges would've smelt something.'

'And you thought it was worth it.'

'I needed the money,' Sam pleaded. 'Not enough work going.'

'Wilf managed fine.'

'He didn't have a taste for the high-life,' Sam said. 'This needn't be the end you know. We can carry on, draw a line and start afresh. You're pleased with my work, always saying so.'

'Don't believe I'm hearing this,' Danny raged. 'You've Wilf's blood on your hands, yet still expect me to press the reset button, forget it ever happened.'

'Yes,' Sam said, as if convinced Danny was being serious. 'It's not as hard as you think. I'll even do overtime, ensure the horses stay A1, make it up to you.'

'Are you for real?' Danny said.'No wonder you've struggled to get more work, fucking deluded.'

'But-'

'Get out of my sight.'

'Tell Ethan,' Sam said. 'And he'll kill me too.'

'Don't tempt me,' Danny said. 'Now get out!'

CHAPTER 20

Danny tapped Ethan Player into the search box but this time he added keywords Royal Marine.

As he scrolled down the result pages, the archived article from the Portsmouth Herald caught his eye. The headline read: *Disgraced Royal Marine pleads guilty to manslaughter.*

Decorated Royal Marine Ethan Player was yesterday convicted of the manslaughter of Jeremy Draper in Brighton Crown Court. Player's legal team entered into a plea bargain with the prosecuting lawyers, changing from not guilty to murder to guilty to manslaughter. The incident occurred at The Star And Garter pub on the evening of Friday 12th January after Player and Draper became embroiled in an argument that flared up after Draper refused to replace a pint that Player alleges had been knocked from his hand.

After the landlord, Mr Clive Royce, intervened, both parties agreed to take their disagreement outside. That is when, out of view from the car park's CCTV, Player inflicted fatal injuries on Draper. The post-mortem revealed Draper had died instantly from a neck broken in three places.

Player will be sentenced in three weeks time and army officials confirm that he has been discharged for life from the armed forces with immediate effect.

Bet he was out in three for good behaviour, Danny reckoned, and closed the web browser.

So much for leaving the marines for a change of scenery. Lying bastard, Danny thought, not to mention murderer.

Why hadn't I performed that search earlier? Before it'd gone this far, near the point of no return.

He wondered how he could look Ethan in the eye without revealing a mix of fear and anger. Fear that he'd let a violent killer into the fold and anger that he'd let it happen.

107

He'd been thorough in every way since setting up as a trainer, leaving no stone unturned in the treatment and training techniques of the horses in his care. Little did he think it was the humans in his business that would let him down. First the vet Sam, who'd done his best to destroy the burgeoning careers of their best jumpers, and now Ethan, the middleman for an investor known only as The Jaguar; the only wild cat capable of killing for the sake of killing. Ethan and this Jaguar appeared to hold similar traits, one of the same. Perhaps they were the same, Danny thought. If The Jaguar was indeed Ethan's alter ego, then he was behind the investment. Fits in with the funds being wired from an account named E-Holdings. It would also explain Ethan's interest, bordering on obsession, with the horses, and the violent streak, resurfacing when results went bad.

Perhaps he'd concocted The Jaguar as an excuse for his violent ways: not my fault, just following The Jaguar's wishes.

He'd no proof Ethan killed Wilf. Only Sam's word and he now knew how much that was worth. He needed more.

Danny sank low in the driver's seat, the Golf's engine idling. He pulled a digital camera from the glove compartment.

His hand went to mask his face. Ethan had emerged from the mouth of Bevan House. He wore a leather jacket and dark jeans, dressed to blend in with his surroundings.

Ethan made for the Range Rover and revved away. Danny shifted into gear and pursued, holding back a safe distance.

He slowed as he saw brake lights flash red. The Range Rover pulled up by a large detached house set back from the tree-lined road in Llandaff. Danny couldn't slow or stop for fear of looking conspicuous. As he drove by, he saw a woman, early thirties, short hair tucked behind her ears. She carried off a knee-length floral dress well. She was pretty.

Danny parked up down the road, jumped out and crept back until able to focus on the pair off in the distance. He checked the coast was clear and zoomed in to snap a few images of the doting couple on his digital camera. They kissed and embraced.

He returned to the car, checking the still images on the tiny screen. Bombproof evidence.

He'd barely settled back in the driver's seat when a glance in the wing mirror made him sink lower. The lovebirds were replaced by a Range Rover in the mirror. His heart quickened as it grew larger. Shit!

Would he clock the Golf? It was at the yard every day. He raised his hand to hide his face as the hulking off-roader roared by, taking the corner ahead at speed. He was gone. Silence. Danny shifted into reverse and drew alongside the house. The source of Ethan's affections was no longer there, gone back inside.

Danny returned the camera to the glove compartment and strode up the straight tarmac drive, well-tended lawn with rose bushes – all bare, brown and prickly – on each side.

No noise came from the doorbell, so he rattled the metal letterbox and stood back. The door was soon replaced by Ethan's woman. Her hair was ink-black with honey-blond roots showing. Her fingers tucked loose strands behind her ears, away from enamel-white cheeks. Her full lips were lobster-red. She had deep blue eyes and an aquiline nose, much like Ethan. Who said opposites attract?

'Can I help you?'

'I'm a friend, associate of Ethan,' Danny said. 'Any chance of a quick chat?'

'Associate?'

'Trainer at a yard he's placed horses with,' he said.

'You've just missed him. Anything I can help with?'

'Maybe,' Danny said.

Her eyes lacked any sparkle as if slightly turned off from the world. Danny couldn't fathom why. Seemed she had it all: life of leisure, fancy house, money and a bloke, albeit Ethan.

She pushed the door wider and stood to one side.

Very trusting, Danny thought.

'He's talked a lot about you,' she said.

'Nothing bad I hope.'

She didn't reply.

He stepped into a cavernous hallway and faced a tall, sweeping staircase. Pictures and certificates coloured the walls. Some were racing scenes, others army regiments.

'Danny Rawlings,' she said, echoing off the walls and high ceiling.

'Yeah,' Danny said. 'He talks to you about work then.'

'Nothing but. It's the only yard he's involved with and he loves the gee-gees, could say I've become a racing widow.' She smiled. 'It's Emily, if you're wondering.'

'Sorry,' Danny said, 'Rude of me.'

'Drink? Tea, or something stronger.'

'No, ta,' Danny said, not keen to linger after what he was about to tell her. But the words didn't come. Couldn't even squeeze a syllable out.

Ethan's seeing someone else, Danny thought, just say it.

But the words that left his lips were, 'You married?'

Emily flashed another smile. He followed her lead into the lounge, substantial, cream carpet with matching leather suite, bathed in sunlight from a conservatory beyond tall sliding doors. 'You've yet to know the real Ethan, clearly. He's not the marrying type.'

'Know he's ex-Royal Marine,' Danny said, fishing for more. 'Unusual switch, army to racing manager.'

'There was a spell at a bookies' HQ. Got into racing from an early age, his mother used to take him. Been obsessed ever since I've known him. Enticed by the risk, the danger. Wanted to be a jockey, but grew too big, then a trainer but too much like hard work.'

'Tell me about it,' Danny said and smiled.

'So he turned to the bookie side of it,' she continued, 'Lucky to get a job, many of his buddies didn't, from the stories he told me. One even topped himself, poor soul. Like doing a stretch inside, I guess. Conditioned to fight, kill, live by a set of rules, and then they're made to readjust to normal civilian life, the real world. I use 'normal' in the loosest sense of the word, you understand, nothing normal about Ethan.'

'And you reckon he has?' Danny asked.

'Adjusted?'

'Yeah.'

'I'd hope so, wouldn't have stuck by him if I didn't.'

'Does he work for himself?'

Emily paused and then . 'No.'

'Who then?'

'Why do you ask?'

'Just like to know a bit more out my owners, help me to help them sort of thing.'

'Don't you think that's a question for him,' she said and turned to fill a crystal glass with some clear perfumed liquid. 'You see, he rarely talks about that side of things, only the horses. Tells me Rule Number One: don't mix business with pleasure.'

'Does The Jaguar mean anything to you?'

'Only the dead one next to the hearth over there,' she said.

Danny glanced over at the animal skin, legs splayed. As his eyes returned to Emily, he caught a flash of some kind of statement on the glass and steel coffee table, inked in red: Final Demand. Was all this flashiness bought on credit? He hoped now more than ever Ethan wasn't The Jaguar. Wouldn't take much for his little empire to collapse like a pack of cards. Bailiffs would come knocking, whisk the horses away to be sold on at a depressingly knockdown price. And with all Danny's spare cash ploughed into Salamanca, he wouldn't be able to snap them up. Stress would explain why Ethan had become agitated, more violent.

She casually went over and sat beside the coffee table, pushing a well-thumbed *Country Life* magazine to mask the offending statement.

'Danny, don't let that cold front of his or the hard-man background fool you, he's a pussycat.'

Don't give me that, Danny thought. 'Speaking of cats, does he own one?'

'No,' she said and shot him a quizzical look. 'That came from left field.'

'Just seems to have an interest in cats, that's all,' Danny said.

111

She let the leather settee take her shapely figure and looked up, 'Ethan was bought a tabby cat as a young child, ten or eleven. He was a bit of a loner by all accounts and doted on that furry little thing.'

Perhaps Ethan had a softer side after all, Danny thought.

'That was, until his dad bagged it up and took it to the local reservoir and … well, you can guess the rest.'

'Why?'

'Leaving hair on the furniture.'

'Could've sold it.'

'Ethan's father was fuming that this little creature had ruined his precious sofa. He wasn't one to mess around, had no problem getting rid. Sorted.'

Like father like son, Danny thought.

'Ethan wouldn't harm animals,' Emily said. 'It's humans he has a great mistrust of. Probably what caused it. He hasn't had it easy, both his parents were murdered not long after. They thought he was quiet before, virtual mute after.'

Emily's full lips pressed tightly together and she blinked, as if forcing back tears. She clearly felt Ethan's pain; they were obviously close. Kelly won't be pleased.

'We all have our crosses to bear,' Danny said.

'His father had enemies you see. And one of them acted on a threat and, well, they were … '

She paused to swallow, as if she was now the one struggling to force words out. 'They were found in bed, necks broken.'

Danny joined her on the settee, more by necessity. Could Ethan be capable of killing his own parents out of revenge for his cat?

'I'd leave it to Ethan to tell you all this but I know he wouldn't, ruin that tough-man act.'

'It's an eye-opener, I'll give you that,' Danny said. 'Feel like I know him a bit better now, help our relationship.'

But she hadn't finished, as if relishing the opportunity to chat, share what Ethan had been through and told her. 'He had to toughen up overnight, after he was left an orphan. Quickly built a

112

defensive front, one that hasn't dropped since, despite my best efforts. Joining the army as a last resort turned out to be a blessing. He needed some discipline, order in his life. The daily routine helped settle him down.'

Could've fooled me, though Danny didn't air that particular passing thought.

'He soon climbed the ranks,' she added, 'made me so proud.'

Would say that, Danny thought, doting partner. He scanned a gallery of photos on the mantelpiece above the hearth.

He went to pick one out that caught his eye, framed in what weighed like solid silver. It was the happy couple. He was in three-piece suit, she wore a hugging red dress. Looked like Ascot's Grandstand in the background, probably the Royal meeting.

He replaced it and picked up another: two children, girl and boy, early teens. Her Bananarama hairdo, back-combed and lacquered to an inch of its life, looked more of a hair-don't now, and his Duran Duran t-shirt and perm was also straight from the Eighties. The boy's arm was over her shoulder, both smiling. Danny suspected those smiles were merely for the camera. Who are they? If you don't mind me asking.'

'That's me and that's Ethan,' she said, needlessly pointing each out.

'Must only be about, what fourteen, fifteen?'

'About.'

'Childhood sweethearts,' Danny said. He didn't think Ethan had it in him to hold down a long-term relationship and here she is, the better half, still in one piece. Perhaps he wasn't such a loose cannon after all. Been wrong about judging characters before, he thought.

There was now some colour about Emily's complexion. Only natural, he guessed, being a stranger.

Danny yawned.

'Coffee?'

113

'Nah, I'm fine, got a little 'un and he's teething. If I ever got any sleep, I swear I'd be dreaming of having a decent night's kip.'

She smiled.

'Any kids yourself?'

'No,' she replied hotly, as if the mere thought was repellent.

Danny was surprised, they certainly had the means to bring them up well. 'The Jaguar must pay good,' he said, trying to catch her out.

She looked at him blankly, as if he was talking in some foreign tongue. He didn't expand; she'd clearly never heard of this Jaguar.

Danny said, 'Ethan hasn't been behaving oddly around you? Stressed or even violent in any way?'

She put her empty tumbler on the glass table. 'Can I see some ID, hope you understand, these questions are getting rather too personal for my liking, no longer feel comfortable.'

Danny fished in his wallet and produced a trainer's racecourse pass. But it didn't appear to settle her.

She said, 'I'd still like you to leave, if it's all the same.'

'Okay,' Danny said, surprised by the shutters suddenly coming down. 'But it might be best if you don't mention to yours truly my calling round, it's merely a harmless chat, nothing meant by it.'

'You can see yourself out.'

Her reception had iced over since he'd questioned her partner's mental state. Perhaps he had in fact struggled to readjust, perhaps he was schizophrenic and in fact The Jaguar. Guessing by the size of that house, he was doing all right out of the deal and when he said to her it was Ethan placing horses with his yard, she didn't correct him.

He didn't know what to think. But he now knew for sure Ethan was playing away from Kelly, or should that be Emily. He appeared settled with this woman and Kelly looked like the bit on the side, ready to be discarded as and when.

Seeing himself out, he noticed a pair of gloves on a hallstand, cut from black leather with unusual beige suede wristbands, too big for Emily's hands. It was a cold day. Perhaps that wasn't Ethan's four by four that'd roared by and he was in fact still in the house? Listening, watching. Danny's eyes flicked up to the corners of the hallway. No cameras.

He climbed into the Golf, parked up opposite. He turned the air conditioner to blow hot, engine ticking over. He felt lucky he hadn't revealed Ethan's love triangle, given the current delicate politics at the yard. It would've stirred up a hornet's nest.

Ethan would soon be on Danny's case for outing the secret, while Kelly might get grief from Emily. Not to mention, if Ethan was influencing this mysterious investor, all the horses would be out of the yard in a flash. Would be career suicide to let that particular cat out of the bag. Either way, Danny didn't want all this hassle, an unnecessary sideshow, putting him off the job in hand, training winners and putting that small yard on the map. He always suspected Ethan might be trouble and was beginning to regret shaking hands with the apparent 'good thing.'

That evening, he gave his very own green and brown striped silks an airing, laying them out on the bed. He ironed them flat with his hands. They'd been mothballed since Silver Belle's enforced retirement. He felt apprehensive returning as a jockey.

A lack of spare cash meant reining in on the takeaways and, along with regular ride-outs on the morning gallops, he'd managed to keep weight down and fitness up. But had he still got it: the bottle and skill to do Salamanca justice?

Perhaps he was being overprotective and was doing the horse a disservice by not booking a full-time pro rider. Nothing on the schooling ground or gallop strip could come near to replicating the pressure and tempo of competitive racing.

He thought about what tomorrow held. His stomach started making strange noises as he sat on the bed next to those silks, yet he wasn't hungry. He put them back. Out of sight and all that. Last thing he wanted was a sleepless night.

115

CHAPTER 21

2.34 PM Chepstow Racecourse. Time Salamanca let the racing public see what Danny could.

Neither fitness nor well-being was in doubt. Yet Danny feared this first run in his colours would go one of two ways. No grey area about this quirky sod, only black or white.

Either he'd canter to post calmly and produce the same fireworks set off on the hunting course in the valleys, or boil over in the paddock, bolt to the start and refuse to take part. He hoped that wild streak was tamed.

Danny fumbled buttoning his silks, finely pressed by the valet. Although this ungainly hulk of a chaser was worlds apart from the nimble and sprightly mare Silver Belle, they both possessed the right aptitude and attitude.

He tugged on his boots, buffed and spotless. He picked up his whip, resting rather too comfortably in one of the ruts on the bench. Curtains without that, he reckoned. It was going to be a grind out there; a war of attrition, testing stamina and mettle of both horse and jockey.

He could feel a tingly film of sweat on his brow and there was now a stabbing pain in his gut. However hard he tried, he couldn't fool his mind into thinking this was just a run-of-the-mill race. Pressure was piling on his strong shoulders. The undulating Borders track staging this established National trial dished up a proper test of jumping and stamina.

Salamanca's chestnut coat shone like a freshly peeled conker. He stood patiently in the parade ring fronting the stands.

Danny knew a win would boost Salamanca's official rating and thereby push him up the weights, improving his chance of making the cut for Aintree, now just a month away. If Salamanca performed like others in the yard, he would be balloted out of the main event. This was make or break.

As the bell tolled for the jockeys to mount, Danny gave the leather tongue-strap a once-over, make sure it hadn't slipped.

Kelly handed him a leg-up on Salamanca, comfortably the biggest in the field, dwarfing a few of them.

Danny held a tight rein as they cantered to take a look at the final fence. Keep him settled, happy. It worked. No bucking or kicking, hadn't even turned a hair.

They returned to join the mingling rivals beside a sea of advertising hoardings on the inner, facing the stands. Danny had sweated up more than his ride.

Two complete laps, covering just over three miles and five furlongs on rain-softened ground, same as the Welsh Grand National course.

Danny knew Salamanca had only a handful of runs to his name over fences under official rules and hoped he'd give them more respect than on the schooling ground. Like driving, as soon as you stop fearing the dangers, accidents happen.

This was a good handicap steeplechase but nowhere near the calibre of opposition he'd face at Aintree. Anything less than a win and he'd save Salamanca for a crack at next season's National when he'd be a year older and wiser. A sensible Plan B but, deep down, he knew Samuel House might well be repossessed by then. He didn't want to even think that far ahead.

A small field of nine circled at the start, about to do battle for the twelve-grand pot. The tape went up as a starter in green waterproofs and clasping a fluorescent flag, pressed down on a lever.

They set off a sensible gallop on the muddy grass and soon negotiated a dip before banking left to face a testing string of five fences down the back-straight. Danny urged Salamanca to take a prominent early pitch, out of trouble. Last thing he wanted was to get brought down early as there were few opportunities to get another run into him before Liverpool.

Danny looked on out wide as the favourite Waterwheel came through to cut out the donkeywork and had soon built up a six-length lead turning to the far side. An early move that fired Salamanca up, competitive spirit taking over, as if keen to show his master how fast he can go. If only Danny could tell the horse there were nearly two laps to go. The horse felt fresh after months

117

off the track and, if nothing else, these exertions would serve to settle him down.

Danny ran a calming hand down the thick chestnut neck. First fence upon them and Salamanca winged it like a top-flight performer. What was the worry?

He kept a handy second as the field streamed over fences two, three and four. The hat-trick seeking Jolly Hockey Sticks moved up his inner, trying to intimidate as they vied for second going over the final fence in the back straight. But Salamanca only had eyes for the stiff barrier of birch nearing fast. He timed it perfectly, jumping like a stag. This was supposed to be an education for the lightly raced steeplechaser but Danny felt like he was the pupil. What a freak!

He tempered that excitement. It was early stages and countless hazards lay ahead. They cornered into the home stretch for the first time. Waterwheel was still trailblazing in a clear lead. Danny was happy to bide his time.

He was content to go in short and pop the seventh fence. Salamanca had other ideas and launched a whole stride early. No way Salamanca would lift that massive frame from the deep ground and clear the fence. Danny grimaced and pushed his weight back in the saddle preparing for a jolt. He needn't have worried. Salamanca's colossal reach saw him home safely the other side. There was a gasp from the crowd.

Salamanca received a couple of gentle reminders with the whip but they barely registered; the monster beneath him wasn't going to be bossed.

A telling mid-race forward move helped make up two places, now tracking the pace. As they approached the fence that would be the last next time round, he caught a flash of long-time leader Waterwheel meander in the hands of Seamus O'Hanlon. Danny pre-empted trouble by tugging the reins. He didn't want Salamanca to be hampered or distracted on the approach. Waterwheel jumped across his path but was clear at the time.

They set off down the back-straight for the second time and three fences into the sequence of five saw a mistimed jump shunt O'Hanlon forward, head-butting Waterwheel's neck.

A more proficient leap helped Danny draw near. O'Hanlon shifted back into the saddle and ran a hand over his mouth, spraying blood Danny's way. He could barely see past the flecks of brown and red, and snapped the goggles away from his face, leaving a clean set beneath.

Salamanca had found a fluent rhythm and was motoring on to the final fence before the bend. Confident stamina supplies were plentiful, Danny decided now was the time to press the button and see what the rest had got.

He took command from Waterwheel and by the time they'd turned the corner, Danny could no longer hear anything behind. He sensed from the muffled commentary, and the collective gasps and groans from the stands that a few had fallen behind. He simply couldn't believe he'd burnt off those useful performers without having to get busy in the saddle. He felt uneasy, as if something was wrong, perhaps the race had been voided and the others had been called back or he'd taken the wrong route. He glanced over both shoulders and saw nearest pursuer Jolly Hockey Sticks was toiling a good twenty lengths back.

Salamanca carried on relentlessly sluicing through the quagmire, relishing the endurance test and blowing less than Danny. A Hollywood performance.

For such a large-framed chaser, he'd handled the ups and downs of Chepstow with ease. And where were the temperament and breathing issues that'd plagued Salamanca's career with George Evans?

Just one more, Danny thought. A clean jump at the final fence would help punch his ticket for the main event at Aintree just weeks away.

Downhill as they approached the wings of the fence. Steady boy … steady.

Whether from loss of focus or he was correcting himself, Salamanca's giant stride began to shorten. Certainly wasn't tiredness.

Danny had rarely seen a rider-less horse hit the deck and decided to let Salamanca deal with it in his own way. He was bred for jumping, after all. Three-two-one.

The gelding cleverly got in tight and scraped the top of the fence but lost no momentum, landing softened by the lush rain-soaked turf.

The crowd showed their appreciation as Danny again checked behind to make sure something hadn't rallied with a late effort. Jolly Hockey Sticks had yet to clamber over the final fence, with the rest nowhere. Danny eased down finishing in splendid isolation, an armchair ride.

He soaked up the roars from the crowd collecting around the winner's enclosure. 'Doesn't get much better than this,' he said down to Kelly before jumping off.

'Wait 'til Aintree,' she said, beaming.

Salamanca eagerly lapped up the water slopping in the yellow bucket held by Kelly, who said, 'Thirsty work, eh boy.'

She then sponged the sweat from the gelding before the race sponsor's cloth was thrown over and smoothed out. Being led away to the stabling area, he was still on his toes, seemingly ready to go round again.

Danny turned to face a gaggle of reporters, eager to get a quote to help fill copy for tomorrow's papers. One asked, 'How's it feel to own, train and ride the new Grand National favourite?'

Good to hear others were as impressed, Danny thought.

He couldn't, however, fathom why the bookies would price up such an inexperienced chaser at the head of the ante-post betting market, an overreaction perhaps. Guess they'd factored in the scope for improvement in this rising star or was it the featherweight he was set to carry at Aintree. Either way, he wasn't complaining, training the favourite for the National was a big deal, good publicity for the yard.

'Favourite you say,' Danny replied and couldn't help smile, setting off a few flashes from those hacks clasping digital cameras.

'Will he be aimed at Liverpool?'

'If you've got the favourite, I guess we'll have to seriously think about it,' Danny said. He knew it was often a mistake to reveal your hand, or make plans known to the press. Nothing can be said for certain that far ahead. And if, whether through illness, injury or drying ground, Salamanca should miss the big event, it wouldn't sit kindly with punters holding an ante-post voucher on the back of Danny's words. Even a day before the race, a runner might not eat up, or get cast in the box. Only when the tape's risen and they've jumped off, it's safe to call a certain runner.

'If you can't keep it vague,' Crane used to say, 'keep it shut.'

A microphone with a 5 Live collar was thrust in Danny's mud-spattered face. It's owner asked, 'What sort of feel did he give you?'

'Can't deny he felt good but Pegasus couldn't have caught him in his homework, so it wasn't a shock, and the best is yet to come.'

'Given his inexperience,' the reported continued, 'do you think he'll be ready and up for the challenge of the Grand National course?'

'Salamanca thinks it's a game, up the ante and he'll say 'bring it on.''

'So you advise punters get stuck into the ten-to-one.'

'Nah,' Danny said. 'Always looking for the headline you lot.'

'Don't rate his chances then,' another piped up.

'Just want to save the price for the stable staff,' Danny said with a sparkle in his eye. The hacks smiled. He gathered up the saddle and gloved fingers hooked through the plastic jaw-strap of his helmet.

He weighed in correctly and got out of those muddy, sweaty silks.

Danny left the track with two races to go. Kitbag slung over one shoulder, he dropped a twenty-pound note in a Red Cross bucket held by a young girl near the exit gates.

'Thanks,' she said.

'Lucky ya caught me on a winning day,' Danny replied. She smiled. For once, everything seemed right in the world.

Light was already losing its battle as he left the track and he didn't risk crossing the busy dual-carriageway to the owners' and trainers' car park. Instead, he descended the chute leading to the subway.

He always felt on edge walking these tunnels, dimly lit by frosted strip lights. He feared an aggrieved punter or rival owner would pounce out at any moment, an irrational thought. He didn't cross any sign of life as he emerged the other end, most staying on for the closing races.

He made for the van, eager to get home and share the good news with Sara. Perhaps Jack would pick up on the excitement too. He was also eager to check the forums on the Internet to see how the punters rated the performance and the post-race reports on the racing website would also be filed by the time he'd kicked off his Reeboks the other end.

He saw a shadow in the driver's seat. Kelly's made good time, he thought, as he pressed the door handle and jumped in.

'You've hosed and watered him,' Danny said, turning the engine over. 'Kelly?'

No answer. Casually glancing over, his hand left the key for the door-handle.

A hooded man sat still, looking out on the seemingly endless rows of horse-boxes and flash cars. His hands were lost in jacket pockets. He hissed, 'Don't you dare.'

'Who are you?' Danny said. A familiar pungent waft of aftershave answered that question. It was Ethan, Danny reckoned. 'How the hell did you get the keys?'

The intruder peeled the hood away. Ethan's eyes were darker, enraged, almost possessed. 'Kelly.'

'Where is she?' Danny asked. 'What've you done?'

'See you've kept the best for yourself,' he said. 'Leaving us the leftovers.'

'Salamanca?' Danny said, 'That's just the way it's worked out.'

122

Ethan's left hand came over and pushed Danny's chest so hard the crushing pain felt like a heart attack. He tried struggling free but one look at those fiery eyes made him stop short.

'Don't give me that,' Ethan said.

'Another year, it'll be you having all the winners,' Danny said. 'Swings and roundabouts.'

'You take us for mugs?' His right hand emerged from his jacket, now gripping a pistol.

'Flashing that thing around,' Danny said, swallowed and then finished, 'won't change a thing.'

'Sure about that?' Ethan said, finger tightening around the trigger. 'Thought it might … clear your mind. Help you do the right thing.'

'Right thing?' Danny asked, wanting this over. 'Where's Kelly?'

'She won't want to hear this.'

'What?' Danny said. 'Why are you here?'

Ethan's left hand kept Danny pinned to the driver's seat as his right pressed the cool barrel against the prickly stubble on Danny's neck. Not daring to move his jaw, his nostrils kept flaring, as his lungs fought to service a thumping heart.

'We want Salamanca,' Ethan growled. 'You owe us.'

'Why should you care? Unless …'

'Unless what?' Ethan snapped. 'I'm The Jaguar?'

It was Danny's turn to look ahead. 'He's not for sale.'

'We're not buying.'

'Well you're sure as hell not taking.'

'An exchange,' Ethan said. 'Straight swap, yours for the pick of ours. You're quick to talk up ours bought at the sales, this will go to prove you mean it.'

'That's unfair.'

'All's fair in-'

'We're not at war,' Danny interjected.

'Yet.'

CHAPTER 22

'What news?' Kelly asked.

'I'm sorry,' Danny said, no longer able to look her in the eye. He slowly turned a glass paperweight on his desk.

'Just tell me.'

'I've found something out about this Ethan Player of yours.'

'Not this again,' she groaned, folding her arms.

'He's more than just a player by name,' Danny said. He drew a breath and added, 'You're not the only one.'

Kelly's laughter died. 'You are kidding.'

'Wish I was.'

'He wouldn't.'

'No? Guess he told ya that did he?'

'Where's the proof,' Kelly said, head tilted, 'apart from your stupid imagination.'

'I've seen him, with her.'

'Who? Where?' Kelly asked, but before Danny could reply, she added, 'You better be bloody sure of your facts, cos if not, I'll never, ever forgive –'

'Emily,' Danny said, 'Her name's Emily. It was at her house, their house. They were … up close and personal.'

'No,' Kelly said, shaking her head. 'This is a lie, to split us up.'

'She made no secret of it,' Danny said and then frowned. 'They're serious.'

'You went to see her?'

'Had to make sure.'

'I can't take this,' she said, now holding her head and doing lengths of the desk.

'Not exactly finding it easy either, but thought it best you knew.'

She stopped pacing and said, 'We've got some history, Danny, and you can't bear seeing me with someone else. That's what this is really about.'

'What history?'

'That kiss.'

'From you!' Danny protested. 'I just got in the way of your lips.'

'Jealous bastard.' She raised her palm, face pink and grimaced.

'Yeah, slap the boss, that'll solve everything.'

'Make me feel damn sight better,' she cried, eyes now glistening.

'What the hell's gotten into you lately?'

She said nothing, hand slowly returning to her side. She sat, as if sapped by the news.

'You're mad with him, I know. Don't use me as your punchbag. This is hurting enough as it is,' Danny said, 'but I had to tell you, before it got outta hand.'

Danny slid the digital camera to rest near where Kelly sat. She stared out of the window behind Danny off to the soft green folds beyond. It was as if she couldn't bear to look down, face up to it. The truth. Her eyes eventually dropped and then widened as they took in what was on that tiny screen. The money shot of Ethan and Emily.

'I don't ...' was all Kelly managed, tear-tracks over flushed cheeks.

'You can do so much better than him,' Danny said, arms open. She stood and accepted the comforter. 'He's not worth it, believe me.'

'But how could ... ? What's wrong with ... ? Am I that boring?'

'Don't beat yourself up. Looks like she was the rock he went home to: do the cooking, keep the house tidy. You were his bit of excitement.'

'Bit on the side, more like.'

'Risking what he has with this Emily, you obviously meant something to him.'

125

'Perhaps he'd leave her, for me,' she said, hope renewed.

Danny's chin left the crown of her head and thumb wiped a tear from her soft cheek. 'Kelly, they've got a house together, they're close, no chance you'd get between them. Been with each other for donkey's years.'

'What a bastard,' Kelly said. Those big sparkly eyes of hers had dimmed, now vacant. 'What a complete bastard.'

'And, you know, he'll always be that way. Alpha male, out for what he wants and will get it at all costs, however many it upsets and destroys.'

'You wait till I see him next,' Kelly said. 'He'll think he's back on tour.'

'What good will that do?'

Kelly didn't answer.

Danny let go of her. 'There's a better way, to get revenge. And it'd do me a favour 'n all.'

Kelly asked, 'How?'

'Next time he's at the yard, don't let on you know about … her,' Danny said. 'Get him to leave his jacket downstairs, take him on a tour of the stables, anything.'

'What good will that do?'

'Think he's hiding secrets from me 'n all,' Danny said. 'Secrets that could affect the future of this place.'

'Couldn't bear losing my job as well,' Kelly said. 'The week from hell.'

'Won't come to that,' Danny said, 'if you do this for me.'

'Don't think he'll buy it,' Kelly said.

'Use your female charms, he'll be putty in your hands.'

Kelly sighed, as if weighing up the pros and cons. 'Okay.'

'Okay you'll do it?'

'Yep, but you know how pig-headed he can be. If he didn't want to, Salamanca couldn't budge him.'

'Try, for Samuel House.'

'I said okay,' Kelly said, pulling a scrunched up tissue from her jeans.

'When are you seeing him next?'

'Was going to be this afternoon, after I'd finished grooming and mucking out.'

'Perfect,' Danny said. 'Give three rings on my mobile when the coast is clear.'

'Don't wait up if I can't.'

'No pressure,' Danny said. 'I'll be up here. Good excuse to catch up on paperwork. I'll join you in the stables soon as I've got what I'm after. Hope it's worth the hassle.'

'So do I,' Kelly said.

'You don't hate me anymore,' Danny said and smiled.

'Hate's a strong emotion,' she replied. 'Too close to love, and I certainly don't love you.'

She wrinkled her nose and left to tend to the horses.

Danny was staring at Racing UK showing the opener at Ludlow though he merely saw moving images and flashes of colour. His focus stayed with the mobile on his desk, now silent for a good hour.

Danny feared Ethan had worked his evil charms on the impressionable young stable-lass and she'd forgiven him everything.

He flicked the telly off. About to give up and check on the horses, the mobile went. One ring ... two ... three.

The subsequent silence made Danny grab it and rush downstairs. Ethan's black leather jacket was hanging on the end peg in the hallway. *Atta girl.*

He unhooked the jacket; a good deal heavier than it looked. He knew anything worth finding was worth hiding and made for the silk lining. He delved deep in both pockets before fumbling across something that most likely gave the coat its weight. His fingers ran over the cool metal shaft of a pistol, remarkably like the one he'd felt pressing his neck at Chepstow. His hand quickly released and withdrew. Fingerprints, he thought, pulling a tissue from his pocket. He wiped it down as best he could and then plunged his hand deep in the other pocket, all the

127

while casting furtive glances at the kitchen and front doors though he'd most likely hear the danger before seeing it.

He soon came across something that felt small and plastic, no bigger than a credit card. He pulled it out and saw a plastic tablet, smooth rounded edges. A thin LCD display ran across its face, black numbers on a grey/green background, like the digital watch he'd got for his eighth birthday that played a tinny version of 'The Yellow Rose Of Texas' for an alarm. Soon got on his mother's wick and had to swap it with a school buddy. Except this tiny screen didn't display the time. There was a ten digit number alongside a stack of black blocks, like those showing his mobile's reception. Though these were vanishing every other second or so, counting down. When all were gone, the number changed.

Looked like a randomly generated code, Danny reckoned. Why would Ethan need access some kind of secure network?

He returned it and delved again. This time he picked out a clear plastic bag, small and square. It appeared to be empty. Similar to those stuffed down metal bedposts in prison but those contained traces of white powder.

Was Ethan a drug runner?

There was also a bookie's diary, familiar to Danny. Used to get loads every Christmas from his various losing telephone accounts in those dark days of reckless betting and boozing. At the time, he was flattered to think they cared. Looking back with a clearer head, it was a cheap way of rewarding their most 'valued' customers, better known as mugs, while promoting the brand on the cover, in this case Raymond Barton.

Danny leafed the pages. All were blank. No surprise as Ethan had an electronic organiser. But the year of the diary, 2004, was less easily explained.

Why the hell would he keep an old diary? Didn't make sense.

Inside the cover, there was a list of company employees, from chairman down to junior traders. His eyes were drawn to the only name circled: Jed Simms. Beside was the number 6342.

Was it a pin number for a betting or bank account?

He plunged his hand one last time, hoping for a lucky dip. His fingers wrapped around something papery the size of a video cassette.

He removed his hand, clutching an open brown envelope stuffed to tearing point with twenty-pound notes. Must be a couple of grand at least, Danny thought, fingers caressing the wad. It was inked in Ethan's hand with an address: 132 Bevan House.

Danny felt Tyler's brass key in his combats pocket. Was this where The Jaguar lived?

The muffled thud of the kitchen door slamming shut made his eyes widen. He shoved the package back and hurriedly patted the coat into shape, flattening the pockets and straightening the sleeves.

He leapt away from the coat pegs just as the kitchen door opened. Sara appeared, cradling a basket of washing.

Danny's shoulders dropped and then shivered. 'Hi, love.'

'What?'

'Nothing.'

'I know you Danny, I know that look.'

'Just thinking, that's all.'

'About what?'

'How lucky I am, to have you. I'll iron those.'

'I'll do it later,' Sara said, 'last time you did them, my blouse had more folds than when it came from the packet. Concentrate on getting a few winners, just passed Ethan out there, completely blanked me.'

'You'll get used to it.'

'And some journalist wanted a quote on Salamanca, they're doing a feature on the National or something. Left his number by the phone.'

'Not another one,' Danny said. 'It can wait.'

Better let Kelly off the hook, he thought.

He found them smooching like lovesick teenagers next to the feed-room, though he suspected Kelly merely felt sick. They'd either already finished the tour or perhaps it never started.

129

'Get a room,' Danny said. Ethan removed his tongue from Kelly's mouth.

'What's wrong, Danny? We're both single. Maybe you should look closer to home before criticising others' love lives.'

'Not this again,' Danny groaned.

'Only passing on what I've seen,' Ethan said and shrugged.

'Don't, Ethan,' Kelly snapped. She turned to Danny and said, 'He's only winding you up.'

'Got to go, flying visit I'm afraid,' Ethan said and sighed. 'Love you.'

'Yes,' Kelly replied.

He kissed Kelly goodbye and was gone as quickly as he'd arrived. So had Kelly's smile. She turned to look Danny in the eye. 'You owe me one, big time.'

'Can't have been easy.'

'Easy?' Kelly said, eyes wide. 'Felt like biting down on that tongue of his.'

'Remind me never to cross ya, Kelly.' The ghost of a smile returned to her face. 'Seriously, you'll get over him in no time and there's always Rhys as a back up.'

'Eh!' a voice came from beyond the stable door four down. Rhys' blonde mop appeared, dappled in the cold sunlight. 'Heard that.'

'Thought you'd gone to Ludlow.'

'My only ride was found lame first thing, not bloody trekking there on the off-chance of picking up a spare.'

'Were you in there the whole time?' Kelly asked.

'Weren't my fault, I was just checking in on The Watchmaker and you two came along, could hardly walk by and wave, feel like a proper lemon disturbing you lovebirds.'

'Only thing disturbing is you lurking in there,' she said. 'How much did you hear?'

'Not a lot, you were too busy playing tonsil tennis. So waited in there until you left. Thank god Danny turned up. Would've been bedding down with the horse before long.'

Kelly turned to Danny. 'Did you get what you wanted?'

'Kinda,' Danny said. 'Came across a few things.'

'What kind of things?'

'What you on about?' Rhys butted in.

'Quiet,' Kelly said.

'Not sure,' Danny said. 'Need to mull it over.'

'Any more favours, call me,' Kelly said.

'Is anyone gonna tell me what you're on about,' Rhys said, louder.

Kelly said, 'Trust us, ignorance is bliss on this, Rhys.'

Danny returned to the study. He ran over what he'd found. A gun was never good news. But what about the clear plastic bag and the out of date diary? Why would he have kept it since 2004, that was years ago? Just didn't add up. And who was Jed Simms? And then there was that code 6342. He clearly had or still worked for Raymond Barton.

CHAPTER 23

'Don't you dare hang up on me,' Danny hissed.

'I've said all I have, owned up and moved on,' Sam said. 'Now leave me in peace.'

'You've left me in seven shades of shit here,' Danny said. 'Some answers are the least I deserve.'

'Or what?' Sam said, bullish.

'I'll find out where you've moved on,' Danny said, 'and make it my business to tell your new clients your record here and why you left, sure they'll appreciate me spilling the beans. I'll be your worst nightmare, a bad smell that won't go away, however far you run.'

Danny stopped turning the glass paperweight as Sam said, 'Go on, be quick.'

'You've known Ethan a while?'

'About four years, became good friends.'

'Did he ever mention the names Jed Simms or The Jaguar.'

'No,' Sam said.

'You're certain, think back,' Danny said, 'lives might be at stake.'

'Would've remembered,' Sam said. 'Who are they?'

'Never mind,' Danny said. He didn't want this getting back to his 'good friend'.

His ideas were stillborn, meeting every cul-de-sac going. He hung up and sat back.

Thoughts of confronting Ethan about this Jed Simms were soon put to bed. He wasn't in any hurry to see that pistol again.

No closer to knowing who this Jed was when he thought of someone who might. He sat forward and swiped his car keys.

He pushed the glass door of Raymond Barton's establishment on Greyfriars Road and walked through a wall of cooling air. He made a beeline for Stony, who was struggling off the chrome and leather stool, new hip clearly giving him some jip.

'I'll put that on for you,' Danny said, 'Got to bend Harry's ear about something.'

'Make sure he takes the price on the bottom horse.'

Danny took the betting slip over to the empty counter and handed it to Harry, who circled the odds penned by Stony and processed it through the till, timing the bet. He then ran it through the scanner as proof to head office.

As Danny handed over a fiver, he asked, 'Ever cross paths with a Jed Simms?'

'Cross paths?' Harry said. 'Used to work with him at the Canton shop years back. Went on to be a trader at HQ.'

'Staying with this company,' Danny said.

'Yeah, wanted more he did, so went and trained as an odds compiler, and I'm still stuck here.'

'And he's still there?'

'Got warned off for something,' Harry said. 'Not like him, I mean, if he was bad news, would've put his hand in the till while working with hard cash in the bookies. Nah, he was honest as they come.'

'It was stealing,' Danny said. 'That got him warned off.'

'Just guessing, he never talked about it, just moved to rival firm Craybourne's. Shame, used to enjoy the banter when I'd call to okay a big or obscure bet with him at head office, lighten my day. A bloke came in asking for a ton on an amateur softball match in some godforsaken country the other day – what sort of a punter bets on that? Jed would've played hell, 'these mugs would bet on two flies up a wall,' he'd say.'

Danny said. 'Anything more about Jed?'

'He took a drop in pay and status from the move, he told me.'

'So you still keep in touch,' Danny said.

'Yeah, well, he hasn't returned my last few calls. Probably doesn't think I'm worthy now he's moved back up the ranks.' He smiled though it failed to tell his eyes. 'Why the twenty questions?'

133

'Need some answers from him.'

'Wouldn't mess with Jed,' Harry said.

'Violent?'

'Big,' Harry said. 'Used to be a prop-half, until his knees went.'

Danny made a mental note.

Face now lit by a mobile, Harry said, 'I can get his number, think he's still on my memory dial. You're in luck.'

'Makes a change for this place,' Danny said.

'Was about to delete him the other day.'

Danny penned down the number on a stray betting slip and returned to Stony with his bet and a few coppers. He'd got what he'd come for and left for Samuel House without even glancing up at the many screens busy with the afternoon's action.

Danny punched Jed's number and swallowed.

'Hello?'

'Is that Jed Simms?'

'Better be important, midway pricing up Chelsea v Man U.'

'Is this being recorded for quality purposes?'

'Who's this?'

'A friend of Harry,' Danny said. 'You used to work together back in the day at Raymond Barton's shop.'

'It's a private line, no recording,' Jed replied. 'What do you want?'

'Don't hang up, but I need to ask you about Ethan Player.'

The silence was soon filled by the soft purr of the dial tone.

Danny redialled.

Jed spoke first, 'Whoever you are, you'll get nothing from me. Do you hear?!'

Danny knew the only way he'd make any inroads was to feed on that palpable fear. 'Ethan's after you, but I can help. I can stop him.' After a dozen or so seconds silence, Danny added, 'Still there?'

'Meet me at five-thirty, there's a gap between afternoon racing and evening sports.'

'At Craybourne's HQ.'

'Yes,' Simms said, 'Feel safer meeting there, and be alone.'

Danny arrived at Craybourne head office. He slowed as he passed a Porsche, Mercedes, Jaguar and two BMWs filling reserved spaces.

Over two floors, its flashy face, all tinted glass, spotlights and flushed steel, was more Las Vegas than Llandaff, and flanked by flags fluttering the company colours green, yellow and blue.

And to think Craybourne's PR guy had the cheek to plead poverty on TV after a few hot favourites won at Cheltenham the other day, Danny recalled.

The doors parted for a big man wearing a salmon shirt with gold cufflinks and black trousers. Small enquiring eyes behind rimless glasses and short strawberry blond hair turning grey at the temples. The man checked his watch and then scanned the car-park, blanking Danny. He then came over. Danny felt scruffy in his leather jacket, blue jeans and Reeboks.

He wasn't certain whether muscle or fat made up Jed's bulk under that loose-fitting shirt. He wasn't in a rush to find out.

'Jed?'

The man nodded. He glanced at his watch again.

'It's Danny. I'm alone, as you said.' He offered his hand but the olive branch wasn't taken.

'I remember you,' Jed replied.

'From where?' Danny asked.

'You were a big player at our shops a few years back.'

'How'd you know?' Danny said.

Jed looked up at the security cameras fixed to the side of the building.

'They're for security, not snooping,' Danny said.

'Believe that if it keeps you happy.'

'What you saying, I was being checked out as I was placing bets.'

'Can't speak for the others, only Barton's. Unlike on the telephones or online where a record of names and bets are logged, any old Tom, Dick or Harry could walk into a betting shop and try get a big bet on. Shop cameras helped us keep an eye who our serious customers were, those treating a five-hundred quid wager as the norm.'

'Using them,' Danny said, now the one looking up at the security cameras.

'We had a photo-board pinned with images of the big players, like those in murder inquiries. We tagged each with a nickname. Your mug was on there.'

'What was mine?'

'Shorty, I recall.'

'Charming.'

'There were worse.'

'Bloody hell.'

'Ever wondered why the RB cashiers went into the back room to get the bets okayed by phone?'

'Thought it was to hear the trader, away from the noise on the shop floor.'

Jed laughed.

'Can't believe they can get away with that, must be against some privacy law.'

'Don't look so stunned, casinos rely on it, cameras homing in on the tables, restricting or refusing bets from those precious few winners. You see, this side of the fence, it's all about knowing who to take bets from. We don't want successful punters, doesn't please shareholders you see. Only industry where it's good business to deal with losers.'

'Could easily come in disguised.'

'Can't speak for other bookies but cashiers at Raymond Barton's could check your handwriting on the betting slip and it's scanned through to head office in any case,' Jed said. 'We always win, you of all should know that.'

'Some go bust,' Danny said.

'They're minnows, taking foolish risks, offering bonuses to steal customers from the big fish.'

'Like you.'

'Squeezes their margins, they struggle to cover overheads, business goes under. Another minnow off the scene.'

'Stinks,' Danny said, shaking his head.

'It's their own fault for taking us on.'

'Bullied them out more like.'

'Gentle push more like, market forces do the rest. We were here before most of those independent bookies and will be long after. Good riddance. It's called business.'

'You had no problem accepting bets from me.'

'Go figure.'

Danny's mouth opened.

'Don't take it personally, you were betting on any-fucking-thing that moved, I recall; two flies on the wall if we gave you odds. 'Shorty' soon left the photo-board.'

Certainly sounded like Harry's friend.

Danny felt his cheeks burn. He wasn't here to rake up his past failings as a punter.

'Be quick?' Simms said, 'What's this really about?'

'You worked with Ethan Player at Barton's years back.'

'Worked under him,' Jed said. 'I was a junior trader, he was a senior, team leader no less.' He pulled out a packet of Silk Cut and lit up.

'You look worried.'

'Can you blame me, this is a past life I've worked hard to forget.'

'Didn't get on then.'

'Not after I'd found something about him and was about to blow the whistle,' Jed said. 'He became a nightmare overnight.'

'Did he threaten to kill you?'

'Might as well have done. Came down on me hard, shook me up, couldn't do my job properly. Finding mistakes out of thin air, blaming me for any losing market we were trading on. It was hell, those few months,' Jed said. 'Then one morning, he pulled me aside and said the company had evidence I was passing on inside info to contacts and punters regarding the markets, complete lies. Even threatened to call the police if I didn't pack up and leave right then.'

'Why didn't you stand up to him?'

'Had enough by then,' Jed said, 'The guy was a fucking nutjob, relieved to get out of there alive. He didn't send you, did he?'

'Knows nothing about this,' Danny said.

Jed then took a lengthy drag on his fag and blow smoke plumes into the cool spring air.

Danny asked, 'What was the secret that kicked him off?'

Another cloud of smoke. 'He clearly hasn't sent you.'

'Well?'

'I promised on my life, literally, that it would stay that way – a secret.'

'Other lives are now at risk,' Danny said.

'That's why I'm lying low. Like you, got a family now,' Jed said, glancing down at Danny's wedding band, 'want the easy life and, if you don't mind, I'd like you to leave as well.' Danny didn't budge. 'Or I'll call security.'

Jed stubbed the fag out with the sole of his leather shoe, black and gleaming. He lit up again.

'Did he mention someone or something known as The Jaguar?'

Ethan looked away and took another drag. 'I shouldn't be saying this but –' He paused as if reconsidering. 'Look, Ethan left his mobile in the office one evening.'

'Go on.'

'I checked to see whose it was,' Jed said, 'Among the names on his memory dial was The Jaguar. Struck me as odd at the time, that's why it's stayed with me.'

Perhaps Ethan wasn't The Jaguar. Danny said, 'Don't suppose you recall the number as well.'

'No chance,' Jed said, 'wouldn't if I could. Like I said, that part of my life is over and want it to stay that way, digging up old skeletons doesn't appeal.'

But Danny found it hard to trust this stranger.

Like dealers at the London Stock Exchange, Danny knew bookie traders operated under intense pressure. Setting the odds for each 'runner' was only half of it. They had to then keep updating those prices as new information came to light. Push the odds out if a key player got injured in a football game, or shorten it up if a horse does a sparkling gallop in the build-up to a big race.

With the advent of in-running sports betting, odds needed tweaking on a second by second or point by point basis and it was up to head traders like Simms to ensure the book for each market was balanced, so liabilities weren't left to build up on one particular outcome. The aim: whatever outcome of the event, the bookies came away with a risk-free profit margin, unlike the majority of punters. No mean task, Danny reckoned, and it needed a sharp mind, along with nerves of steel.

Jed wasn't showing the latter right now. He was in bits. Danny's arrival must've been the catalyst. What the hell did Ethan do to this man?

'What makes it worse,' Jed added, 'just weeks after that bastard made my life hell, driving me out of the firm, he goes and leaves as well. By that time, I'd got a post here back at junior level in the trading room. The first rung, having wasted four years climbing the ladder at Raymond Barton's.'

'When was this?'

'2004.'

Danny's mind shot back to the Raymond Barton diary in Ethan's coat. Perhaps he'd taken it as a parting gift.

'Police came asking questions, didn't they,' Jed said

'About the bullying?'

'About the robberies.'

'Of the bookies'?'

Jed gave him a look and said, 'What else?'

'They suspected you.'

'I said questioned, not arrested.'

'Do ya reckon Ethan's behind it then?'

'I'll tell you what I told them: no comment.'

'Do you know a guy called Tyler?'

139

'Tyler Shaw,' Jed said, 'yeah, through work.'

'With you at Barton's?'

'God, no,' Jed replied. 'He was the enemy. Works, or should I say, worked at Wheeler's, big rival.'

'He quit as well.'

'Could say that,' Jed replied. 'His body was found, swollen twice the size and tangled in reeds, in the River Taff.' He took another drag. 'Don't look so shocked, it was on the news and everything.'

'Drowned?' Danny asked.

'Broken neck's what did him, must've been dumped there.'

Danny leant against the bonnet of a BMW. Jed frowned. 'When was this?'

'Two or three weeks back,' Jed said, 'that's when they found the body, God knows when he snuffed it.'

'Did Ethan know Tyler?'

'Don't think so,' Jed said. 'What's this fascination with Tyler? Only met him twice.'

'Reckon he'd suffered like you,' Danny said. 'Only you got out in time.'

Jed said passively, 'Lucky me.'

Fearing he was losing Jed's trust, he fired in a compliment. 'See you've done okay since.'

'Hard work and clever trading, no luck there. Head the team now, got my own parking space,' Jed said. 'One of the perks of the job. Haven't been this happy in years and then you turn up.'

'What about Bevan House?'

'What about it?' Jed asked.

'Thought you could tell me.'

Jed pushed his glasses against the bridge of his nose. 'Whatever wild goose-chase Ethan's sent you on, I'd leave it well alone. I have.'

'One more thing and I'm gone, promise.'

'Quick.'

'Does 6342 mean anything?'

140

'Where did you hear that?'

'I'll take that as a 'yes'.'

'My trader number,' Jed said. 'At Barton's. How the hell –

'Looks like Ethan had your number,' Danny said.

Jed looked up at the security cameras fixed to the building and then down at Danny. Was he about to raise the alarm?

Danny was going to leave when Jed said, 'Come with me, there's something you should know.'

Danny was led to the shady side of the building.

Looking both ways, Jed said, 'The thing is …'

He paused and then turned, grabbing Danny by the jaw. He raised his free hand.

Danny could feel the heat from the orange end of the cigarette, gritting his eyes. 'Leave alone, get it into that thick fucking skull. If I see your ugly mug, there'll be no warning next time. Clear?'

Danny blinked.

'Clear?!'

'Yeah,' Danny said and raised his right leg. He kicked out, Reeboks connecting sweetly with Jed's knee. Danny saw the cigarette drop to tarmac and Jed bend double, holding his leg. 'Little shit!'

'Don't dish it out then!'

Jed sucked in air and was now upright, still grimacing.

'Ethan's not after you,' Danny said, restoring balance and poise. 'I'm after Ethan.'

He turned, making good on his promise to leave.

Jed called after him, 'Beware of them.'

Danny relived the moment he'd clicked on that email: Beware of them.

Was Jed the unnamed sender? Warn Danny before he'd got up to his neck in it. Too late now.

He half expected a firm hand anchor his shoulder. But the faint hiss of the glass doors parting again suggested Jed had already moved on. Given their Jekyll and Hyde character, Danny was surprised Jed and Ethan hadn't bonded better.

141

Before leaving, he went over to take a closer look at the small white signposts hammered into a grassy bank, fronting those flashy cars. Moving down the line, he stopped at the one inked Jed Simms, facing a polished sky-blue Jaguar X-type.

CHAPTER 24

Danny had suspected the words before they came from Ethan's mouth. 'We're removing our horses.'

'No,' Danny said reactively, still seated. 'It would only unsettle them.'

'But we're near the end,' Ethan said. He stood staring at the trophy cabinet nearby.

Probably admiring his reflection, Danny thought, as there was next to nothing in it. 'End of what?'

'The money,' Ethan said, 'there's little left to burn.'

'You knew the risks. Results haven't been good, but –'

'Enough excuses,' Ethan said. 'We've sent four horses plus three of your buys and not a penny prize money in return.'

'Cos of Sam! And now he's rooted out, things –'

'First you blame Wilf, now Sam,' Ethan interjected, 'Point the finger at anyone but yourself. Sign of a weak, desperate man. And it no longer washes with my boss.'

'So, what? That's it?' Danny said, 'Rip up the contract before the ink's dry?'

Ethan now faced Danny and adjusted the shades hooked over the V-neck in his duck-egg-blue pullover. 'Nearly four months, this decision wasn't rushed into.'

Danny knew a sudden exodus of the best horses would seal his fate as a trainer. He was struggling to balance the books as it was. 'Can we meet halfway?'

'All or nothing.' Ethan went to the window, pushing back the heavy red drapes. 'You've done all right by this, we've had sweet FA. We need to free up cash from the sale of assets, the bloodstock down there.'

'We can still make this work, there must be a way.'

Ethan didn't react. Was he making Danny stew, suffer?

'What do ya want?' Danny asked. 'See me beg?'

'You've tried your best,' Ethan said. 'I'm sure you'll find work as a stable-lad, no disgrace in that.'

With no qualifications, Danny knew Ethan was feeding off his fears. Racing was his life and Ethan must've known he'd just struck a chord.

Was this good cop, bad cop routine unmasking both facets of his character? Ethan and The Jaguar.

Danny didn't know what to think anymore, willing to accept any compromise, as long as they stalled the removal of his best hopes from the yard, keep the training dream alive. He couldn't rely solely on Salamanca producing the goods, nothing to fall back on if he picked up an injury pounding the drying spring ground at Aintree.

'This will finish you,' Ethan said.

Was he getting some kick out of this?

Danny filled his lungs before he said something he couldn't take back. 'We were doing just fine before you came on the scene.'

'But you've let a few owners drift away since.'

'Cos I was giving your horses the time of day,' Danny said. 'That's got to be worth something, loyalty.'

Ethan stayed looking out the window though he probably couldn't see much through those lace curtains.

'We owe you nothing,' Ethan snapped.

Danny didn't want another blade at his neck and said, 'Wasn't asking for anything more, just stick as we are.'

'Not possible,' Ethan said.

'That's it then.'

'There's another way,' Ethan said, turning. 'A way for you to make amends.'

'Go on,' Danny said. 'All ears.'

'Fix the National.'

Once Danny's laughter died, he said, 'That's insane, you're insane.' Ethan remained still as a mannequin. 'No … no way!'

'No other way for you.'

'Lotteries can't be fixed, too many variables, too many pitfalls. And I'm not gonna pull Salamanca, over my dead body, he's primed for the race and I'll be made for life if he does it, winner pockets a million. No glory in cheating, can't think of any reason why I should.'

'Can think of a million reasons,' Ethan said, eyes narrowed. He turned to that window again. 'And who said anything about throwing the race?'

'What then?'

'Said yourself it's a lottery, let's increase the odds of you winning.'

'No need, Salamanca's the favourite,' Danny said.

'He's shortened to five-to-one,' Ethan said, 'We both know, there's over 83 per-cent chance you'll lose. We can reduce that.'

Ethan's experience as a trader was showing.

'But why should I risk all by cheating? If rumbled, the scandal would go down in history and drag me with it, we're talking the World's Greatest Steeplechase here, a global audience.'

'You thrive on taking risks,' Ethan said. 'It's in your blood.'

'What's that supposed to mean?' Danny asked.

'Like I've said, I know all about you.'

'Wish I could say the same about you.'

'That's not what you're paid for.'

'Look, I believe in Salamanca, jumps like a stag and stays all day. What you're asking goes against all I'm about. You can take your needles and potions. No chance you'd get away with it anyhow, drug tests would flag it up before the winner's cheque clears.'

'Nothing like that.'

'Then how?' Danny asked, merely out of curiosity, 'outdoor motor?'

Ethan removed his hand from a pocket and slowly raised an index finger.

145

'You'll point me in the right direction, great,' Danny said and then laughed nervously. 'Yet to ride the National course, but I've printed out a course map, reckon I'll know the way round.'

'Look closer,' Ethan hissed, patience seemingly threadbare.

Danny closed, eyes squinting. He could make out a shiny patch, either flesh-coloured or transparent, no bigger than his fingernail. 'What is it?'

'An earpiece.'

'You are joking.'

'Do you see me laughing. It's the latest in surveillance technology and will dissolve without trace within an hour of losing contact with skin.'

Probably nicked it before chucked out of the army, Danny reckoned. 'And what, I'll follow a running commentary?'

'Getting warmer,' Ethan said, 'orders will be sent down this, help pull off the mother of all betting coups. We'll clean up.'

Ethan clearly had this prepared months in advance yet it came over as a Plan B thought up on the spot.

'As I said, I'm on the best horse in my eyes and the punters don't need no gizmos to win.'

'But you also said, the National is fraught with pitfalls,' Ethan said, 'brought down, hampered, even meeting Canal Turn at the wrong angle can unbalance the best of chasers. I'll simply guide you to victory and we'll both be in clover.'

'And if I don't?' Danny asked, 'accept I mean.'

Ethan turned from looking over the gallops and said, 'You know what's at stake.'

'The fate of Salamanca.'

'The fate of Samuel House,' Ethan replied. 'Get cold feet and the horses will be gone by Sunday morning and who in their right mind would send their pride and joy to a trainer on the decline? Yesterday's news.'

'Why the National?'

'It's the race that stops the nation. A massive bet would be a mere drop in the ocean, no eyebrows raised, no investigations or enquiries,' Ethan said, 'It's also the one race where this technology will come into its own. You said yourself, luck in running is vital. With this,' he continued, eyeing the earpiece, 'we can make our own luck. No other race we can gain such a tactical edge.'

Clearly once Ethan knew he couldn't take Salamanca, he'd concocted all this. If you can't beat 'em, join 'em.

Ethan seemed calmer than normal, more receptive. Perhaps he was making an effort to seal the deal, ensure Danny came on board.

'This is too much,' Danny said. 'Can you hear yourself?'

He knew he was being bribed but was backed into a corner. Although his name was above the door at Samuel House, it dawned on him he was no longer in control. The Jaguar held the majority share.

'But above all, if this is to work, you must get rid of the earpiece before jumping the fourth last fence.'

'Why then?'

'You're setting out on the run for home, the business end, no tactics involved, just point the beast and go. And there'll be camera's picking up everything. If this is discovered, we're all in the shit. Amazing something so small could end your license and training career.'

'What if they spot me flicking it out? Camera's will be pitched up all over the course, even the back-straight.'

'You lot are always adjusting goggles, chin straps,' Ethan said. 'And even if they suspect, by the time the search party is sent out, the earpiece will be no more. Finding this fingernail-sized patch in the grass within an hour, well, good luck to them, like a needle in a haystack.'

Ethan appear to have all the answers; this was no passing idea.

'This is too much to take in.'

'The clock is ticking, poor results have gone on too long, The Jaguar wants out.'

Danny stood and leant against the desk. 'Say I was guided a trouble-free passage, Salamanca still mightn't be up to it, no certainties in racing.'

'But you said he's indestructible.'

'Yeah and what did they say about the Titanic.'

'Relax, they've trimmed the size of those hedges and filled in the drop sides, less likely to crumple on landing.'

Danny inspecting the tiny device. 'And this will dissolve once I put it down. What if it slips out?'

'Make sure it doesn't,' Ethan said. 'We'll hold a practice run, reduce the risk of any fuck ups.'

'I dunno,' Danny said.

'I'll leave a spare one for you to try out for size and comfort,' Ethan said, placing a tiny plastic bag on the desk. It looked like the one he'd come across rifling through Ethan's pockets weeks back. Seems this plan had been a long time in the making.

'You'll see sense soon enough. And when you do, I'll fax the set of codes you'll need to learn, relaying a command at points of the race where split seconds make the difference. Should be no problem given your photographic memory. Every eventuality covered.' Danny stood looking at the clear packet. 'Why the worried face? Learn the codes and follow my word, we'll come home ahead. First military adage drummed into me at Sandhurst, the seven Ps: Prior Planning and Preparation Prevents Piss Poor Performance.'

'No way, can't do it,' Danny said, 'couldn't stoop that low, no pride in winning that way. Can't believe you thought I would. Take my own chances out there.' He put the patch down and could now see a vein throbbing on Ethan's temple.

'Refuse and Salamanca won't run.'

'That's bollocks. He's entered, made the weights, you can't stop us.'

'Think Shergar,' Ethan said.

Danny suddenly felt sick. He knew Ethan wasn't referring to Shergar's stunning Derby win but the subsequent kidnapping, never to be seen again.

'You wouldn't,' Danny said, mindful of Emily's words, *Wouldn't harm animals, it's humans he mistrusted.*

'Try me,' Ethan said.

148

'Get out,' Danny said. 'Get out!'

'Sleep on it,' Ethan said, 'if you're able to.'

'Just leave, get out of my sight.'

'Shouldn't I be saying that, given results?'

'Like you said first off, it's my name above the front door, I make the calls round here.'

'Say goodbye to Salamanca.'

'Get out!'

And with that, Ethan left. 'Remember, Danny, the fourth last,' came echoing down the hallway, seemingly convinced Danny would come round to the idea.

The front door slammed shut though the atmosphere remained. It fell eerily quiet. Danny left alone with his darkening thoughts.

This smacked of a premeditated scam, planned meticulously. Probably after Salamanca had produced a demolition job in his prep race, Danny thought, propelling to the head of the Grand National betting markets.

They were getting a piece of the action by betting big on a strong contender, made all the stronger by this tiny gadget in front of him.

He still couldn't get his head around how Ethan could be so sure Salamanca could do business. Nothing riskier than the National.

Perhaps Ethan was already in financial straits, beyond the point of no return, and this was the last throw of the dice. Shit or bust.

Either way, the mere thought of having to cheat in a race where the eyes of the world would be looking on made him sick. Yet Ethan left no doubt in Danny's mind what would happen if he either refused outright, or didn't follow orders in the race. All the best horses would be chucked out of Samuel House, closely followed by Danny and his family, by the bank. They'd have to find a safe house someplace far away. And he'd have to sell Salamanca. Couldn't risk Ethan taking his anger and revenge out on the horse.

Kiss goodbye to the only career left to him in racing, say hello to sleepless nights and financial ruin.

Going to the police or the racing authorities weren't options, either. What evidence did he have? Just a tiny earpiece, probably found in any reputable spy shop. Nothing in writing or any taped conversations.

Danny felt he'd been blackmailed into a no-win situation; his hand was forced. He removed the phone from its dock and looked at it, making sure in his mind that the answer he was about to give was the right one. He made the call.

'Yes?' came down the line.

'I'll do it,' Danny said.

'Knew you'd finally see some sense,' Ethan replied. 'No talk of this on landlines from now on, I'll fax through the race-riding codes.' The line went dead.

He reached into the top drawer of his desk and delved under yesterday's *Racing Post* and fished out a bottle of single malt, only a third left. He slugged down two fingers, winced and then refilled. See why Crane turned to drink, he thought. He knew it wasn't the answer, but perhaps it would turn his thoughts positive, more constructive. It didn't.

CHAPTER 25

Danny felt like he was in the War Rooms planning the main event with military precision, now just forty-two hours away.

He'd fanned his arms to make some room on his cluttered desk and flattened a blown up Aintree course map he'd printed off the Internet. It'd been defaced with notes penned with fence heights and the yardage between each. He'd also inked a trail with arrows, like a treasure map, reminding him the best path to take, save ground on bends and when to go wide on certain fences.

He studied the dimensions of the hedges, the breadth of the water hazards, where and when to dare go for a big jump, what angle to take the sharp turns on the track. His obsessive, compulsive streak ensured no stones were unturned. He couldn't afford any mistakes. He also watched recent renewals of the race on a video sharing website and visualised himself being there in the thick of it.

Nimbleness wasn't Salamanca's main asset and Danny needed to have him spot on at fences like the Canal Turn so as not to lose momentum. He even marked down where the crowds were positioned around the track as he knew Salamanca was easily worked up and that wasn't a place to be riding a flighty animal of his size.

And then there were Ethan's six riding codes called upon if they were in a tight spot requiring a quick instruction:

1) Rein back
2) Move sharp left
3) Move sharp right
4) Get rid of earpiece and abort plan
5) Keep a true line, danger on left or right
6) Charge forward

He'd hoped doing all this research and planning would take his mind off the actual task ahead, keep him relaxed. But by 3AM, he found himself staring at Salamanca's box on the CCTV screen, make sure Ethan's threats were empty.

Danny's phone went minutes before the alarm was set to bleep.

'Hello?' Danny croaked.

Sara stirred under the sheets.

'Good time for a trial run,' Ethan said.

Danny blinked his dry eyes open. 'Where are you?'

Flashes of white filled the window like sheet lightning. Danny jumped from bed and lifted the lace curtain. He could make out the dark shape of Ethan's Range Rover parking up.

'Give me a minute,' Danny said, muted. Sara turned over silently. He slipped on his fleece and tracksuit bottoms. Booted up, he joined Ethan outside. 'Bit late to be seeing if it works.'

'Not worried about the earpiece,' Ethan said, 'it's you I don't trust. There can't be any fuck ups. The seven Ps.'

They headed for Salamanca's number one box. His giant head was lolling over the metal V in his stable door. 'Time for a freshening spin, stretch those legs,' Danny said, tacking up.

Danny mounted and urged Salamanca to the schooling ground. Ethan followed some way behind, adjusting a headset to a comfortable fit. Danny prodded at his left ear, pushing the tiny earpiece deep inside. He tightened the neck strap of his riding hat.

'What about the right,' Ethan said, catching up.

'Got bit of tinnitus in that one, standing at the front of too many gigs as a kid.'

'Is it secure? Tilt your head.'

Danny did so and the earpiece held firm.

'Good,' Ethan said, 'now take him over some fences.'

'It might work fine out here in the wilds,' Danny said, 'nothing to scramble the signal but another story at Aintree, air will be thick with signals.'

'It's tuned to merely pick up one frequency,' Ethan snapped. 'You just stick to the riding.'

'But –'

'Do it!' Ethan snapped and then checked his watch.

Danny turned Salamanca on a sixpence to face the first of four regulation fences. He knew his ride needed one last confidence-lifting schooling session before the main event, keep him sharp and enthusiastic. But to have the distraction of a nagging voice in his ear wasn't the ideal prep and clocking Ethan in his periphery made his muscles tense, like driving with a police car filling the rear-view mirror.

The image of crossing the line triumphant dominated his dreams and spurred him on.

Danny and Salamanca held their ground as Ethan walked beyond earshot. He adjusted the tiny head-microphone. 'One-two, one-two,' came loudly into Danny's left ear. He shouted, 'Not deaf!'

'Better?' Ethan said, quieter.

Danny gave a thumbs up.

'Go on, then,' Ethan added, 'let's see what all the hype is about.'

Danny knew the earpiece was one-way traffic and whispered in Salamanca's large pricked ears, 'Okay boy, nothing fancy, just four clean jumps.'

He slid a calming hand down Salamanca's mane before kicking him in the belly. Salamanca got the message and took off. They galloped strongly into the first fence.

'Jump!' blared through the earpiece, breaking Danny's focus. He asked for another short stride but Salamanca was having none of it, leaving the rain-softened grass and ballooning the four-feet six-inches of tightly packed birch, just short of most Grand National fences. They landed the other side, partnership intact and on an even keel, ready for the second fence just strides away.

'Jump!' came in his ear yards from the planned take-off, once again taking Danny off-guard. He stalled on his trusty mount, transmitting mixed messages down the reins but Salamanca looked after him, adjusting his stride accordingly, sturdy legs clearing the fence with no bother.

They'd now found a rhythm and Danny let Salamanca do the rest, clearing the final two practise obstacles. He was about to rein him in and return back the way when, 'Six!' crackled in his left ear. Danny instantly knew the code to mean 'charge forward'.

'But I've jumped all four,' Danny said under his breath, 'test run over.'

'Checking the range,' Ethan said. 'Keep going until you stop hearing me.'

Ethan began to count without taking breath. He'd reached sixty-two when it then fell eerily quiet.

Good job, Danny thought, as they were closing in on the boundary hedge.

Danny afforded a glance over his shoulder, earpiece still in place. Ethan was a mere dot on the grainy horizon. Behind him was the orange hem of the dawning sky.

They must've covered a good six or seven furlongs of sloping field. He slowed to a stop and turned to trot back to the schooling ground and Ethan, who said, 'Ought to be enough range, I'll be relaying info from somewhere in the stands.'

Danny was in no mood to prolong their meeting and dismounted, dragging the reins over Salamanca's head to lead him back to the stables. 'And we don't need to be told jump at each bloody fence, we both know the drill.'

'I was checking the earpiece worked mid-jump, in full flight.'

Danny sensed the atmosphere had cooled and felt gooseflesh spread up his forearms. Ethan's murky past was never far from his mind. Anyone capable of snapping another's neck over a spilt pint was always liable to 'snap' again.

'Clear on where we stand,' Ethan said. 'Follow orders and we'll all prosper from this. Back out and it's over for you, and the end for this chap.' He slapped Salamanca on the neck.

Danny didn't reply.

'Next time you hear my voice, you'll be lining up.'

'Not gonna wish me good luck then,' Danny said.

'Won't need it,' Ethan said, pressing another plastic bag into Danny's palm. 'Not with this. And remember, before the fourth-last fence is where we part ways.'

CHAPTER 26

Jed was alive, Tyler was dead. Danny couldn't fathom why.

They both worked as traders for rival bookies. They both were men in their thirties. They both lived in the Cardiff area. They both had something on Ethan.

What set them apart?

Tyler knew of 132 Bevan House.

Is that what sealed his fate that night, by the river?

Danny felt his jacket pocket for the key shape.

Was he next on the list? Should he respect Tyler's final wish and hand it over to police? But would that make Danny prime suspect for murder, being the final person to see Tyler that fated night.

He had nothing else to go on, only that bloody key. It was time to pay the tower block a visit.

Danny parked up safely away from the infamous Newtown Estate on the outskirts of Cardiff.

Could fill a *Crimewatch* from this place, easy, he thought.

Clearing a low wall, he clocked a gang of hooded youths, hanging out on bikes between an empty steel half-pipe for skaters and a line of lock-up garages. Some resting on handlebars, others with their hands lost in chip wrappers, all staring Danny down. Their adolescent build and stance were no threat alone, but in the safety of a group there was no telling.

The smell of salt and vinegar was carried his way, along with the words, 'Eh, you.' He felt the eyes on his back. 'Good for some gear?'

'Nah, sorry mate,' Danny replied, voice deeper.

He briefly glanced over in the general direction of the gang, avoiding eye contact.

He pushed his shoulders back, strong arms hanging away from his body in a swagger, like a threatened iguana.

Not daring to look over again, he made a beeline for the second of two tenement blocks. BEVAN HOUSE in black, above a sheltered entrance.

Both lifts were cordoned off with red and white tape. Danny made for the dank stairwell. Patchy yellow walls met concrete, blackened in parts and damp. He climbed the flights, swerving cider cans, carrier bags, crumpled tinfoil, a headless plastic doll and needles.

As he stepped on to the seventh landing, he stretched his lungs with musty air.

Surely the bloke bankrolling the yard doesn't live here, Danny thought, unless it was a decoy address to fool the taxman.

He followed the walkway. To his left, makeshift washing lines sagged with wet kids' clothes above a rusty railing. He stopped at an unmarked door between flats 131 and 133.

His knuckles rapped the peeling blue paint, setting off a thunderous gunfire of baying barks. Danny took a step back.

The dog was soon drowned out by a man's gruff voice, booming, 'Zeus!' I'll ring ya fucking neck, get in there.' A loud squeal. A door slammed.

Danny took another step back, elbows now hanging over the railing. He heard a cry far below, 'Jump!'

Danny looked down. The gang of youths had continued loitering near the lock-ups. All of them joined in, like an eerie tribal chant. 'Jump! Jump! Jump!'

Danny brushed it off with *don't think much of the locals*, though he could no longer pretend he didn't feel threatened. He wasn't keen to hang around. Come on, answer.

As a door chain was pulled, Danny glanced up where the walkway of floor eight met the wall. There was a small camera, caged with lens directed above Danny's head. Not that bloody short. Clearly this Jaguar had bigger enemies to fear. Needing a camera and guard dog told its own story. He was surprised the camera hadn't been nicked long ago. They'd have also taken the cage if it was worth anything.

157

The door opened, until anchored by the chain. Half a jowly face bearing a week's growth, topped by thinning brown hair, filled the gap. His Johnnie Walker eyes had glints from the gold hung from his thick neck. 'This better be good.'

'I'm looking for someone,' Danny said.

'Aren't we all.'

'The Jaguar.'

The man groaned, as if tired of the same old question. 'Try London Zoo.'

The door clicked shut.

Danny knocked again, and again. But nothing came of it. He simply couldn't leave with more questions. See if Tyler was true to his word, he thought, and removed the brass key from his jacket. He forced it into the lock.

If it turned, he wasn't sure whether he'd dare push and enter. But it didn't. The key wouldn't even disappear all the way.

Not keen to bust the lock or snap the key, his only link with Tyler, he carefully pulled it free.

He looked up at the camera. Was he now being watched?

He returned to ground level. The youths had moved on, clearly bored by the lack of reaction they'd got.

Danny sped back to Samuel House.

The sweet smell of cake mixture filled the hallway. The kitchen light was on.

'All right, love,' he said, dropping the Golf keys on the pine table.

'Good day at the track?' Sara said.

'Left Kelly in charge,' he said. 'Good experience for her.'

Sara opened the oven and another waft of baking cakes filled the room. Danny filled his lungs. It sent him back to school holidays as a youngster, maybe five or six, when he'd help his mum in the kitchen though he didn't pick up many tips, face normally lost in the mixing bowl. 'Where've you been then?'

'Newtown Estate,' Danny said.

Sara looked up from inspecting the cakes. 'Why on earth would you want to go there?'

'Didn't want to, had to,' Danny said and then dropped onto a pine chair. 'Something bugging me needed settling.'

'Don't think I want to know.'

'I reckon this Ethan owns a flat there.'

'Can't see Ethan somewhere like that, even if there's a penthouse, wouldn't be seen dead there I'd imagine.'

'That's what I reckoned too,' Danny said.

'So why do you think he lives there.'

'Didn't say live,' Danny said. 'Just owns, some caveman looks like he's flat-sitting.' He sat up and nabbed a cake, still piping hot from the tray. 'You reckoned they could be robbing banks to fund the yard.'

'I wasn't serious,' Sara said.

'I'd feared you were close to the truth.'

'What changed your mind?' Sara said. She rubbed the tip of her nose with the back of her hand, leaving a spot of flour, and then picked up the cooling tray.

'When I had a big win as a punter,' Danny said, 'was told to come back once they'd got the funds in.'

'Where's this going?'

'They don't hold more than a thousand cash at any one time in the shops.'

'And?'

'Can you see them bankrolling this place at a grand a throw,' Danny said. 'Would need a raid a day to keep up.'

Sara shrugged.

'No,' Danny added. 'It's something else they're up to. Something they're not too keen on sharing.'

'I was right, didn't want to know,' Sara said, placing the tray to cool by the window. 'But I think the police will.'

'I'd be laughed out of the station with what I've got, probably get charged with time-wasting.'

Danny's fingernails strummed the table. He hoped telling Sara would be a problem halved, but it'd more like doubled. He stood, restless. 'Another thing, why would this guy have a security camera?'

'It's a rough estate,' Sara replied, seated again. 'Think I'd have one.'

'You haven't seen the size of him,' Danny said, marking with his hand someplace well above his head, 'and don't get me started on his dog.'

'Any of the other flats got one?'

'Nah, that's just it, the odd satellite dish, makes no sense.'

Sara looked up, eyes narrowing.

'What've I said now?'

'Not looking at you,' Sara replied, 'the clock.'

Danny paused, glacier-blue eyes wide. 'That's it.'

'The clock?'

'No,' Danny said, 'Maybe the camera's not filming the walkway.'

'Where then?'

'Dunno for sure,' Danny said, grabbing his jacket, 'but reckon I will soon.'

'Danny, you're not going back there,' Sara sighed, 'not at this hour.'

'This can't wait, love,' Danny said. 'Too much on this.'

'Take your mobile,' Sara called after him. 'And don't be long.'

He rushed up to his office and picked up a big paperclip from a tray on his desk. If the key didn't fit, there were other ways.

He slammed the front door. He climbed into his Golf, checked for a torch and revved away, swallowed by blackness.

He parked his Golf on the edge of the estate and walked the rest. It was cold and he pulled his jacket collar up and tugged at his sleeves.

He stopped near the half-pipe, bathed in the flickering orange glow of a street lamp. No sign of the hoodies. Was the camera directed over there?

He looked up at the towering Bevan House. A good dozen landings lit soft yellow and windows, some black, others flickering grey-blue from tellies watched by those unable to sleep or with little to get up early for. He heard a barrage of distant dog barks, loud enough to be Zeus.

He homed in on Flat 132. He hoped the camera had no night vision.

Behind him, a long line of lock-up garages. Were they the star of the show?

He was about to run down them, see if any were numbered, when a high-pitched voice came from nowhere. 'What you after?'

'Not aggro,' Danny said.

'Not looking for any,' replied the voice. A kid, early teens, rolled his bike under the streetlamp. 'I'm not one of the Newtown Crew.'

His small, spotty face was faintly familiar to Danny. 'Swear your mug was among them when I was here last.'

'Only cos it makes life easy,' the boy said. 'Would be well-fucked if I wasn't.'

'Who owns these?'

'They're rented out to those in the tower blocks,' the kid said, 'ones that can afford it, like.'

'Any used by the big bloke in Flat 132.'

'I can tell ya,' the boy said and smiled, 'but it'll cost ya?'

Danny sigh formed a ghostly cloud.

'It's for me mam's tanning sessions.'

Danny sighed again. 'Tenner.'

The kid paused and then said, 'Twenty.'

'Better not be lying.'

'Lived here since I was a toddler, know all there is to know about the place. Mam reckons they'll flatten it all soon enough, once the council find someplace for them all to go,' the boy said, outstretched palm, like a beggar.

'Not yet. Show me the way.'

The kid wheeled the bike to stop beside a lock-up on the left, four in. It's white shutter was shinier and plusher than the rest, as if someone had replaced the original council one.

'You sure?' Danny asked.

161

'Yeah, definitely Trev's, swear on mam's life,' the kid replied, extending his palm.

Danny kept the note safely from grasp. 'Heard any noises inside, or seen anything, people coming and going.'

'That'll be more.'

Danny pulled another note from his pocket.

The kid snatched both up, beady eyes lit by the moon. 'Nah.'

'Nothin'?'

'Not even Trev,' the kid said.

'Why so sure it's this one?' Danny asked.

'He's a face on the estate, don't mess with Trev, or his business.'

Danny glanced up at Bevan Place. He tested the padlock that held down the metal shutter.

'Go,' Danny said, looking over at the kid straddling his bike, 'and you've never clapped eyes on me, yeah?'

The kid held his hand out again.

'Don't push ya luck,' Danny snapped. 'Now hop it!'

'Don't need telling,' the kid replied, 'If Trev found out, I'd be dead meat.'

Danny crouched and flashed the torch at the lock, built in to a thick strip of metal at the base. He placed his finger over the keyhole. He killed the light, mindful it would attract locals like flies to shit.

With his other hand, he removed the paperclip and hooked the end, before inserting it where his finger had been. He expertly twisted and turned the lock, a skill he'd picked up on a stretch inside. But it wasn't budging.

Danny dropped the wire as it suddenly struck him. The key! Tyler's key.

He recalled that moment it was handed over by the river. Did Tyler mean the 'lock-up' not the 'lock, up' in 132 Bevan House?

He fumbled in his jacket and removed the key. It glided in. Perfect fit. He held his breath as it turned. The click was like music to his finely tuned ears.

He slowly raised the shutter, grimacing as the clatter of metal on metal filled the night air. He pushed it up until his arms stretched high, only to be faced by another one. Danny wondered what the hell was important enough to need two shutters. Perhaps leftover loot from the bookie raids.

He turned the key again and raised the second shutter. He picked up the torch and shone light into the black hole. He edged in, now safely from view of the tower block. He turned and pulled down the shutter.

There was a wooden trapdoor set in the middle of a smooth concrete floor. Car inspection pit, Danny reckoned. His grandpa built one similar. He'd turned his hand to kit cars to fill the time after a forty-year stint down the colliery.

But, unlike his grandpa's garage, there was no stink of grease or oil. Couldn't even pick up a trace of Zeus. Clearly Trev didn't come down here with guard dog in tow, he thought, if at all. The air was as clear as the wooden shelves fixed to the breezeblock walls either side. More like an office than a place for storing or DIY jobs too big for those cooped-up flats nearby.

Scanning the room he noticed a desk pushed against the far wall, near a naked bulb. He went over, flicked it on and put the torch down beside two laptops and a steel carry case on the desk.

He lifted the lid of one laptop. As it booted up, he clicked open the carry case, expecting guns. Resting on the foam lining were two mobiles and an electronic card, no bigger than a bleeper.

Not as incriminating as he'd hoped, but then looked closer.

The card felt and looked like the one in Ethan's jacket, smooth rounded edges and thin LCD display filled with changing digits. It was the link Danny needed. He was tempted to leave but he wanted more. Were they hackers?

A loud dog bark made him turn on his heels, eyeing the shutter. He instinctively rushed over and flicked off the light. He stopped breathing. Listen out for footsteps, voices. Nothing.

That feeling of terror gave him a rush and shot him straight back to days as a housebreaker during his wayward youth, stuck on the landing as the owners came home too soon.

The light returned and he switched on a mobile, slotting its lead into a USB port on the side of the laptop.

Hook up to the Internet, Danny thought. As he waited, he turned over the other laptop. Inked in black marker on the base was *Property of Wheeler's Bookmakers Ltd.*

He looked closer at the phone too, same model as the Pay As You Go his mum used to have, no need to register a name or address. Probably why they chose it.

His index finger skated over the censor pad on the keyboard, moving the cursor over the desktop icon *RB Secure Network* above an open padlock symbol. He double-clicked. A grey box popped up. Danny clicked on the first of two white windows within that box. He held the One button down. The white bar soon filled with four asterisks. A four-digit code. He'd come back to that. He clicked on the second window. It was longer. He pushed the one key again. This one filled with ten asterisks.

Danny looked down at the digital tablet. The randomly generated number was also ten digits long.

His focus returned to the first window. The only four-figure code he could summon was Jed's trader ID found in Ethan's diary. He deleted the stars and typed 6342. His furtive eyes flicked between the digital tablet and the keyboard as he input the current ten figures on that tiny LCD screen. He clicked on the OK button. Danny could hear his heart banging away as he waited.

Another grey box appeared: Attempt 1 of 3 failed. Access denied. Please try again.

What memorable number might Ethan use?

Danny thought back to that diary. The pages held no clues, but perhaps the cover did. He punched in 2004 into the first box and then the current sequence of digits lit on the security card. He clicked OK and held his breath. He had no back-up plan if this didn't work.

He could barely bring himself to read the new grey box that flashed up. When he saw the words: Secure encrypted link successful. Trader logged in: Jed Simms ID 6342.

He inked the code on the back of his hand. If he didn't make it out alive, he hoped the police would discover his body and see this clue before it'd decayed.

Looked like Ethan had stolen Jed's trading identity and kept the account open, even years after both had left the firm in 2004. He tilted his head back and clicked his neck. Last thing he needed was to pull something the night before the big race. The tiny muscles surrounding his eyes were bubbling, didn't know if tiredness or tension. He blinked.

He clicked on the Enter button and the menu screen shone white, lighting up Danny's face all silvery.

1) Personal details
2) Live Betting Markets
3) Trading Room
4) Recorded Bet Settlements
5) Mail Box

Danny punched the four key, checking if Ethan had in fact been laying off the yard's runners. Columns of boggling numbers and words darkened the screen. Danny's eyes scanned down the list. On the left, dates and times told Danny when the bets were settled. The middle column gave the selections in the bet, either horses or sports. The right column showed whether the bet had won or lost and the returns due.

The stakes were in hundreds, occasionally thousands. The list was topped by a £6,000 bet placed at the branch on Greyfriars Road in Cardiff. Danny's local. It was on an evens favourite on the card at Kempton this evening. Result: WON Return £12,000 *Cash Request*. Payment due to be delivered: 11/4.

So the cash would be sent to the Greyfriars shop day after tomorrow, Danny thought.

He searched his jacket and pulled the folded newspaper article he'd saved, detailing the bookie raids. He flattened it out with his palm on to the desk and eyed the date Raymond Barton's shop in Barry was targeted: 17th December.

He clicked on the link at one side for recorded bets in December. He scrolled down the list, most were losers in black font, returning £0. But there was one in green that caught Danny's eye. It was a £1000 treble on the horses. Result: WON Cash request. Return £26,450. Payment delivered 17/12. The date of the armed robbery.

Crafty fuckers, Danny thought, they were clearly swooping in whenever there was a big cash payout. No wonder the police hinted it might be an inside job in that crumpled article.

But surely the police would make the link by now, he reckoned, know they're a bit slow and all that. But perhaps … if Ethan had stolen and taken command of a former employee's account that was assumed by the rest of the workforce to have been shut down years back. Chances are police stuck to interviewing the current crop of staff there, not suspecting past head traders or sleeping accounts. An inside job being operated from the outside, from the security of a lock-up linked solely to an assailant in Flat 132, paid good money to keep his trap shut.

The metal shutter suddenly rattled. He bolted upright and waited. Too late to hide and he was trapped. But it soon fell quiet again, must be a gust of wind.

He returned to the newspaper cutting. The previous raid on the list was a Sketty branch in Swansea on December 4th. He checked the screen and saw there'd been a bet of £8,000 on Man U at home to beat Arsenal. Odds were 5/4. Result: WON. Return: £18,000. Cash Request. Payment delivered: 5/12.

Danny had seen enough and logged out. He clicked 'Shut Down' on the start menu.

He'd only just picked up the crumpled article when voices made him freeze. Two men, muffled.

He scanned the room and picked up the torch. He flicked off the naked bulb and rushed forward. As he flashed the torch, he tugged at an iron ring on the trapdoor. It creaked upon. He leapt into the black hole. An eerie falling sensation for a moment as if missing a step, not knowing when he'd meet the bottom. Falling into an abyss. He landed awkwardly on the stone floor but bit down the pain.

He stood and lowered the trapdoor on top of him, praying they'd not yet raised the shutter. He heard the industrial clatter of metal. The voices came clearer now. 'Warned you time and again to keep this fucking locked, pay you decent money and you still fuck up.'

Sounded like Ethan, Danny thought.

'I swear on Zeus' life,' the other voice replied gruffly. 'I checked it.'

'You're in luck, they've not taken anything,' Ethan said.

'I swear –'

'Shut it. Enough excuses.'

Danny peered up through a slenderest of cracks between the wooden planks of the trapdoor as light filled the lock-up above. He feared Ethan would feel warmth from the laptop, or he'd notice things were out of place. A clumping boot came down on the board, blocking Danny's view. He waited in hiding, little else he could do.

The boot shifted forward. Danny could now see Trevor, wearing string vest, pyjama bottoms and slippers, standing by Ethan in front of the desk, both studying figures on the computer screen.

'Bingo,' Ethan muttered.

'How much?' Trevor asked.

'19K due in Sunday, late afternoon, we'll strike 5PM, trade will be winding down by then, fewer civilians about,' Ethan added, 'Customer requested cash payment, clearly wants it earning interest right away, than wait for a cheque to clear.'

'Result,' Trevor said.

'It might be small change if that simple fucker doesn't balls up in the biggie at Aintree but still beats a day job.'

Simple fucker! Danny fought off primal urges and didn't rise to the insult.

'Need any help?' Trevor said.

'Want the job done properly,' Ethan said and turned. Danny looked on as Ethan turned off the laptop and looked somewhere in the direction of Trevor, who was now gone from

167

view. 'Just keep your eyes peeled on this place. Do that and we'll all be winners, not rocket science.'

'If anyone goes near, I'll set Zeus on 'em,' Trevor grunted.

'Good to hear it,' Ethan said, slapping Trevor on his broad hairy shoulders. The metal shutters rattled twice and then the lock-up fell silent.

Danny could feel his ankle now. He hoped it wouldn't swell. He pushed the trapdoor and climbed from the pit. He ran the torch up and down the sides of the shutters. Better be some kind of internal release lever, he thought. Must be somewhere, prevent getting locked in.

If he was trapped there, it didn't bear thinking about, missing the night before the big race. Ethan would go ballistic.

He pulled at a metal lever at the base where a thick steel band met with concrete. The door clicked. Danny rolled both shutters to waist height and ducked under.

He turned Tyler's key in the padlock and hobbled from the scene.

CHAPTER 27

'Think I'm set,' Danny said. 'Bag of frozen peas helped the ankle.'

'Good, I'll need them for supper,' Sara said. 'When you return safe and sound.'

She sat Jack down on the playmat and planted a lingering kiss on Danny's dry lips. Sara always kissed him before he left for the races. It had become a sort of good luck ritual. No words spoken, her serious, unblinking eyes told him enough.

He guessed it was hard for her to say goodbye, living with the constant nagging fear he'd not return in one piece, like loved ones of a deployed soldier or a fireman off on a shift.

He guessed those fears would be magnified as this was the Grand National. But he couldn't offer reassurance by telling her that he'd have his very own guardian angel in his ear, guiding his safe passage over the two laps and thirty gruelling fences. Although he trusted she'd keep it a secret, he couldn't bear her getting embroiled as a witness if rumbled by the BHA or police.

'Got to do this, it's for the little 'un's future … our future,' were Danny's parting words.

Kelly had already loaded up the yard's two runners entered for the prestigious Aintree meeting. He slung his kitbag in the holdall on the side of the van and joined Kelly in the cabin.

'Ready?' she asked.

'Hope the traffic's light, knackered before we've even left. Pity this Jaguar's budget didn't stretch to a driver.'

The weighing room was beside the parade ring. Cream walls and dark wood panels. The tables were lost under piles of saddles and their cloths. The smell of veneered wood and sweat took Danny back to gym class at school in Rhymney. A smell of leather also clung to the air, now thick with tension and anticipation.

A few jockeys were slapping the back of Ronnie Mason, riding in those familiar colours of leading owner Marcus Sowers; the Scottish cowboy. He'd read reports Mason had been sidelined with a broken collarbone some months back and his peers were clearly welcoming him back from the wilderness. Big ask to make a comeback in a race like this, Danny thought, lacking match-fitness.

Minutes later, the weighing room had thinned to a smattering of jockeys. The quiet before the storm.

Tom James was one and called over, 'You could smell the fear in here just now.'

'So that's what it was,' Danny said and grimaced.

Tom smiled, as he tied the colours to his cap. He'd been riding jumpers for donkey's years, as long Danny could recall anyhow. A veteran of the weighing room. Despite this, the pair had barely spoken a word to each other. Funny how sharing a daunting experience opened people up. A kind of bonding, he guessed, all in this together, Dunkirk spirit.

Rhys was another lingering, putting off the inevitable. He approached, cap yet to be tied and goggles hanging from his neck. He placed one hand on Danny's tight shoulder and their palms met. Serious eyes and flat mouth, he said, 'Daniel, may the horse be with you.'

'Cheers,' Danny said, forcing a smile.

Rhys appeared to pick up on Danny's nerves and added, 'Seriously mate, have a good one out there, come back safe.'

'And you.'

Danny bent to pick up his goggles and whip. He turned but Rhys had already gone, a flash of his red and yellow colours slipping through the door out to the parade ring.

He paused for a moment, trying to stay in the here and now. He scanned the room, wanting it to himself, reduce the risk of being caught inserting the earpiece. He knew that wouldn't happen. The valets, now tidying up, would most likely stay on to watch the race on the TV fixed to the wall.

He was the last jockey to leave. He couldn't stall any longer as he was already late for a group photo with all the jockeys set to line up in this year's renewal. He slipped behind one of the many pillars and from a pocket in his britches removed the tiny, flesh-coloured receiver. He peeled off the wrapper and, as he'd done on the morning gallops, pushed it deep into his ear. He pulled the neck strap tight, hoping it would hold secure in the rough and tumble out there. Last thing he wanted was it to work loose and need prodding back in on the approach to the first fence. He'd have enough on his mind by then.

He shiftily looked around and then emerged from the shadow of the pillar. One of the valets, fortyish and balding, looked up and said, 'Too late to chicken out now.'

Danny matched his grin and left to meet Salamanca. On the nervous walk to the parade ring, he passed a bronze bust of legendary commentator Sir Peter O'Sullivan. His stomach turned again as he sucked in the smell of greasy burgers held by a group of young lads, all shirted in pastel shades and steadying pints of lager with their other hands. Loud, yet harmless.

Being one of the taller jockeys, Danny was positioned in the middle of the back row in the huddled ensemble for the race photo, a patchwork of colours. Faces white with fear and fake smiles as the camera flashed. The jockeys soon dispersed to go meet their bosses.

He could now hear the clop of hooves on the asphalt ring framing a grassy area, already packed with connections, very few able to stand still. The other thirty-nine jockeys stood out like exotic birds in their bright colours against owners and trainers wrapped in earthy tones.

The enclosure was filled by countless connections; trainers going over last-minute plans and tactics with jockeys while owners looked on nervously, helpless.

Despite the congestion, he'd quickly clapped eyes on Salamanca, could hardly miss the brute. He was on his toes, alert, all eyes and ears. Kelly kept a good grip on his rein as she led him round. Not long ago, he'd have needed two handlers, proof the horse had settled since joining Samuel House.

Kelly said, 'He's right on the edge, Danny, hope the bell goes before he boils over.'

Danny ran a reassuring hand down his mount's neck, wiping some of the white off. The sweat was no concern, a family trait.

A loud metallic clang told jockeys to mount and begin filtering through to the track and the pre-race parade for the cameras.

He boarded the colossal chestnut. Kelly looked up and added, 'Looks super though, doesn't he?'

'It's not a beauty contest,' Danny said.

'Only saying,' she said, frowned and then stared vacantly ahead.

The icy silence was filled by chattering racegoers standing shoulder to shoulder around the ring.

'Sorry,' Danny said. 'Bit stressed that's all, he does look well.'

Danny drew a lungful of cooling air. He blew out hard, trying to ease his cramping stomach. They were led single file under a tunnel cut into the Grandstand and splashed by sunlight emerging the other end. He barely heard the bugler's fanfare as they spilled out on to the track, parading for the thousands of fans to admire.

Salamanca was now arching his neck and flaring his nostrils, ready to do battle.

Danny's grip on reins and stick tightened. Another lungful. He felt sick, not from excitement.

The forty runners began to circle in racecard order as a young man went down the line with a Steadicam, allowing the commentators to go through the runners, riders and colours for the viewing public. Danny looked across at a sea of heads packing the series of tiered grandstands to his left.

Kelly let go of the reins and smiled, though it failed to tell in her eyes. No words were exchanged. Danny urged the buzzed-up Salamanca to join the others in a hack canter at the start.

Scudding clouds cast dappled shadows on the swirling grass and the spring sun gently warmed the nape of his neck. He bit his gloves taut and made final adjustments to the length of the stirrup leather. He shifted his weight in the saddle and boots in the stirrups until settled. He was going to ride with reins long, allowing plenty of leeway to adjust if the pair ploughed through a fence or knuckled on landing.

He clocked the starter climbing his rostrum on the inside of the track. His heartbeat picked up as his finger briefly pressed against the strap of his helmet, securing the fingernail of an earpiece in place. Goggles up and a few dry swallows. This was it. *Showtime.*

Since slipping the flesh-coloured patch into his ear, he hadn't heard a peep from Ethan. Perhaps he never would, with all the TV and radio signals scrambling the air.

All he could hear now was the rumble of a helicopter's rotor blade high above, beaming aerial shots worldwide, and the thud of his racing heart. Not only was he about to take on the same daunting Grand National course he'd watched in awe on the TV beside his dad as a kid, he was also about to cheat, against all he stood for.

'One, two, three, testing,' came into his ear, little more than a whisper above crackling interference. It fell silent as if the feature presentation was about to start and then the voice returned louder and clearer, 'Ethan clocking on, if you can hear me okay roll your neck once now.'

Danny reluctantly did so.

Ethan said, 'Good.'

Danny didn't react any more, aware this was a one-way device. His eyes fixed firmly on the jowly face of the starter, now lost behind a large megaphone, allowing him to assert his authority on such a large field of geed-up jumpers above a full house packing the stands.

'Get yourself organised, jockeys,' the megaphone blared, voice slightly digitised. The runners began to trot, circling faster and faster, like a whirlpool, anticipation growing. Jockeys and horses, both athletes coiled like a spring, primed to produce their A-game for the richest steeplechase in the world. 'Want a clean start jockeys, hold back … wait!'

The runners spread across the breadth of the track, walking forward, making some sort of order. Danny shook his reins and kicked Salamanca in the belly, urging him to go with the flow, sitting just off the likely pacesetters.

'Turn at the back,' growled the starter to someone clearly facing the wrong way. 'That's better, move in, we're ready. Go!'

The tape rose. The wall of sound from the racegoers struck Danny as he sat low, pushing the powerhouse beneath him to gain a good pitch.

The one-hundred and sixty hooves thumped the drying ground, like the rumble of distant thunder, as the twenty tons of horseflesh made the cavalry charge to fence one, leaving the towering Grandstand behind.

Danny spotted Rhys' vibrant red and yellow silks on a lively hope called Bright Lights a couple of lengths ahead as he continued to persuade his street-fighter to go with this frenetic early gallop. They streamed over the brown Melling Road cutting the course, tanking now. To his right, growing spectators perched on a grassy bank yelled and cheered in delight, carried along by the stampede.

The massive field gathered momentum on the lengthy 420-yard stretch to the first fence over a velvety carpet cut into striped and chequered shades of green.

Glossing up on the race, Danny had read boffins at some university reckoned runners were seven times more likely to come a cropper at this than any other ditchless plain fence on the course because of the sheer speed of the approach. Danny reined Salamanca in, fight that trademark exuberance. Yet his giant stride still ate up the ground on the approach. Three-two-one. He dwarfed the four foot six wall of fern, clearing the fence as if it was a hurdle.

The perfect marriage of man and beast as they streamed over, though three became divorced; one faller and two unseating. Danny heard a gasp from the crowd.

A market leader must've tipped up, he reckoned, though his eyes remained fixed ahead.

He could see the majority of the field group towards the centre of the course, possibly searching for the best ground. Danny wasn't interested. Keen to steer clear of trouble, he drifted across to the far rail, lying about twelfth, a few places behind second favourite Layabout.

Danny felt Salamanca had become a bit flighty, perhaps upset and buzzed up by the growing roar of the crowds lining either side. He needed settling. He managed to find some cover behind Cocktail Surprise, who he knew was a safe jumper, no concerns about getting brought down.

'Move out to centre, more space there,' Ethan's voice came down the line. But the second fence was upon them. 'Now!'

Danny did as he was told, mindful of Ethan's threats. He yanked hard right, sending Salamanca's hulking frame off kilter as the pair left the ground. His barrel skimmed low through the forgiving fence, sending foliage up in the air. No energy or momentum lost, Danny felt.

Behind, he heard a few shrieks from jockeys fired into the firming Liverpool turf. No casualties in front.

A rush of cool spring air and Danny picked up the sweet smell of freshly cut grass.

He'd made a few places as the field headed towards a big ditch, with its yawning six-foot gap on the take-off side. A stretch for most jumpers and it was where previous winner Party Politics, a similarly giant chaser, fell in 1996, though it proved no problem for Salamanca, who negotiated it with aplomb and had now found a decent rhythm for one so young. He also met the fourth and fifth, merely plain fences, on a good stride. Jockey and horse needed to understand each other instinctively, like an old married couple. Danny knew it was his job to deliver the gelding to meet the fences right. He also knew Salamanca was a clever jumper and, if they made a mistake, it was most probably Danny's fault. You rarely see a rider-less horse fall.

As soon as he'd found some space on the inside, a loose horse darted up his right flank. Danny tugged on his left rein to swerve the rudderless runner; a potential banana skin, mindful of the upcoming Becher's Brook - the most famous steeplechase fence in the world - named after the jockey Captain Martin Becher, who fell there in the first official Grand National and took shelter in the ditch. Danny was once told in the weighing room

175

that Becher had reflected after, 'Water tastes disgusting without the benefits of whisky'.

God knows, Danny felt like a stiff drink right then but he knew the fear helped sharpen his mind and give the fences the respect they deserve on this white-knuckle ride. Its steep drop-side was a good deal lower than the take-off, taking many less experienced horses and jockeys by surprise, expecting the ground to arrive quicker than it does, an eerie falling sensation, like missing a step.

'Take him right,' Ethan's voice growled. But Danny feared that'd put him on a collision course with the loose runner. He guessed Ethan wanted him to tackle the brook wide as the drop side is less harsh that side of the course. It went against all his instincts. Danny hesitated.

'Pull him right!' Ethan said. 'Three!'

Danny obeyed the code number, sending Salamanca off a true line, baulking the diminutive rival aside in a barging match just strides before the daunting fence. Salamanca lost balance from the altercation and his normal fluent stride began to stutter. The gelding's large head tossed left and right, clearly upset. He cocked his jaw. He wasn't liking this.

Danny felt like flicking the earpiece out there and then. It wasn't helping. But Ethan's words returned to haunt him, the fate of Samuel House is in your hands.

Danny gathered up the reins to get his charge organised and then pushed on into Becher's, keeping both their minds on the job, while gathering momentum. The ground fell away. He pulled on the reins and shifted his body weight back in the saddle to act as ballast as Salamanca skimmed off the top layer of fern, bracing for impact the other side. He feared Salamanca's legs would buckle under the force of half a ton hitting the turf on impact the other side. But they were strong and cushioned the blow with ease. Unlike one of the 200/1 no-hopers to his right, skidding to a stop yards after the fences, jockey curling into a ball like a threatened spider, as the pursuers desperately sidestepped the stricken pair.

All the while, Danny could hear the snorts and heavy pants from both jockeys and horses, above the rumble of hooves.

Danny barely had time to adjust his goggles when the Foinavon fence came upon them; named after the only horse to jump the fence at the first attempt, swerving the ensuing pile-up behind, en route to glory in 1967.

Danny knew Salamanca would struggle with a sharp left turn into the straight after the fence. He edged out into the middle of the track to avoid having to jink soon after the jump, saving momentum. He cut the corner fine and avoided another loose horse. No such melee this year. Salamanca's ears were now pricked. So were Danny's as he waited for the next command.

He let the handbrake off and the response was instant, moving up a place and drawing alongside Tom James on his inner. He heard the veteran ask, 'What you got left?'

Danny looked across, surprised he cared. Turned out the veteran was asking another jockey on the rails, masked from view. He wouldn't have answered either way, mind too consumed by the shoddy orders fed through the earpiece.

He could picture the press hounds slating him for having a crack at the 'big one' on such an inexperienced chaser. Scarring him mentally and physically by taking on such a mammoth task, rather than taking the softly-softly approach with future campaigns in mind. He'd stick two fingers up at the lot of them; Salamanca was his and he knew more than anyone what the chaser was and wasn't up to. They were low on the list he needed proving wrong. Topping that list was Danny himself. Winning on Salamanca would not only rate a pinnacle of his stop-start riding career but cement his credentials as a trainer and further confirm it was Sam behind the faltering start to his rookie campaign at Samuel House.

He'd now made headway to track Ronnie Mason, catching a flash of his face, now a glistening beetroot, and got a nose-full of stale sweat as that rival jockey's arms continued to flap away on his equally legless mount, Mason's injury layoff clearly now taking its toll.

Danny was coasting, sitting motionless, but he knew there was an even sharper bend in the course after clearing the next – the Canal Turn. He was about to deploy similar tactics as at Foinavon, hand tightening around his right rein. But the voice returned, 'Stick to left rail. Too much traffic on your outer.'

Danny's vision had become blurred. One swift motion, he peeled off the outer pair of goggles, now covered in dust from the spring ground.

There was no time to see how bad it was on his outside and, toeing Ethan's line, he tracked the rail, going the shortest way. Although Salamanca was built like a tank, he steered like one too and, after clearing the Canal Turn and the brook on its drop-side, he was forced to slow to a hack-canter as he persuaded his ride to bank a near ninety degrees left, avoid veering wide on a collision course with a pack of runners taking a more orthodox route on his outer.

Soon, momentum returned.

'One!' came down the earpiece. Danny processed the code in a flash, yanking the handbrake on, fearing a loose horse was about to cut him up. Pulling on the reins, Salamanca's head reared up, wanting to go faster. The stunt cost them three places. But where was the loose horse, nothing ahead but clear seas.

'Fucking useless,' Danny shouted, though he knew Ethan couldn't hear. Was he playing games?

'Nowhere near ya,' came from his inside. It was Irish jockey Colm Maguire, easing off as his mount was already spent, legless having helped force the early gallop.

'Not you!' Danny shouted, though he felt bad taking out his pent-up frustration on an innocent passer-by.

He pushed on again, tapping into Salamanca's seemingly limitless reservoir of stamina. He swiftly made up any lost ground and a few places, now a handy sixth.

But he knew any more stunts like that would scupper dreams of winning. What was Ethan's plan? Barge and bully the rivals into submission? This isn't a fucking Stock Car Derby!

178

Valentine's Brook was up next, similar to the Canal Turn with over five foot of ditch to clear on landing side and not as dangerous as Becher's.

Danny's nostrils pricked at the smell of wet grass carried on the freshening breeze; the clerk of the course had clearly watered this stretch to prevent jarring ground.

Salamanca found a trademark leap, front feet landing clear of danger, restoring some welcome confidence.

The following straight sequence of five-footers allowed Danny to collect his thoughts and Salamanca to regain equilibrium. He was amazed the colossal gelding hadn't lost his leg action and gone lame, all that he'd been through.

Nothing daunting about the first in the straight named Thorn Fence in front of the Sefton Stands. Not for Salamanca, who lifted his shoulders, flexed knees, conjuring a massive jump, to clear the fern with daylight spare. His landing gear came out and they were on to the next.

It was a similar story at the upcoming Booth fence. Straightforward by all accounts and Salamanca again made it seem that way. He belied inexperience to clear the six foot ditch preceding the five foot of vegetation, those laps on the hunting ground now paying dividends.

He now held eighth of the remaining thirty-one surviving runners as they ploughed on to the twelfth fence, what will be the third-last next time round. Another fluent jump, unlike Toby Eaton on Carpetbagger, who'd been moving sweetly just ahead only to overjump and fire Toby into the air. Danny didn't have chance to look back, see if both had got up, as the thirteenth fence was up next, the first in the home-straight. Danny would feel happy once he'd completed a circuit. No more hidden surprises, he hoped.

'Jump!' Ethan said, catching Danny off guard. Thankfully Salamanca couldn't hear the same and winged it, now seventh.

The final fence next time round was upcoming. He jumped it almost too big and bold, as if to impress the sea of racegoers packing the stands. A roar came as he pushed the punters' favourite into fifth, the highest ranking he'd been since flag-fall.

But Danny knew they were merely halfway – and what had his baby left to give? Having suffered interference on the first circuit, he suspected not a great deal. No time for a mid-race assessment as his thoughts quickly turned to the mighty Chair, one of the most daunting fences ever built. Danny kept low urging his mount to find some kind of rhythm. An orange board at its base encouraged the horses to take off early. But it didn't work for the pacesetter Red Letter Day. Danny couldn't help but witness the car crash as the long-time leader failed to get his legs up, rooting the fence.

Head down, Salamanca appeared to eyeball the stack of fern, taking it on with relish rather than shying away. He got over a little low, but the fence came off worse in the argument. George was right, *what a tank!*

The sixteenth was only negotiated once. Danny knew it was a low fence, standing just below three feet, but it needed to be, as there was a near nine-foot channel of water the other side. More of a long jump than a high jump. It provided a magnificent spectacle in front of the main stands as the field gathered the speed necessary to get the length. Danny growled in Salamanca's ears, hoping he'd recall the times he'd cleared the brook at home on the hunting circuit. They left the ground and came down clear of the water hazard.

The rival at four o'clock from where he was positioned didn't, splashing his hind legs in the water, four faults and earning a slap down his flanks as a wake-up.

Most of the massive field had survived a circuit and had set off to do it all again. No surprise, given the drying ground. There was less emphasis on stamina this year and more on accurate jumping and an ability to go flat out from the get-go.

Salamanca's raking stride stretched out on the run to the next, making stylish headway into fourth. 'Ease off,' Ethan said, 'It's a marathon, not a sprint.'

Danny took his foot off the gas, sending out the wrong message to Salamanca, who got in close and breasted one of the easier fences on the track. He got a slap on his rump as a reward.

'Focus!' Danny growled, though he knew the fault lay solely with him for taking notice of Ethan.

Fence nineteen, a six-foot ditch overlooked by houses. A couple of proven stayers had made a forward move, demoting Danny to eighth. Another slap on that powerful behind yielded no response this time, other than a slow drift towards the far rail, handling even heavier than normal. Was this the beginning of the end?

'Come on!' Danny said, asking for a big one to help keep in contention. Like a marathon runner, Salamanca had hit a flat spot and was struggling to keep up pace and fluency. Hopes were fading with every shake of the reins and sloppy jump.

Fence twenty-three was Foinavon for the second time, where the course narrows. He'd now lost touch with the leaders, but could make out Rhys' vibrant silks on Bright Lights up ahead. His bobbing yellow cap was lost the other side. Danny's concern had switched to his stable jockey.

He steered Salamanca wide. Landing safely on the drop side of the fence, he glanced over to see Bright Lights struggle to his feet before carrying on the pursuit, while Rhys had scrambled to safety and then whipped the rails, like a child having a tantrum.

Danny's relief from having negotiated the sharp turn was soon wiped as Ethan commanded, 'Push your way through, boss them.'

Couldn't get a cigarette paper between those, Danny reckoned, tucked in behind the rear-end of two rivals riding tandem.

He did as he was told and forced his way between the runners, featuring last year's runner-up Tailor Trade. Salamanca was the meat in the sandwich. His brute strength and gladiatorial spirit bullied his way through. There would only be one winner in this tussle.

'What the fuck!' came from his left.

'Jesus!' from his right.

Danny hadn't the time or inclination to hold his hand up. He was more concerned by Valentine's just strides away, the first of a line of four on the side of the course. Vital to meet this right, garner confidence for what lay ahead. But Salamanca had lost some zest since playing dodgems and his stride shortened. Was he finished?

Danny could do little but brace himself as Salamanca paddled through the fern, brushing off the crown of the fence and sending the green stuff flying. He did well to find a leg the other side. Danny was shunted back but managed to stay on board. He switched to the outer, affording some space and time.

It was now Danny's stamina, rather than Salamanca's, being called into question. He'd never ridden beyond three miles and was entering unknown territory. He knew he'd have to cross new pain barriers to last the distance.

He sat lower and asked for more, but the answers still didn't come. No surprise, after all Danny had put the gelding through. The next was a regulation fence though there was nothing regular about any of those walls of vegetation. Another low jump. This wasn't the Salamanca that'd won Danny over.

Perhaps it was time to cut losses and pull up. Ethan would have to understand. It just wasn't their day and there would be others.

As if able to read Danny's thoughts, Ethan called. 'It's a lost cause. Ease down.'

He was surprised by Ethan's apparent concern for the horse.

Danny could see the fourth last fence grow larger. It was nearly time. Soon be on his own, cut adrift. But lying a distant eighth, well off the pace, he knew the plan had backfired badly.

He'd just about come to terms with that final order, ready to wave the white flag on Salamanca, a bright prospect who didn't deserve being beaten up. But still it went against his competitive spirit and he stalled on quitting until after the fourth last, just in case Ethan had a late change of mind, or had seen a pile up ahead, giving him renewed hope.

The earpiece fell quiet. Had Ethan jumped ship already? Given up the ghost, like Danny had.

He then heard, 'Almost time to part ways, Danny, just enough to thank you for guiding Salamanca blindly into trouble.

We've laid you big-time in the place market on the exchanges. Salamanca finishing out of the front four means we collect, finally some return from our investment. You've done well. And now we part ways.'

Danny saw red. He flicked the earpiece out and cried, 'Fucker!'

No wonder he'd yet to hear code-six: charge forward. But he no longer needed telling. Fired on by sweet revenge, he growled and shook the reins, slapping Salamanca's powerful behind with a couple of sharp reminders.

Fire filled his belly and eyes on the approach to the fourth last. There was still a chance, however remote, he could foil Ethan's massive bet and pick up some much-needed place prize money as a kind of severance pay. It wasn't too late to grab something positive from this though he knew Salamanca had been through the wringer and was still toiling in a remote eighth.

Most horses would've called it a day several fences back, petrol gauge flashing red. But Salamanca wasn't like most horses. He caught a glimpse of rivals up ahead meandering, punch-drunk. This gave Danny hope.

He set about the chase. Sitting lower in the saddle, he rousted the brutish street-fighter beneath him, and drew an instant response. One he hadn't expected after previous requests had failed. He asked for a big one at the fourth last fence, gain some impetus. With a wet sail, he would soon eat into the deficit.

Being an alpha male, Salamanca came up with the goods and more. Almost jumping too big, he cleared the six foot ditch at the Booth fence for the second and final time with ground to spare, though he pitched slightly, throwing Danny's weight forward. He quickly shuffled back and wasted no time rousting his charge, who appeared to respond to the sudden injection of urgency from the saddle, finding a second wind.

Danny couldn't kid himself. He knew exacting revenge on Ethan by finishing in the top four was a long shot. But merely making him sweat for his ill-gotten gains would be worth the effort and spurred him on. While there was breath in both their bodies, he'd try his damnedest.

The horse in seventh was Jolly Hockey Sticks, who they'd thumped by twenty lengths at Chepstow. Danny was confident he could uphold that form. Easy pickings for the rejuvenated Salamanca, who gained a place with a quick and low jump at the third fence from home, last of the quartet of five-footers.

A good half-mile journey before they saw the penultimate fence, Danny reckoned.

As they crossed the Melling Road again, he felt Salamanca pick up speed, as if sensing they were on their way back to the stables. The horse currently in sixth, Time Please, was still a good seven lengths away and not stopping, as those ahead banked left into the home-straight on a lung-burning gallop for the line. He felt like he was wearing a suit of armour.

Having asked a question and got an immediate answer, Danny couldn't let his stable-star down. Not now. He could sniff the sweet smell of revenge and any prize money from ranking highly would help keep Samuel House in business for another season. He'd take home a hundred grand for third or fifty grand for fourth, seeing as Danny would also keep the ten per cent normally deducted for both the trainer and jockey. He no longer cared about Ethan's threats. Deal with those as and when.

They'd closed to within five lengths from Time Please, four lengths, three. He'd built up a full head of steam, unlike those in a protracted duel up front, now on their last legs.

Buoyed by taking sixth place, his arms and legs moved as one with the motion of the horse, finding a rhythm to maintain momentum. A clean leap at the second from home would see him go fifth, passing the colours of Yellowstone Ranger, who was now paying the price for a tough race in the Gold Cup the month before. His wishes were answered, Salamanca taking off on an accurate stride at this fairly routine fence, if there was such a thing round there. He skipped over the fern as if it was one of the baby fences at home. But he knew Ethan would collect if Salamanca finished out of the front four. He needed to catch a runner in front, either Tailor Trade or See No Lies involved in a private battle a good eight lengths ahead. It was a big ask but his sights were blinkered and the gruelling 494 yards dog-legged run-

184

in after the final fence had proved a fortune-changer over the years and would afford him some leeway in the chase.

Keep going kid, Danny thought, as Salamanca started to shy away from the raucous cheers given off by the packed stands away to the right. His thoughts had fragmented, as if he'd sunk a dozen pints, no longer sure of his surroundings, the sun-kissed crowd merely brushstrokes of colour making white noise.

Danny asked for one last heroic effort to clear the final fence. He'd gathered the reins and pushed Salamanca's plaited neck forward. Beyond, he saw the shadowy shapes of those up ahead, led by Marmalade who'd struck the front. The second and third paddled through the fence, despite its low stature.

Three-two-one. Lift those sturdy legs one last time, he hoped.

Salamanca appeared to catch sight of the orange take-off board and slowed, getting in close but popping it nicely. He landed running. Nothing flashy. Salamanca knew best. Two furlongs to go and work to do. He could no longer feel his limbs, as if he'd slept on them overnight. Yet he could feel his lungs sting, burning with every stuttering breath. He knew there was an elbow where the racetrack steered the legless runners from going out on another circuit. He yanked down on the right rein and Salamanca went with the flow, no energy left to rebel. It was if he'd switched to city-steering in his Golf.

A furlong to go. Driven on by the desperate need to exact revenge on Ethan, who'd just robbed him the chance of glory, an entry in the history books and the half-a-million prize that goes along with it.

The many speakers blared, 'Marmalade wins the National.' The eighty-thousand racegoers roared.

He was jealous. That partnership could now ease down and drink in the adulation whereas Danny's job was far from complete.

His head throbbed, like the morning after a heavy night in town. His couldn't feel his arms and legs as they flapped away, driven by instinct.

185

The finish line appeared to shrink with every shortening stride. He started seeing red spots. One of them must be the lollipop stick marking the finish.

Every oxygen-deprived muscle working on fumes, barely up to keeping him balanced. He blew a ball of choking bile away, though a snail's trail flew back in his face. He didn't care. Vanity went out of the window as he now had those in front firmly in his sights.

He felt himself slide off kilter to the right and needed all his reserves to stay on board, left boot pushing down on the iron, helping to right the pitching ship.

Come on boy, Danny thought, dig deeper.

Salamanca started making a noise, struggling to fill those huge lungs to fuel that Bentley engine of his. Had the tongue-tie worked loose or was it sheer exhaustion?

The pair kept finding more from somewhere, now within spitting distance of the fourth and fifth placed horses.

Picturing Ethan's whitening face drop in the stands somewhere drove him beyond any pain barrier he'd had to clear.

This was torture. He slapped Salamanca's shiny rump one last time, eke out any last untapped energy from his partner though he knew he was scraping the barrel.

He'd drawn alongside rivals Tailor Trade and See No Lies, invading their battle for the minor money.

The commentator bellowed over the racecourse, 'Yards from the line and Tailor Trade grimly holding on for third, but See No Lies won't go away and here's Salamanca from the clouds nearside. It's on the nod, that's close, a three-way photo for the placings, with Yellowstone Ranger, a distant fifth and looking back to Showman, who's come from nowhere to take sixth.'

They'd flashed past the line. Danny didn't know whether he'd galvanised his horse to snatch fourth, or maybe even third, in the dying strides, a Herculean effort from man and horse.

He collapsed forward, clinging to Salamanca's thick neck as his body switched to standby. He now felt his weight shifting to the left. He was a spent force and was about to pass out when Kelly came running up the track and gave him a shove in the right direction. Danny gulped in another lungful of clear spring air, like menthol. Lifted by adrenalin, like the winning side of the Boat Race, but still gripped by an all-over stitch.

'What a finish!' Kelly shouted up, above the cheering crowd. 'Where did you find that from, mister?'

Danny wasn't sure who she was talking to, but suspected it was Salamanca. He wasn't begrudging.

'No longer a talking horse,' Danny puffed, holding his side, shiny reddened face creased. 'He's arrived.'

'You bet,' Kelly said, patting Salamanca on his withers.

Danny didn't dare dismount as he wasn't sure his legs could carry him back to weigh in.

Led by Kelly, they veered off into the spot marked third and Danny's boots hit the asphalt. Has the result been called?

'One of the hacks,' she paused, panting, 'they said …'

'Wha –?'

'They reckoned you'd got up for third,' she said, all eyes and teeth.

Danny didn't like pre-empting the judge and said, 'Hold fire.'

He looked on as connections, TV cameras and journalists swarmed around the 25/1 winner Marmalade, who stood proud in front of the growing crowds around the winners' circle, soaking up the applause.

Next year, Danny thought, you just wait. He leant forward, gloved hands resting on Salamanca's glistening neck, 'A year on, we'll both be older and wiser. Won't know what's hit 'em.'

Three chimes came over the Tannoy. 'Here's the result of the photograph for third place, third number twenty-three Tailor Trade.'

Shit, Danny thought. He started doubting whether they'd even made fourth. Perhaps Ethan had in fact collected on the bet at the expense of Danny. Please say thirty-six, please say thirty-six.

'Fourth number thirty-six Salamanca and fifth number sixteen See No Lies.'

Danny's hand made a ball and punched the air. He unbuckled the girth to take the saddle to the sheltered weighing area. He stepped on to the steel plate and Kelly looked down at the digital display, showing 10st4lb, and gave Danny the thumbs-up. He knew the prize money would keep the bank manager quiet for a while and help fill the hole left by the inevitable exodus of The Watchmaker, Pepper Pot, Pick Nick and co.

CHAPTER 28

Danny dropped on the wooden struts of the bench framing the weighing room, back against the wall. The BBC cameras had come in and were pointing at the winning jockey, now drenched in champers.

Danny barely noticed any of it, alert eyes skimming over a backlog of texts, mostly titled congrats or hard luck. He only opened one. It had no caller ID. His eyes widened and lips parted as he read. 'Say goodbye to wife and child.'

Danny fumbled to find the memory dial and picked out Samuel House. 'Hello?'

'Sara, it's me.'

'Hi, Danny, we watched the race, well, I looked away at the fences, couldn't bear it.'

'We?' Danny said. 'Who's with you?'

'Jack, who else? He was pointing at the screen when –'

'Sara,' Danny jumped in, 'listen to me, did you ever talk to Ethan about your parents, where they live?'

'No, why should I?'

'I need you to go visit them, now. Don't pack, just take Jack, use the Golf, no time for a taxi.'

'You're worrying me, Danny,' Sara said. 'What's happened?'

'I'll explain later, once you arrive, stay there and wait for my call. Don't go back to the yard, clear?'

'Please, tell me what's going on Danny. Are you in trouble?'

'Just go, speak soon, love you both.'

Danny hung up and stuffed his soiled silks into his kit bag. He forced the zipper shut and slung it over his stiffening shoulder. On the way out, he slapped Rhys on his back protector and said, 'Take the morning off.'

'You sure?'

189

'Safer there.'

'Eh?'

'Just stay at home, my treat. You'll thank me in the morning when your legs are killing.'

'Speak for yourself, granddad.'

'Seriously, Rhys. Stay at home.'

'Okay, boss, don't need telling twice,' Rhys said and turned.

Danny sprinted feelingly on tender legs to the van.

Leaving three races before the end of the meeting, he avoided the inevitable crush pouring from the track after the last. Only a smattering of punters who hadn't paced themselves, either staggering off drunk or sloping off skint.

He was glad to be out of those silks, certain plenty of punters would want to string him up after his dubious riding tactics on the favourite up until the fourth last fence.

Not being a household name, it was doubtful anyone would clock Danny's face, allowing a hassle-free escape.

Kelly was sat checking something on her mobile. 'Horses already boarded and ready to go.'

Perhaps that text was merely another one of Ethan's empty threats but he couldn't take the chance. Stakes were too high. The van skidded away.

One look over at Danny and she said, 'You okay?'

He didn't reply.

'Know he was the favourite, but you must be pleased with fourth,' she said. 'It *is* the National, stuff of dreams.'

'I'm happy.'

'Can you tell the face then?' Kelly said.

'Things on my mind.'

'Care to share?'

'Not really.'

'Whatever it is, quit driving like a maniac Danny,' Kelly shrieked, thrown forward in her seat. 'Got all night.'

Danny lapsed into another silence, eyes blinkered on the road ahead.

'I'm serious, what the hell's up with you? Upset the horses,' Kelly said, above the roar of the engine, yet Danny kept his foot down. 'Danny?!'

'Gotta get back,' Danny said.

'If you don't tell me,' Kelly said, 'I can't help.'

'Got a text,' Danny said, blinking his watery eyes.

'From?' Kelly asked.

Danny glanced over. 'Lover-boy.'

'What the hell did *he* want?'

'Sara and Jack dead.'

'Wha –' Kelly's hand left her lap to cover her mouth. 'Fuck … he's not serious. Some kind of sick joke. He wouldn't.'

'No?' Danny asked, tossing his phone over. 'You sure about that?'

Kelly scrolled down the text. 'He's a bastard, but no monster.'

'Trained to kill,' Danny snapped. 'And wants revenge.'

'For what?'

'I betrayed him,' Danny said.

'When?'

'On the track, refused to play ball.'

'On Salamanca?'

Danny nodded. 'Okay to keep my foot down?'

She no longer protested.

He dropped Kelly off en route and soon found himself cranking up the handbrake alongside Samuel House. All the windows were black as soot and, once he pulled the key from the ignition, it fell perfectly silent, merely the distant whinnying of a youngster in the stables out the back.

He circled the cottage but it failed to allay Danny's fears. If Ethan was lying in wait, he'd hardly make it known.

He heard the patter of his heartbeat as he turned the key in the front door. The hallway was cool and dark. He silently crept forward on the slate floor and slowly opened the door leading to the lounge. He flicked the light on. The room was just as empty, everything was in its place.

He picked up the yard's shotgun from the top shelf in the locked alcove under the stairs and, room by room, he gave it the all-clear. He returned to the lounge and downed a settling measure of whisky, resting the gun against the desk.

The horses! He rushed outside and set about unloading the precious cargo. After such an ordeal on track followed by the lengthy drive, it pleased Danny to see Salamanca still on his toes.

'Next year boy, we'll show 'em.' He suddenly felt very tired, barely able to keep his eyes open. 'Come out of the race better than me.' He checked there was feed and water and bolted the stable door sporting the nameplate Salamanca.

'Goodnight, Tank, sleep well.'

He returned to the cottage and retired to bed, thankful Ethan's threat appeared to be just that – a threat, nothing more. He didn't regret telling Sara to flee, as an added assurance. He made a mental note to phone her, knowing she'd be worried sick by now.

Danny's eyes opened as if stunned by a taser. He lay there perfectly still, ears pricked, tangled in sheets.

A muffled thud and then a crash came from the room below, the lounge.

He levered himself from the soft mattress and made for the window on his toes. He parted the lace curtains and looked down at the owners' parking spaces in rear. One look at the roof of Ethan's Range Rover and he was fully awake. Through the gloom of first light he also caught some shadowy movement in the stable block.

He'd better not be messing with the horses, Danny thought. He pressed his face against the pane and made out the shapely figure of Kelly. What the hell's she doing here?

He had to confront the intruder downstairs before she did.

He went back to the bedside to collect the shotgun and called upon the warm mattress for support when it dawned on him where he'd left it.

He braced himself before feelingly descending the wooden staircase in the dark. He waited behind the lounge door and drew another breath. His hand rested on the brass doorknob, silence the other side. Three-two-one. He twisted and pushed.

Ethan had frozen, stood there in the middle of the room. He let a glass vase, a present from Sara's mother, crash to the woodblock floor and filled his left hand with Danny's shotgun. He stepped over files and notepads lying next to the upturned desk. 'Careless,' he said and took aim.

'Why trash the place?' Danny broke the stalemate.

'They're not here.'

'Who?'

'Sara and Jack. You'll never find them.'

'I'm not after them,' Ethan said. 'This is to cover my tracks, make it look like a burglary gone wrong.'

'But your text,' Danny said, 'say goodbye to wife and child.'

'As they will never see *you* again.' Ethan said, 'would never kill innocents.'

'Explain Wilf, then.'

'He was a cancer that needing cutting,' Ethan said.

'But he did nothing wrong,' Danny snapped.

'I trusted your word,' Ethan said.

'I was wrong,' Danny said. 'Sam lied to me.'

'Blood tests for the horses came back all wrong,' Ethan said.

'Seems like Sam lied to you too,' Danny said, 'Your precious vet was behind those flops, not me.'

'No more shifting the blame,' Ethan said, 'It's over!'

'You didn't stop at Wilf, though. Did you?' Danny said.

Ethan's grip tightened. 'This isn't helping your cause.'

'Do you want me to spell it out?' Danny stepped into the room. 'T-Y-L-E-R, remember? The one you left to balloon with water from the River Taff. You were there that night, on Riverside Bridge. I saw you.'

'Bullshit.'

'Don't give me that, he named you.' Danny edged closer. 'Why do it? What had he done to you?'

Ethan's shoulders lifted slightly, as if unburdening himself of a secret, 'He hadn't done anything, it's what he was about to do.'

'Reveal your secret?' Danny asked. 'Even if he'd told me, it would've gone no further.'

'Don't give me that. If you hadn't visited him by the river, he'd still be alive, after-timing of the highest order.' Ethan's eyes screwed up as if taking aim. 'And let's not forget your foolish reaction in yesterday's race cost The Jaguar everything and, for that, you must pay the ultimate price.'

'Wait,' Danny said. 'Did my side of the bargain, rode the race to orders you wanted.'

'But not the result.'

'How was I supposed to know, cut me adrift before the fourth last fence,' Danny said. 'All bets were off from then on.'

Danny noticed the drapes had yet to be tied back. He briefly scanned the room, absorbing every detail: the files strewn across the floor, the upturned sofa, the floored widescreen TV, the phone off its cradle, Jack's toys. It was like a war zone.

'You won't find another weapon here,' Ethan said.

But Danny wasn't looking for one. Ethan's finger was now pressed firmly against the trigger, barrel pointing between Danny's eyes. He didn't doubt the ex-marine was a good shot.

With time running out, he asked, 'Don't let me die without knowing who The Jaguar is?'

It served to take Ethan's eye off the ball for the briefest moment. Danny's left arm slapped the wall, killing the lights.

He dropped to the ground, guessing Ethan would fire a pot-shot. He was right.

Danny called upon his photographic memory to skirt the desk and sofa. Neither said a word, afraid to reveal their whereabouts. Danny was aware he held a tactical edge and, when he heard the thunderous clatter of the fan-heater go flying, he knew exactly where Ethan was and charged forward, shouldering them both to the ground. His weight pinned Ethan down. He heard the clunk of the shotgun fall somewhere nearby.

Danny leant over and pawed the floor like a blind man though merely grabbed air. As Ethan wriggled and writhed, Danny's fist came down like a hole-punch but knuckles came off worst with the wooden floor. Ethan had moved his head to one side and, drawing upon superior strength, broke free from Danny's hold. Despite the searing pain from throbbing fingers, Danny jumped to his feet and turned, bracing for an attack.

Something made him sense a presence off to his left and threw a hopeful swing that way. The looping uppercut connected with something hard. Ethan's jaw, perhaps.

Both groaned from the crunching impact. There was a thud, as if Ethan's fall had been broken by the table on its side. If that was the case, Danny knew the table lamp was nearby, strewn among debris.

He knelt and fingers soon made contact with the conical lampshade. He flicked the switch on its base, hoping the plug was still connected.

The yellow light revealed Ethan, out for the count and propped up by the table. Danny closed in and leant over, extending his arm from a safe distance to place the back of his hand near Ethan's mouth. Nothing. Not even the faintest brush of air.

Danny's stomach turned over. Ethan dead posed even more problems than alive. He was about to back off from the corpse when Ethan's face lunged forward and strong jaw snapped shut, strong teeth gathering up loose skin on the back of Danny's hand.

Danny howled and instinctively pulled away but was held by Ethan's piranha grip, as if his jaw had locked. His eyes wide and fiery.

Danny cried out, 'Let go, fucking freak.' He made a fist with his free hand and a swift right hook made contact with Ethan's temple, breaking his hold. Danny fell back and cradled the open wound. 'Fucking animal.'

Ethan spat out some skin and blood.

If he wasn't The Jaguar, he acted like one.

Ethan shook his head, as if to clear a punch-drunk mind, and then struggled to his feet but needed the table edge as support, Danny's fists having made some impact. Ethan made for the door, slipping on loose leaf paper and stationery as he went, leaving a trail of red.

'I'll be seeing you,' Danny called out confidently, mindful the Greyfriars Road raid was planned for tomorrow. He got to his feet and picked up the shotgun. He rushed to flick the hallway light on. But the front door had already slammed shut. Danny went to the bowl to grab his keys but Sara had taken them. He slipped on riding boots in the hallway and went in pursuit. Stood on the front doorstep, he could see distant flashing red dots as the shrinking Range Rover snaked the driveway. Wielding the gun, Danny ran to the stable block, check Kelly was okay.

'Morning Danny,' Kelly said, 'thought I'd look in on our champ to be. He'd eaten up and looks fresh as a daisy.'

'Good, get a saddle on him,' Danny said.

'I said he's well, but he's earned a day off, no?'

'Ethan was here, didn't you see the Range Rover.'

'I was mucking out.'

'Help me tack-up, quick!'

'What the bloody hell are you doing with that thing?' she shrieked, spotting the gun.

'No time to explain,' Danny said.

He tugged on the reins as Kelly was tightening the girth.

Kelly sucked in air. 'And your hand?!'

'Just a surface wound,' Danny said though it didn't feel that way as he bit back the searing pain, adrenalin only helping so much.

He knew it would take at least five minutes to circle the farmland by meandering country road and, taking the fields as the crow flies, Danny reckoned he could cut Ethan off before the junction. There was time, just.

He walked Salamanca out. He turned right before mounting and urging him forward.

'Haven't woken up?' Kelly asked. 'The schooling ground's down there.'

'Taking the scenic route,' Danny called back. 'Has to earn his holiday first.'

As soon as they met the green stuff, Salamanca went from a walk, to a canter to a gallop in a matter of strides. He cruised at racing speed with surprising ease, no sign of stiffness, or any hangover on the morning following the afternoon before.

It felt like Salamanca had already enjoyed a summer's rest in the lower paddock. His giant stride effortlessly covered the ground. Bouncing off the dry farmland, they'd soon crested the rise. He still held out hope they'd meet the road in time. The broken fence marked the boundary of his land. His grip tightened on both rein and gun as he pushed on. Salamanca floated over the wooden barrier, spring-heeled like a show jumper. He was clearly up for it.

Salamanca threaded between the mature oak trunks, flew the snaking brook and low stone wall, tackling the familiar route with relish, as if it were a game. After the Aintree assault, this was child's play. They ploughed through lush grassy thickets to crest the rise and then, as the ground fell away, he began the decent.

Off in the distance, through breaks in the hedgerow, he could see flashes of shiny bottle green. Danny asked Salamanca for full throttle down the slope. The pair quickly gathered momentum. But Salamanca was a creature of habit and instinctively banked left, off back to the yard on their usual practice lap. Danny fought off this urge by yanking hard on the reins to stay on course for the road below.

He feared such a large horse may become unbalanced and injured changing tack on such a steep slope. The gelding didn't deserve that, not after the heroics at Liverpool. He eased off slightly, letting Salamanca freewheel.

Momentum from the hill helped keep up speed as they met flatter ground, galloping alongside the hedge. He glanced over his shoulder and saw glimpses of the Range Rover pass him. Up ahead, another large hedgerow. Danny wasn't sure what lay the other side. He was running out of real estate.

He lifted the shotgun and kept glancing to his left. The breaks in the hedge were less frequent now. He took aim at the wheels, but the barrels were lolling this way and that. Not keen on another murder charge, he lowered it to rest beside the saddle. He caught the briefest glimpse of Ethan's grinning face as he sped away.

Danny eased off and Salamanca drew to a stop, blowing jets of steam in the cool morning air. He felt like firing an air shot to vent his anger and give Ethan a scare, though it would only serve to make the gelding bolt. And Ethan wasn't worth risking the well-being of his pride and joy. He turned and cantered back to the yard.

CHAPTER 29

4.14PM. Danny entered Raymond Barton's bookies on Greyfriars Road. T minus forty-six minutes. His eyes had grown accustomed to the lipstick red interior. He was relieved to see it was business as normal. A handful of middle-aged gents engrossed by the bank of monitors, while the three gaming machines were flashing and playing tinny tunes as punters fed them coins. Stony was at his usual ledge. Basil was straightening a spoke on his bike. Harry was busying himself, probably counting out the cash delivery.

The in-house announcer came over the speakers, 'We're still running late at Wincanton for the four-fifteen. Looks like we're going to clash as they're almost all in the boxes for the four-twenty at Doncaster and that's where we'll go for commentary.'

No sign of Ethan or any armed raider. He wasn't sure if he felt relief or dismay. This was perhaps his last opportunity to catch Ethan in the act red-handed.

He went over to urge Stony to leave early but his mate was having none of it.

'Go have a drink on me,' Danny said, waving a tenner. 'Please.'

'Having a rare good day,' Stony said, 'gonna make the most of it. Can't quit on a winning run, like gold dust for me. What's with you today anyhow?' He then smelt his armpits, 'Had a shower this morning.'

Danny gave up and joined others watching the closing races on the afternoon cards though his eyes were trained on the tiny digital clock in the corner of the screen, not the action unfolding.

As the seconds ticked, his stomach grew tighter. He was the only one aware of the potential carnage impending, yet he couldn't call the police on merely a hunch.

T minus four minutes. Danny was back with Stony.

'Dodgy stomach,' he said. 'Gonna take a load off my mind.'

'Too much detail,' Stony said.

'You're looking peaky, Stony, get some fresh air,' Danny said, one last try.

Stony gave him a look and said, 'Air is air.' He returned to the form-sheets pinned to the wall.

Danny hadn't an answer for that and left for the gents. He stood there, waiting.

He splashed some water over his burning face and turned when he heard noises the other side of the door. Sounded like a scuffle, or fight kicking off.

He edged closer, face near the black paint of the door. Ever so slightly, he pulled the handle. Was it merely an argument between two punters or had they gone ahead with the raid?

Staring intently through the finest of gaps, a finger of light ran down his face, over his alert eyes. He saw two figures brandishing guns. They wore black with balaclavas.

The tall one leant over the red counter and pushed the barrel in Harry's ashen face, shouting, 'The safe, open it, and the tills.' He then turned to the punters. 'Everybody down and you won't get hurt. Down!'

Only one didn't. Basil remained on his feet and blurted out, 'What's it all about, Alfie?'

Danny no longer needed to ask why he kept saying that. Clearly couldn't help it, some kind of Tourette's, probably brought on by stress.

'Hello, we've got a wise guy,' the raider at the counter growled. Basil just stood there, his bald patch shining under spotlights.

Probably thinks Basil's taking the piss, Danny reckoned.

'Sort him,' the raider told the shorter accomplice wearing a baggy top, who paced over and, with the butt of a gun, made sure Basil joined the others on the floor. Basil didn't even react or flinch as the gun came down in an arcing blow on his neck. The side of his glass eye; a blind spot. The pain in his neck was probably the first he knew of it.

200

Bodies lay strewn across the bookies' floor, like no man's land.

He saw Stony's creased face look up at the gap in the door and his hand was shooing Danny away. It only served to catch the eye of the lookout of the raiding party. Danny let go of the door to rest shut. Trapped. Shit!

He heard a muffled, 'Go check.'

Danny made an about-turn, away from danger. He glanced up to see if he could slip through the clerestory windows high above. No time.

He turned to the cubicles for refuge, two stalls ahead. He closed the left door and slipped into the one on the right, also shutting that one behind him but he didn't slide the lock. There was no roof to the stall, just seven-foot walls, linked by the bar forming the top of the doorframe. He jumped on to the toilet seat, and then cistern before hoisting his light frame up. His arms and legs took the strain as they spread, low and wide, straddling the stall above the toilet bowl. His hands and feet gripped the top of the cubicle walls, perfectly balanced, like a pond-skater. Drawing upon the agility and balance honed from years in the saddle, he waited, eyes entranced by the door ahead, primed to pounce.

He knew the main door would soon burst open, any second now. He slowed his breaths as he heard the thud of the black door, dulled by a rubber buffer on the wall. He hoped the smaller of the masked robbers would go deal with him. Seemed likely, given the other was busy bagging the loot. He kept fully focused on the inside of the cubicle door ahead. The rhythmic smack of leather on ceramic tiles ran right through him.

His limbs started to shake, overloaded by a mix of physical strain and tension. Can't hold this much longer, he thought. He hoped those morning runs and lifting weights at night would now pay dividends.

He spotted the top of the left door swing open and lowered slightly, making sure the armed raider couldn't see him crouched high above and across, hidden by the cubicle divide. His muscles tensed like a coiled spring.

As the door ahead then blasted open, he pushed forward with his feet, like a sprinter from the blocks. His hands reached for the metal strip connecting the cubicle walls.

Feet first, he swung forward like a gymnast on the high bar. He kicked the masked robber in the chest, both crashing to the shiny floor.

The gun skated to rest under one of the sinks. Danny looked over but didn't go after it, wary of being implicated in the robbery.

He made a break for it and burst on to the bookies' floor. The robber at the counter turned the gun from Harry to Danny but didn't say anything. Perhaps it was Ethan, afraid to reveal his true identity to Danny.

Danny held his breath and made for the glass door; the only way out. He leapt and swerved the floored bodies though knew he was an easy target if the trigger was pulled.

'Stop!' growled the robber. 'Down or you'll die!'

Danny took hold of the vertical metal bar on the glass door. He glanced across and saw the masked raider raise the gun, finger poised. The black sleeve rode up his extended arm to reveal black gloves. Except these had a suede wristband. It shot Danny straight back to Ethan's hallway.

'Said I'd see you again,' Danny said clearly. He made sure those looking on would pick up on this, hoping police would run through all of Danny's associates and stop at Ethan.

Those sharp blue eyes narrowed in the holes cut from black cloth. It was the reaction Danny was after.

'It's over!' came back.

Danny pulled on the bar and called back, 'Don't bet on it.'

He was struck by a strong spring breeze whistling down Greyfriars Road. He sprinted away on block-paving, past a white van parked up. Was it their getaway?

The briefest shoulder-glance saw the black shape of the robber, gun now concealed, on his tail.

Whether to make his escape down Queen Street, or seek cover in the castle grounds or head for St Mary Street, via St

David's Way? Instinct made him opt for the last option, more side streets with nooks and crannies to hide.

Danny's lungs and thighs felt the burn as he pushed on down St David's Way. Expecting a bullet in the back any stride, he was propelled by the image of Sara's face opening the door to police removing helmets, braced to deliver the bad news.

Up ahead, he saw the statue of former mayor John Batchelor. Too risky to dive for cover. Would be a sitting duck if found.

He also clapped eyes on the widening mouth of Morgan's Arcade, a shopping mall for the Victorians. He'd often used it as a shortcut to St Mary Street. It was a chance to slip his pursuer. As he jinked into the opening, he pushed past a security guard bent double unbolting a metal grille pinned to the wall. Danny called back, 'Sorry.'

'You're too late, son, I'm locking up!'

Danny didn't look around as he followed the arcing parade, lit by the grey sky filtering through a pitched-glass roof high above.

His Reeboks slapped the rough patchwork of flagstones. The snaking line of shops, juice bars and art galleries a blur.

His heart sank and pace slowed as he turned into the home stretch. He could see a mix of office workers carrying shoulder bags and briefcases, and shoppers weighed down by bulging plastic carrier bags. But they were safely beyond a metal grille. The guard had clearly locked up. A dead end.

He didn't believe it, or didn't want to, and ploughed on. He reached down to try and lift the shutter. Perhaps the guard had yet to bolt it down. The metal lattice work rattled, echoing back the way, as he shook with a rage. An immovable iron cobweb and Danny was the fly, trapped, awaiting death.

'Help! Please help!' His eyes were wild as he shouted out to passers by, most kept their head down and carried on their way, as if afraid to even acknowledge the actions of a madman. He turned. Face it like a man. A loud crack of gunfire pinballed off the glass walls and flagstones. Danny shuddered. Had the security guard got in Ethan's way?

A shadow spread, like a growing slick of oil, along the sweeping line of shop displays to his right. Like a hunted animal, survival instincts took over and he rushed to the window crammed with cameras on tripods, below the shop banner Fowler and Sons' Visual and Audio Shop. He glanced across and saw the masked robber appear into view, gun raised and closing fast.

Danny cranked up his elbow and, like a battering ram, jabbed down sharply at the shop-front, sending glass flying. He leapt through the jagged hole he'd made and waded past the display stock, knocking cameras like dominoes and crunching on a carpet of broken glass.

He noticed a multiplex of plasma TV sets to his left, all showing the same screensaver. He leapfrogged the counter and crouched into a ball the other side, head resting against a silver box that looked like a digital set receiver, probably linked by the shopkeeper to those TVs. He hoped the raider would return to the loot while there was time.

He winced at the screeching alarm high above on the wall behind the counter. He looked down and was shocked by the blood. For a moment, he couldn't believe it was his. Adrenalin masking the pain. Shit! In the soft green light from the glass display cabinets, he checked each limb and soon found the source. His left arm was leaking.

He needed to get out of there while physically able. He glanced over the counter and swiped a display model of a handheld video camera screwed to a tripod. He dropped as he saw the masked man appear, legs ballooning over the glass fangs of the shop window. Another deafening bang and the alarm died.

He listened intently for the crunch of glass, telling him the trigger-happy raider was nearing, the distant roar of buses and taxis from St Mary Street a reminder of routine life unfolding just yards away.

He weighed the tripod as a potential club. He looked over at that silver box with a red LCD light glowing on its face and had an idea. He pulled the wire from the input socket on the back of the box and replaced it with the one coming out of the camera. His hand went to cover the lens. He heard another crunch, louder this time, the gunman clearly not giving up having come this far. Danny half-expected the masked head to loom over the counter and finish him off.

From where he crouched, warmed by his own juices, he could see an edge of the final row in the bank of TVs. The screensavers had been replaced by ghostly grey shadows.

'Don't be shy, Danny. I won't kill you,' a voice sounded. Ethan. 'I mean, who'll we find to train us winners?'

Danny didn't rise to the bait. He just got onto his haunches, ready to strike. He turned the camera on himself and got psyched. Three-two-one.

He whipped his hand away and stood. Ethan swivelled to face the sixteen screens, all showing a close up of Danny's face staring back, like something from Orwell's 1984; the only book that'd left an impression on Danny at school.

Ethan fired three panicked shots, killing three of the screens. He appeared confused, transfixed by the bank of faces, like a Warhol print. Reminded Danny of tennis fans on Henman Hill waving at the big screen before realising the camera was behind them.

Danny didn't stand and stare. He dropped the camera as he cleared the counter and lunged forward in one swift motion.

Ethan had now turned on his heels to face Danny but hadn't the time to aim and fire. Danny shouldered him to the ground.

Straddled on top, he anchored Ethan to the carpet of glass. He grabbed the wrist of Ethan's gun hand and squeezed like a boa constrictor.

Ethan grunted. Danny's free hand came up, splashing blood as he swiped the gun from Ethan's loosening hold. Knowing the gun would shortly be hot property for the police, Danny tossed it to settle somewhere beneath the TV screens.

He scrambled to his feet and fought off the giddiness from getting up so sharply. He made a concerted effort not to look down, inspect the damage. He'd probably pass out if he did. He glanced over at Ethan on all fours, searching for the gun. He looked up and said, 'You were right about that text.'

The only recent text Ethan had sent read, 'Say goodbye to wife and child.'

Distant sirens were growing louder. The net was closing.

He retraced his path out of the shopping parade, slower this time. He unzipped his jacket and concealed his bloody arm. His free arm pressed down against that side of the coat, cutting off the trail of blood behind him.

He saw the guard curled into a ball, clutching his chest a few yards away from the mouth of Morgan's Arcade. Fearing he'd taken a bullet or blind panic had brought on a heart attack, Danny leant down and said, 'Help is coming.'

He looked both way before heading back up St David's Way. With previous form, he knew how all this would look and didn't want to hang around at the scene of the break-in and shooting. He suddenly felt weak, legs trembling, fit to drop. As the sirens grew and blue flashes were projected up the face of St David's Hall, he knew the police would soon be swarming the area. He vanished between black railings, staggering down some steps like a drunk and fell through a door marked Gents/Dynion.

His good hand turned both taps. He made for the paper towel dispenser and drew a fistful. He stooped over the sink and looked down.

The blood was everywhere.

CHAPTER 30

Danny stepped into the squinting light. He wasn't sure how long he'd been down there but the charcoal sky told enough. As a crutch, his hand called upon a mock-Victorian lamp post. He glanced up at a nest of CCTV cameras looking down, mostly at him. Star of the show, or was paranoia taking over?

He felt more light-headed and out of it than some of those boozy nights in town as a teen.

He struggled to track a straight line as he set off for Queen Street. More blue flashes and a squad car swept into view. He didn't know whether to feel dread or relief.

Head bowed, he kept on moving. But the car slowed to stop nearby, outside St David's Hall.

The window lowered and a shadowy face shouted, 'You okay, pal?'

'Yeah,' Danny managed. His good hand came up to shield from the torchlight.

'You don't look it.'

Danny's eyes followed the path of the torch. On the paving, he saw a galaxy of red spots where he'd been stopped. He blinked, but they were still there.

'We'll get you patched up, pal,' the officer said. 'Save the questions for later.'

Danny couldn't recall arriving at the hospital, nurses saying he'd passed out on the trolley waiting for emergency surgery.

He spent the next two days recovering though it felt like a fortnight. Among the highlights: clockwatching and sculpting dried mashed-potato round the plastic plate to fool the nurse he'd actually eaten some.

Wednesday 3.47PM. Two officers entered. One uniformed, the other suited.

Danny levered himself up, propped by pillows.

The suited one scraped a plastic chair bedside and said, 'DCI Barnes, come to ask you a few questions, we'll need a full interview once you're checked out if that's okay.'

'Not really,' Danny said.

'Doctors have assured us you're ready,' Barnes said.

'Will it take long?' Danny sighed, 'Feel weak and got people I actually wanna see.' He glanced through the wall-length window looking on to the corridor where Sara stood chatting on the payphone, no doubt reassuring his mum.

'Sooner we kick on, sooner it's over,' Barnes said, leafing through a notebook.

'What's it about?' Danny asked, though he knew. He remembered Barnes' name from the newspaper article about the bookie raids.

'We're investigating the latest raid on a Raymond Barton bookies,' Barnes said, 'on Greyfriars Road.'

The other officer flipped open a pad

'Can I take you back to Sunday, late afternoon,' Barnes said.

Danny groaned and said, 'Do we have to?'

'I'll take that as a 'yes',' Barnes continued. 'A man fitting your description was seen, along with an armed accomplice-'

'No accomplice,' Danny snapped.

'You weren't with him.'

'No!'

Barnes's colleague turned over a page on that notepad, clearly a quick writer. 'We'll be more thorough and take a statement once you've left this place.'

'Something to get better for.'

'It's to eliminate you from our enquiries. You're a key witness to the armed robbery. Good info from you could lead to us catching them before another strike, prevent future casualties. Anything you can give us, however insignificant it may seem, could save lives Danny. Bear that in mind.'

'I was at the bookies,' Danny croaked. 'And before you kick off, it's my regular. I remember going to the toilet.'

'In the bookies,' Barnes said.

208

'Then heard something was up on the shop floor.'

'What exactly?'

'Shouting, like a scuffle. I was about to rush in, break up the fight, got friends in there you see, when I heard above it all 'Get down!' or something along those lines. Knew then this was no barney between punters.'

'So did you?' Barnes asked.

'What?'

'Rush in.'

'No. Thought it best to hold back, see what was going on before getting involved.'

'At that moment,' Barnes said, 'what did you think was going on?'

'Occasionally get raised voices between regulars. Normally just harmless kidding around, handbags at dawn stuff, particularly when the bookie's busy. But this was different. Deep, booming. Made my blood run cold it did. Anyway, peered through a gap in the door and saw it was an armed raid. Before I had chance to back away and call you lot, they'd spotted me. Dead man walking I was, trapped in the bogs.'

'How did you escape?'

'Managed to barge by the second robber and ran through the bookies. Pure chance the gunman at the counter didn't blow my head clean off. Best bit of luck I've had in that place.'

'Might've been a replica,' Barnes said.

'It was real all right.'

'How can you be so sure?' Barnes said, eyes narrowing.

Danny came up with, 'You could see it a mile off.'

The answer didn't appear to satisfy Barnes. 'Some sort of expert are we?'

'No,' Danny replied, 'but seen enough stuff on TV to know the difference.'

Barnes said, 'So you ran out?'

'And my luck ran out 'n all, as the gunman came after me. Couldn't believe it.'

'Quite,' Barnes gave a knowing look. 'Why do you think he did that?' Danny hadn't even chance to open his mouth when

Barnes added, 'After all, he was bagging the money, that's what he came for. You were nothing to him, why not let you go? He was masked, and he wasn't taking hostages, not their style.'

'Perhaps he feared I'd raise the alarm.'

Barnes laughed off Danny's suggestion and said, 'Think the bells going off in the bookies' would be enough.'

Danny suddenly felt uncomfortable and tried shifting his weight. It did no good.

'Moving on,' Barnes said, 'You got to Queen Street and then?'

'Legged it towards the castle, before banking left down St David's Way, past the Owain Glyndwyr pub, towards the new library. Reckoned there were more places to hide down there.'

'With the robber in pursuit.'

'Never ran so fast in my life,' Danny said. 'Managed to duck in Morgan's Arcade but it was locking-up time and I was cornered again.'

'You'll have seen the guard then.'

'And he'll have seen the fear in my eyes and also got a good look at the gunman, just ask him,' Danny said.

'He's dead.' Danny's eyes met the bright white paper on the desk. 'Danny, no one in their right minds would chase an innocent bystander halfway across Cardiff in broad daylight.'

'Can't control what others do,' Danny said and shrugged feelingly.

'Unless you knew them.'

'But I didn't, already told ya that.' He didn't want to reveal his association, not stuck here with Ethan free to take revenge on Sara and Jack or Salamanca.

His memory was fuzzy in parts and he wasn't comfortably certain it was in fact Ethan behind that cloth mask. Even if it was, it would sound the death knell for the yard.

'I don't believe you,' Barnes said. 'I've been in this business for over thirty years and, aside from the added wrinkles and raised blood pressure, it's given me a good sense of smell. Can sniff bullshit out from a mile off.'

His quiet colleague briefly stopped writing notes and smirked.

'What are you two, Chuckle Brothers?' Danny said, feeling his own blood pressure rise. 'This isn't bullshit.'

'That was the ninth raid on Raymond Barton's branches in the region alone in the past year and, together with recent raids at Wheeler's bookies in Cardiff, they all have similar profiles.'

'So?' Danny said.

'At no point do the raiders go chasing after any customers on the shop floor. Quick, efficient, in and out in the shortest possible time, smacks of experienced pros.'

'And?'

'It would take an almighty incentive for them to alter their usual plan of action, leaving the second robber in the lurch.'

'And let me guess, you still managed to let the other one slip through your grasp.'

Barnes said, 'That one had the van and took the backstreets from the scene.'

'And the one chasing me?' Danny said, stalling short of saying Ethan.

'Thought you'd have a better idea of that.'

'Wouldn't know, took cover behind the counter before he had chance to gun me down. Made my escape and last I saw of him, thank fuck.'

'Rest assured, we'll be running over the tapes in the camera shop with a fine-tooth comb. What did you have that he wanted so badly?'

'I dunno,' Danny said, blinking his eyes. 'Look, think we've already had your *few* questions.'

'Did you take some of the loot. Don't be shy, Danny, we'll treat your case with leniency if it leads to the conviction of the ringleaders.'

'No!' Danny said, now fully awake again. 'Those in the bookies will say as much.'

'Ah yes,' Barnes said. 'Your friends.'

'They wouldn't lie as witnesses,' Danny said, 'not even for me.'

'Well if it's not the money, what is it?'

'Like I said, dunno.'

'Perhaps, it was intellectual property he was concerned about, what you knew.'

'Don't understand,' Danny said, though he had a good idea.

'You knew him,' Barnes said.

'No!' Danny said, 'How many times? You're worse than water-boarding.'

Barnes reversed in his seat, scraping loudly, running right through Danny like nails down a chalkboard.

'Something I said?' Danny said, looking ahead.

'We have enough, for now,' Barnes said and then stood before threading his arms through coat sleeves. 'But I'm sure you have more to offer us, so don't go booking any holidays.'

'In this state?' Danny said, raising his arms slightly.

'Yes,' Barnes said, forcing a smile that didn't reach his eyes.

He gave his mute colleague a look and they were gone.

The cloying aftershave had yet to fade and the door barely had time to click shut when Sara burst in. Her eyes and nostrils were stinging pink.

'All right love, where's Jack?' Danny asked. 'He's okay?'

'Still with my parents,' Sara said, 'and he's fine, blissfully unaware of all this.' She leant over, mindful to give a wide berth to his left forearm swathed in soft bandages, and kissed him on the lips. He savoured the moment's respite from the pain, like another shot of morphine.

She sat on the seat warmed by Barnes. 'What the hell happened Danny?'

'You were right.'

'Then I'd rather have been wrong,' she said. 'What's this about?'

'It's a long story,' Danny said.

'I'm not going anywhere,' Sara said. 'You were caught up in the raid, I know that much, told you going to that bookies was no good for you.'

212

'It's Ethan,' Danny said. 'You're a good judge of character, better than me any road.'

'Is that why you told us to leave the house after the race, because of Ethan?'

Danny nodded, wetting his lips with water from a clear plastic cup on the bedside table.

'But why did you go back there instead?' She looked down at Danny's bandages. 'If you knew this would happen.'

'Didn't think he was after me and needed stopping. He's capable and willing to kill, if something got in his way.'

'Could've called the police.'

'Needed to be certain.'

'Of what?'

Ethan's parting words in the camera shop flashed back: 'You were right about that text.'

Knowing Ethan a bit better now, he couldn't put it down to merely an empty threat. He wouldn't put it past that psycho sinking to such murky depths.

And as Ethan was lying low, he couldn't risk revealing any more as he knew Sara would be straight down the cop shop.

'Nothing,' he said.

Danny didn't have enough evidence to nail Ethan, just circumstantial. And what if he was wrong? What if it wasn't Ethan behind that cloth mask?

'At least you're still breathing,' she said.

'Painfully,' Danny said past cracked lips.

'Was worried sick. Even Jack picked up on something was wrong.'

Danny groaned as he tried to move. Pinned to the bed by crackling starched white sheets, it felt like he wore a deep sea diver's suit. 'Sooner I get outta this place the better.'

'What did the police want?'

'Ask a few questions, what I saw, harmless stuff.'

'They didn't seem happy as they passed me out there.'

'When are they?'

'Is that it then?' she asked, reaching out to touch Danny's good hand. 'Ethan's behind bars?'

213

'Gotta get out of here,' Danny said, glossing over her questions.

'Stop saying that,' Sara said. 'Doctors will tell you soon enough when they're happy.'

Danny held a deep mistrust of doctors, ever since they'd left a swab inside him after a routine appendectomy as a twelve-year-old.

'I got scared,' Danny said. 'Not of dying, but the thought I'd never see you or Jack again. Too painful and I don't mean this cut.'

Sara tightened the grip on his hand. 'Soon have you out of here,' she said. 'Cook you a nice fry-up first meal back.'

'Cheers, but reckon I'll be dragged down the station before I have chance to put my feet up.' Sara loosened her grip and eye-line dipped. 'I didn't do nothing.' Danny tried to sit up. 'Honest, I was just in the wrong place at the wrong time, you do believe me, love.'

'Yes I do,' Sara said, grip firm again. 'Of course I do.'

Danny's face stretched to accommodate a satisfying yawn.

'Get some rest,' she said. 'And promise me you'll stop worrying.'

Danny mumbled something, eyes now shut.

The next day, he was allowed to leave, freeing up a bed for a backlog of patients. He left knowing he'd be back to remove the stitches.

CHAPTER 31

'You were the hunted?'

Danny looked DCI Barnes straight in the eye and nodded.

'Speak for the tape,' Barnes said. He wore a grey suit, champagne shirt and navy tie.

'Yeah, I was,' Danny said. He dried his palms on the dull grey veneer of the table.

'But you knew the armed assailant and that's why he ran after you through Cardiff.'

'Cos he feared I'd be a witness.'

'The thing is, I don't believe you were being chased,' Barnes put to Danny. 'You both were in on the raid and got scared off by distant sirens. We were coming and you both panicked.'

'Sure we'd leg it with a getaway van parked around the corner.'

'It was stolen only last week,' Barnes said, 'You're no stranger to trouble, you knew only too well that a vehicle check would see you both picked up before you'd sped from the scene.'

'I wondered when that'd come up,' Danny said, sat back, arms folded. 'That was years ago, I've settled, got a business, a young kid. Wanna see him grow up, so I'm keeping my nose clean.'

'But we've looked into your 'business', a racing yard that's not produced any winners this season. Managing to pay the bills are we?'

'As well as the next man.'

'Tell us about your stable's recent results.'

'Didn't have you down as a gambling man,' Danny said.

'Must be hard to cover bills and keep owners sweet, with no winners to your name.'

'Like I said, doin' okay,' Danny said, leaning forward. 'And what's that got to do with why I'm here?'

'If it were me,' Barnes said, 'I think panic would set in, then depression. I'd soon crack, only natural.'

'And resort to desperate measures,' Danny snapped, 'is that what you're angling for?'

Barnes also loomed in large, shadow sweeping across the table. Danny could feel Barnes' coffee breath brush over his flushed cheeks. 'You needed money. Playing a part in these raids was a quick fix to the problem, 18K from this one alone. Where will that money go? New gallops, perhaps, CCTV system.'

'No!' Danny protested. These guys had done their homework. A bit too close to the mark for comfort.

'Well who is it then? Who are you protecting? Names!'

'Ethan,' was about to escape Danny's lips when he put the handbrake on. What if he was wrong? What if Ethan went through with his parting threat? He was a man on the loose, ready to kill. Seemed like Sara, Jack or Salamanca were all high on his list and, even if he spared them, it would be career suicide, accusing the middleman working for the main man behind the influx of money into the yard. A sign of betrayal whether or not Ethan was the mastermind behind the raids.

'I've been stitched up,' Danny said, 'good and proper.'

'Tell us why you think that,' Barnes said, looking down at notes, 'give us names.'

Danny swerved it by saying, 'Even you lot reckon it's an inside job, said so in the local rag.'

'Don't believe everything you read.'

'Well?' Danny asked, sitting back for an answer.

'It's one line of enquiry.'

'But I've never even worked for Raymond Barton.'

'You've spent more time in their shops than those that do.'

'More than I care to mention,' Danny said, 'tell me how that'd give me access to the loot.'

'Befriending staff.'

'Only mates with one.'

'Name?'

'Harry.'

'Would that be Harold Waters?'

'Yeah.'

'Harry to his close friends,' Barnes said. 'Remind me how you just referred to him.'

'Harry,' he replied. 'And it's Danny … but I'm no friend of yours.'

'Is this the same Harry you asked several questions regarding the procedure that bookie uses to deposit large sums of money to pay out big winning bets? And let's see,' Barnes said, 'this was just a week or so before the armed raid took place at that branch.'

'Several questions?'

'In his statement, and I quote: 'Danny asked me where and when the cash payments were made, how much was kept in the safe. Went all quiet when my boss came back.' Barnes gave him a look and a show of teeth as if he'd just backed a winner. 'Being 'mates', you trusted he'd keep his mouth shut.'

Danny sighed. 'But why on earth would I ask where and when the drop-off would be made, shortly before the raid? Not stupid.'

'Quite. And something else your friends have told us.' Barnes called upon the sheet again. 'Moments before the raid took place, you were 'acting oddly', urging them to leave the premises early.'

Cheers, Stony, he thought.

'Odd indeed,' Barnes added, 'why would you do that?'

'No comment.'

'I mean, if you knew when the raid would take place, it's the least you could do for a friend.'

'I knew …' Danny snapped. 'All right, I knew. Happy now?'

'Now we're getting somewhere,' Barnes said. 'If that was the case, why didn't you call us? That is, unless you were part of it.'

'I feared it might take place. Didn't want them involved *if* I was right. It was a hunch that's all. Couldn't be certain who's involved either.'

217

'You consistently deny knowing those involved, yet,' Barnes looked up, appearing to relish the sight of Danny squirming, 'several witnesses recall you shouting over to the ringleader, before you both left, 'I said I'd be seeing you again.' Not something you'd usually say to complete strangers, is it Danny?'

'Another hunch, trying to get a reaction,' Danny said. 'But I tell ya, no way was I one of them.'

'You're full of hunches,' Barnes said, 'What's your hunch on this?' The suited chief held up a brass key settled at the bottom of a clear plastic evidence bag.

'That's got nothing to do with this.'

'So what was it doing on your person?'

'It was a key for an old house.'

'That you kept.'

'No comment.'

'What do you take us for,' Barnes said.

'No comment.'

'Do you know, or have you ever met Tyler Shaw?'

Danny pursed his lips and said, 'No.' He was aware how the meeting at the Riverbank that night would look.

Barnes picked up the same evidence bag and said, 'Is this what he gave you that night, by the river?'

'No comment.'

'An eyewitness has given us a description that matches yours.'

'Along with thousands of others,' Danny said, mind thinking back to the twitching curtain of the house opposite the water.

'That's where we have a problem. CCTV shows you on St Mary Street, in a rush. Anxious about something, were we.'

Danny sighed. He didn't know for sure if they were bluffing but there wasn't a flicker of doubt behind those steely brown eyes of the chief.

Barnes added, 'Why drag Tyler to the riverbank?'

'I didn't.'

'At night, few people around, perfect place to finish him off and let the river take it away.'

'No comment.'

'According to forensics, he was most likely killed around that time and dumped in the river. You were the last person to see him alive and were at the scene, makes you our prime suspect. So talk, clear your name.'

'He dragged me there, all right!'

Barnes leant forward again, eyes wider, as if about to reel in the catch.

'Confirm for the tape, it was you with Tyler at the River Taff that night, January 12th.'

'Yeah,' Danny said flatly, now resigned. They seemed to have more than enough evidence to place him there without the need for his say-so. 'He left a message.'

'Where?'

'On my answer-machine.'

'Is the recording still there?'

Danny pictured the answer-machine in bits by the wall. 'No.'

'Why did he want to meet?'

'To warn me.'

'Of what?'

'Didn't say.'

'Was he threatening you? Is that what happened? He attacked, you defended, he came off worse. Would explain why you ran down St Mary Street in some blind panic.'

'No! We just talked and went our separate ways. He wasn't threatening me, just warning me, there's a difference. He was on my side, gave me some advice.'

'Did he give names?'

'No,' Danny said. It was now Barnes that sighed. 'He didn't need to.'

Barnes looked up. 'Who was he whistle-blowing?'

'Someone we both knew,' Danny said, still reticent in naming names.

'Enough of the cryptic clues, Danny. Names!'

'Ethan!' Danny said. 'Ethan Player. He's an owner's rep at my yard.'

'Is this another hunch?'

'One of my better ones,' Danny said and shrugged. He felt his shoulders loosen slightly and the tiny muscles around his eyes settled.

Barnes smiled and scribbled a note to the officer beside who promptly read it and left.

'From that look,' Danny said, 'I'm guessing he's already on your shortlist.'

He only hoped they'd track Ethan down before the ex-marine had got word who'd grassed him up. He was now more concerned about the safety of Sara, Jack and Salamanca.

'But some things don't add up,' Barnes said, 'Why would Tyler bother dragging you down to the city centre and tell you something that could take seconds over the phone.'

'He also gave me something.'

'What?'

Danny's gaze fixed on the evidence bag again.

'For the tape.'

'The key in that bag,' Danny confirmed.

'Now we're getting somewhere,' Barnes said. 'Wasn't painful was it.' He slid the evidence bag over to rest in front of Danny. 'From a receipt found at Tyler's apartment, we know he got a key cut of this type a day before you met on the banks of the river. We also know something changed hands that night. Can I confirm it was the key in evidence bag 142?'

'Yeah,' Danny said. 'Didn't hang around passing it on then, clearly.'

'Why?'

'Dunno,' Danny said. 'Keen I handed it over to you lot if he died.'

'But you didn't.'

'Thought about it, last wishes of a dead man walking and all that, but, it's like witnessing a gang crime, you don't want to get involved, knowing it would put me and my family in danger, end up like poor Tyler.'

'You think Ethan masterminded the bookies' raids.'

'Can't be certain,' Danny said. 'The mask covered his face and muffled his voice.'

A flat-screen TV was wheeled alongside the table. Barnes' face was first to back away.

'Perhaps this'll jolt your memory.' Barnes clicked the telly on and a box beneath began to whirr.

They all stared at the slightly fuzzy monochrome video footage, like the moon landing. From the shadows, he could make out a place he hadn't wished to see again. It was an internal view of Fowler and Sons'. It appeared to be a still shot and the shop window was still intact.

'Look closer,' Barnes said. 'What do you see?'

After eavesdropping in the lock-up, he was convinced Ethan was behind these targeted raids but he couldn't place him for sure at the bookies. He had no concrete proof to give them.

Barnes tapped a button on the remote. 'We'll move forward to the money shots.'

Danny's slim silhouette appeared at the window. Barnes punched another button and the footage returned to play at normal speed. On the screen, Danny's elbow came down, shattering the window, now sharpening those faded memories.

'How is the arm?' Barnes said.

Danny didn't reply. Barnes wasn't genuinely concerned, merely underlining the fact it was Danny in the picture.

They both sat still. Danny looked on as he saw his own image leap over the counter, sheltering out of view from the masked raider now slowly revolving in the centre of the shop floor, gun held at arm's length.

'Wait, go back,' Danny said, waving his bandaged hand, 'there!'

As the screen froze, so did Danny, entranced by the shadows on that grainy shot.

'What is it?' Barnes said, also looming closer to the screen.

Danny's sharp eyes caught a glimpse of something.

221

As the masked raider turned sharply, searching Danny out, a slender strip of flesh appeared between jacket and balaclava. Only visible for a few frames.

'What do you see?' Barnes added.

'There,' Danny said, urgency firing his voice, as he prodded the screen.

'That black blotch, it's a jaguar.' There was no longer any doubt in Danny's mind. It was Ethan.

'How can you tell?' Barnes said, inspecting closer.

Danny didn't want blood money funding Samuel House and added, 'I've seen it close up.'

'Where?'

'On Ethan Player.'

'What else do you know about Ethan?'

'He came to me at the start of the season, not long after I'd been granted my full licence. Said he was working for a reclusive owner.'

'Called?'

'Only knew him as The Jaguar.'

'The Jaguar?'

'Like I said, he's reclusive, if he even exists at all.'

'You've never even met.'

'No, all dealings were through this Ethan.'

'Didn't that smack you as suspicious.'

'He paid the bills and left me alone to train them my way, the perfect owner.'

'You say they've invested heavily in the yard.'

'Well into six figures.'

'Where does the prize money go?'

'Back to an account called E-Holdings.'

'Have you had a cold?'

'Why?'

'Because this reeks, Danny.'

'Of what?'

'Money laundering.'

'These guys clearly like their racing, invest in a promising trainer and wait for a return with new untraceable banknotes.'

222

'But they've not had a return, not yet, results haven't been great.'

'Explains why the gaps between raids have shortened,' Barnes said. 'What else have you got on Ethan?'

'He used to work for Raymond Barton. He pushed out a colleague called Jed Simms, fellow trader there, and Ethan left soon after, stealing Jed's identity as a trader. There's his ID.' Danny raised the back of his right hand where the faded 6342 was inked.

'What's this got to do with the raids?'

'Everything,' Danny said. 'He was logging in to head office accounts to find out where and when to strike next. That's why I asked Harry, confirm my fears these weren't just random raids. They were targeted where they knew hefty cash winnings were being sent down. Like you said, an inside job. Didn't bank on them raiding that shop soon after.'

'But you did,' Barnes said, 'you were present at the raid.'

'I came across inside info soon after,' Danny said, 'Logged into Jed's account.'

'How?'

'Seems Tyler was on to the same thing, somehow managed to get one of Ethan's keys cut. Probably on one of his threatening visits to Wheeler's bookies.'

'This one,' Barnes said, fingers pressed down on the evidence bag.

'It's for a lock-up on Newtown Estate where they do their 'research', plan where and when to strike next. Probably felt they were pushing their luck raiding just one company, feared one day they'd be second-guessed. So they were hassling this Tyler, who worked as a trader for Wheeler's.'

'To hijack his log-in details and do the same to their branches.'

'You said yourself they've already started raiding them, broadening their horizons.'

'Using Tyler's account, now he's dead.'

'Guess so.'

'Is there any link between Ethan and this lock-up?'

223

'Nothing on paper, it's leased to a guy living in Flat 132 Bevan House, Trevor's his name, that's what the local youths call him anyhow.'

'And he works for Ethan?'

'Paid cash to look over it, make sure no one breaks in.'

'Because that's where they keep the money from the raids.'

Danny wanted to swerve where the money had actually gone, into Samuel House. 'Computers and Internet access, like I said, that's where they hack into the system.'

'Do you believe Ethan will visit this lock-up again soon?' Barnes asked.

'Doubt it, they space the raids out, lying low for the next big winning punt.'

Barnes wrote a note and passed it to his colleague, who promptly left the room, taking the bagged key with him. 'We're going to check if this adds up.'

'It will.'

'It's in your interest as much as ours to catch Ethan Player at this lock-up. We may need you to cooperate in an undercover operation.'

'A sting.'

'Yes.'

'What's in it for me?'

'Living your life in the knowledge he'll be safely behind bars.'

Danny shrugged. 'It wouldn't work. Why would Ethan want to visit me at the lock-up? Set off the alarm bells don't ya think, he'd be jetting out of the country before we'd set the sting up. He's no idiot. He must know it's odds-on I'd be here talking to you by now, either by choice or not.'

Barnes pressed his thin lips together, looking down at some forms in front of him. 'Is there anything else we could use to entice him there?'

'Honeytrap?' Danny's eyes lit. 'Could try Emily.'

'His wife?'

224

'Girlfriend,' Danny said, 'but got him wrapped around her little finger from what I've seen. Perhaps you could say she'd discovered the lock-up and lure him there, squeeze a confession out of him. Got their address written here somewhere, must be in my wallet.'

'Would she go along with this?'

'Dunno, but once she finds out what Ethan's been up to, what with the two-timing and armed raids, reckon she'd be more than willing to turn him in.'

'We'll leave it there for now,' Barnes said and wrapped up the interview. Danny was led to a cell and left to wait, stew over what he'd said and what Ethan was up to. He couldn't believe he was cooped up in this small, grey room while Ethan was out there, no doubt on the war path.

CHAPTER 32

Danny shifted his weight in the back of an unmarked police van, running over the dos and don'ts he'd been told by a plain-clothed officer called Steve. Short cropped hair, more grey than black.

Barnes was also there and asked, 'Do you want to call your wife in the safe house?'

Danny considered his answer. 'No, she'll only try to talk me out of this. Only upset us both. Let's get it over, plenty of time to explain things after.'

'There's always an element of risk volunteering for police undercover operations,' Steve said. 'We'll need you to sign this consent form.'

Danny said, 'To cover your back if it goes tits up.'

'Just sign,' Barnes said.

'Remember the codeword – Likelihood – in case the mission needs aborting,' Steve said. 'This will pick up everything clear as day.' A wire was duct-taped to his chest and he was strapped into a bulletproof vest with Velcro.

They climbed from the van, parked in a shady side alley beyond the perimeter of the Newtown Estate.

Danny had often looked in awe at the undercover footage in TV programmes like *Fly On The Wall*. How the hell can they keep their nerve wired-up with a hidden camera amidst ringleaders of organised criminal gangs?

He was now about to find out first hand. He pressed his palm against his chest, making doubly sure the wire was stuck firm.

'Don't,' Steve said. 'Forget it's there. Pressing your chest isn't a natural gesture, unless you've got indigestion or having a heart attack,' he added, smiling, as if picking up on Danny's growing anxiety.

'Feels like I've got both coming on,' Danny said.

'Just nerves.'

Barnes added, 'Remember, you're meeting Ethan's girlfriend behind his back and revealing to her what he's been up to.'

'And that's supposed to settle me,' Danny said.

Barnes continued, 'I'm saying, she'll expect you to be nervous, it's only natural.'

'And if I say the codeword, you'll be there in a flash. Cos if she does manage to entice Ethan to come and he smells the faintest whiff of this, I'm dead.'

'Good luck,' Steve said. Barnes clicked the van door closed and returned to the squad car. Danny stood there in the cold and dark. He filled his lungs, trying to stave off being sick in front of the officers.

If the wire was as sensitive as they reckoned, he'd be surprised it would pick up anything above the thud of his speeding heart.

Trying to burn off some of the adrenalin building, he paced to the lock-ups.

He checked his watch. 10.16PM. Less than quarter of an hour until they were due to meet. Danny wanted to be prompt, gain Emily's trust. He turned into the long corridor of lock-ups, grip tightening around Tyler's key. No sign of Emily, or Ethan.

He stopped four doors down; the newer one linked with Flat 132. He faced away from Bevan House.

Danny was confident Emily would be enough to attract and snare Ethan. But that confidence waned with every second he waited there alone, shivering.

He was about to check his watch for the umpteenth time when he caught sight of a silhouette passing near the light from the street lamp beside the half-pipe.

As the figure neared, he could make out feminine curves under black top and jeans and a canvas holdall slung over her shoulder.

It was Emily. She broke the silence by asking, 'What's this about?'

'Does Ethan know you're here?'

'No,' Emily said. 'You said not to.'

227

'Good.'

'Why?'

'You'll see,' Danny said, crouching down. He turned Tyler's key and lifted the first shutter. He pulled up the second metal barrier, eager to get out of camera shot.

'Is this yours?' she asked. 'I'm not happy about this.'

'Brace yourself, there's more bad news on its way,' Danny said and flashed the torch around the lock-up, get his bearings. The beam struck her, illuminating those blue eyes. He caught a glimpse of blotchy purple bruises at the base of her neck. 'You sure Ethan treats you okay?'

He hoped she'd confess and add counts of GBH to Ethan's list of charges.

'He wouldn't harm me for the world.'

Danny flicked the naked bulb on and the torch off. He felt now was the time to play the trump card in a bid to get Ethan to the lock-up and admit all to the wire. 'I'd say take a seat but there aren't any.'

'Why?' she asked.

'The thing is, Ethan's been seeing someone, a girl at the yard.'

She said, 'You've mistaken me for someone who gives a fuck.'

Clearly they've a more open relationship than she first let on, Danny thought, ruing the missed chance to reveal that sordid secret when they'd met at her house.

Plan B, Danny thought, still surprised by her lack of interest in the revelation. Had they argued or separated? Maybe Ethan had already let on about Kelly.

'There's another thing you should know about your beloved Ethan.'

'What?'

'The raids on bookmakers in the area.'

'Where's this going?'

'They were masterminded here, on the laptops over there.'

'And?'

'By Ethan.'

From the soft light thrown off the bulb, Danny could make out her pretty face remain unmoved. 'Did you hear me?'

'Yes,' she replied calmly. 'And what do you want me to do about it?'

Was she in shock?

He said, 'Couldn't believe it at first either, but I heard them, plotting the Greyfriars raid, from down there.' Danny's gaze dropped to the trapdoor. 'It was definitely Ethan, certain of it.'

He felt an inward mix of surprise and disappointment. Having unveiled both of Ethan's secrets and not even produced a gasp, he felt a film of sweat on his brow and palms; there was no Plan C.

Emily wasn't rising to the bait.

She removed a phone from her blue coat and its tiny screen up-lit her face mint green. She pushed her hair behind her ear and held the phone there.

'Calling the police?'

'I'm checking Ethan's on his way,' she said. They both looked off to the left as the metal shutters rattled and again, before rising to reveal a silhouette in the mouth of the garage doorway, followed by a rush of cool night air flooding the lock-up. 'But needn't have bothered,' she added. 'Speak of the devil.'

'Thanks my sweet,' Ethan said, stepping into the guttural light. 'You did well to call me.'

Must've made the call shortly before this rendezvous, Danny reckoned.

Danny turned back to Emily and instinctively stepped back. The phone in her hand had been replaced by a handgun, barrel pointing his way.

'Do it, my Jaguar,' he said. 'Do it!'

Danny raised his palm instinctively. Ethan had blocked the only way out.

Her aim suddenly turned away from Danny and on to Ethan, who said, 'What are you doing?'

'It's over,' she said.

229

'You're not serious,' Ethan pleaded and then forced a shaky laugh.

'Deadly,' Emily said, 'Over there, move!'

Ethan remained stood, rooted to the spot, whether from fear or stubbornness.

'Go! By your trainer!'

'But think of all we've been through,' Ethan said.

Danny presumed he meant the several raids.

'They've closed the net,' she replied. 'We both knew this time would come.'

'But we've moved on to Wheeler's branches, given us some breathing space, shake the police off our tail.'

'Don't fool yourself, it's the end.'

'But we'd face the end together, you promised.'

'You were never in my plans,' she said. 'Wouldn't get through passport control, given your criminal record.'

'But I did it all for you,' Ethan said, voice breaking.

'No one forced you,' she said. 'It was in your interest as well, so you thought at the time.'

'What will you do?'

'After killing both of you,' Emily said, 'leave your bodies to rot down there.' Her eyes flicked to the trapdoor. 'Until that Neanderthal's wretched dog smells out your decaying corpses.'

'Why are you talking like this?' Ethan said and stepped forward.

'Back!' she shouted. He obliged.

'By then, I'll be sunning myself, with enough to retire on from what's left after this one,' she said, waving the gun at Ethan but looking at Danny, 'foolishly invested in your doomed yard. Get out while the going is good.'

'There's nothing left,' Ethan said.

'What do you mean?' she replied, head tilted slightly.

'I mean there is nothing left.'

'You're lying, why tell me this now?' she said, frowning. 'To buy you time? Well it won't work.'

'I couldn't find the right time to break it to you, now seems perfect,' Ethan said.

'No,' she said.

'Don't believe me then,' Ethan said, 'but you'll find out soon enough when you try to shift money from your account.'

'E-Holdings?' Danny asked.

Ethan didn't correct him. 'It's all gone Emily, you're right, it's over.'

'I knew you were thick as pigshit but you've outdone yourself, gambling the lot!'

'Did everything I could to fix the outcome of a race,' Ethan said, 'cover the losses from our horses.'

'There's 60K here,' she said, clinging to the holdall. 'Siphoned it off to my own personal account as I feared this would happen. Enough to get a foothold abroad. I'd written off the fortune you blew on that deadbeat yard of yours.' Danny was again staring down the barrel 'You could never resist the horses, how you expected to get a return let alone a profit is beyond me. This will be sweet revenge.'

'No! Em, please!'

Ethan said, 'It's not in you, said so yourself, that's why you needed me to carry out the dirty, Tyler remember, also leant on Jed heavily, couldn't have done any of the raids, either.'

'Don't kid yourself,' Emily replied. 'Could've let anyone partner me in the raids, even Trevor.'

The bruises on her neck, Danny thought, where he'd kicked her escaping from the Gents in the bookie.

'But I cared for you, only one who'd look out for you after mum and dad died.'

'Didn't ask you to.'

They were siblings? Danny thought, struggling to process this. Same deep blue eyes, aquiline nose, her black hair showing blond roots, even her Home Counties accent. The likeness seemed obvious now. But it's less easy to see something when you're not looking for it.

'But I did,' Ethan whined. 'I made good that promise. My Jaguar. Please think about what you're doing.'

'I have, for years. And don't call me that!' she said, and turned to Danny as if needing a sympathetic ear to vent her frustrations. 'Mother and Father bought that bloody cat to try and entice you out of that shell of yours.'

'And it did,' Ethan said.

'You pointed at the tabby cat and said 'jaguar'. First word he'd spoken in over a year. The name stuck. When dad killed the wretched thing, little sis became the replacement, didn't I. Treated me as a plaything, since our parents had gone. I want my own back, my life back.'

Danny felt hot and cold, sweaty and weak. The predicament was worsening by the word. He felt it was time for *that* word and said, 'Any likelihood you'd let me go.'

She laughed, 'You're just as guilty in this mess. Your failings as a trainer were put in the shade by that shining performance in the Grand National.'

'Could've gone elsewhere,' Danny said defensively.

'Ethan forced my hand, as usual. I watched as he ploughed the winnings into your wretched yard.'

Danny felt like pointing out it wasn't their winnings in the first place but thought better of it.

'We could hardly hide it under the bed, or store it here,' Ethan said. 'And properties and shares were on the slide, too risky.'

'Too risky!' she scoffed. 'What about the horses? You thrive on risk. It's what got you started, nicking sweets to buy friends at school.' She glanced at Danny and added, 'Father didn't believe in pocket money.'

'They were bright jumping prospects,' Ethan said and swallowed. 'Don't blame me, it's him.'

'Whoa,' Danny said, 'it was you who introduced Sam.'

'My Jaguar,' Ethan whimpered.

'And you know what jaguars are capable of.'

'You're not thinking right, put the gun down,' Ethan said, firmer now, as if trying a different tack.

Emily hissed, 'Don't you dare tell me what to do. He's always controlling me.' Her eyes shifted back to Danny, as if to seek more assurance.

'I watched over you,' Ethan said, 'it's what Mum and Dad would've wanted, expected. We had no other family, us against the world.'

'Wasn't allowed out on my eighteenth, even my twenty-first, no friends, let alone boyfriends.'

'I feared you'd get into trouble, led astray.'

'Like snapping a neck over a spilt pint.'

'That was different.'

Getting two confessions in one, Danny thought, praying the wire was picking all this up.

'Don't do this,' Ethan said. 'I'll let you go, do your own thing.'

'Was going to anyway, flights are booked.'

'Where?' Ethan asked.

'Anywhere but here,' Emily said. 'Start afresh.' Her grasp tightened around the leather holdall clutched to her chest. 'I knew you'd blow the rest.'

'My precious Jaguar.'

'And you treated me like an animal. To think, I'll never have to hear you call me that again.'

'But –'

'I'm human,' Emily cried, for the first time flustered, as if releasing long-held frustrations, 'not some pet to look after. And do you know the first thing I'll do?'

'Wha –'

'Get rid of this,' she said, eyes glistening in the half-light. She rolled up her sleeve to reveal the tattoo on her arm. She then turned to Danny and said, 'He pinned me down and burned this on me, in one of his fits of rage. A manipulative bully. Always were, always will be.'

Danny felt like backing away into a dark corner while this domestic was going on.

What the fuck was holding up the police, he thought, were they stalling to get more from the wire to nail them?

She released the safety catch.

Fearing this was it, Danny had an idea. He noticed her grip on the gun. It was loose, the gun wavering slightly. He could tell

233

she was a novice. Like a non-smoker holding a cigarette. She'd most probably fire at the bigger target of his torso, rather than his head. He turned to Ethan, whose ashen face shimmered like silver in the dim light. He whispered, 'Six.'

Ethan met his gaze and replied, 'Six.'

'What did he mean?' Emily snapped. 'Ethan?!'

They both charged forward, Danny taking the lead.

'Stop!' she cried.

Their feet trampled over the groaning wood of the trapdoor. Danny's eyes cut through the gloom and saw her fingers tighten round the trigger. A piercing crack filled the lock-up. Danny felt a crushing blow in his stomach. He was winded yet kept on.

Another shocking bang and flash of light. A sickly shriek, a dull thud. Had Ethan taken the second bullet?

Danny didn't turn to find out.

Emily let slip the gun as Danny shouldered her to the ground. Her long nails, like talons, clawed at Danny's face, drawing blood.

Danny pushed her away. She reached out for the gun. He extended his legs and kicked it beyond her reach. She struggled to her feet. Danny looked down, no sign of blood where the bullet struck. The vest had done its job. He looked over. Ethan hadn't been so fortunate. He lay there in a growing red pool, loosely holding his torso, jacket now glistening.

What the fuck was holding up the police? The deafening gunfire must surely have been picked up by the wire, unless the bullet had severed it.

A tinny ring filled his ears as he looked up at Emily. Her fiery eyes fixed firmly on Danny as he struggled to his feet, biting back the pain. He briefly glanced at Ethan, who, grimacing, reached across to the handle on the trapdoor of the inspection pit. He let out a primal roar as he lifted the door.

Emily remained unmoved as if assuming the noise was the last gasp of a dying man, no apparent concern, despite it being her own flesh and blood. Danny saw his chance to trap The Jaguar; a black rectangle in the concrete.

He pounced forward, taking Emily along with him. She screeched as she was swallowed by the hole. Danny grabbed the edge of the pit, halting momentum. He felt himself following her in when a leg came out. It was Ethan. He grimaced, 'One.'

Danny figured he meant the codeword One. Rein in. Ethan gave the ghost of a smile as his eyelids came down over dulling eyes.

Danny let the wooden door drop with a loud thud and a cloud of dust. The wood shook as her fists hammered the underside, like a caged wild animal. But the weighty door wouldn't budge. She was going nowhere.

As the shutters came up, flashes of light and several armed officers, with salivating police dogs, flooded the place.

Handcuffs were slapped on Ethan as he was whisked away in an ambulance standing by. Emily was lifted from the pit and, after the briefest of struggles, was taken from the scene in a police van.

The remaining medics carefully peeled off the bullet-proof vest. It had done its job well. No wounds, except for old battle scars.

Barnes came over. 'It was a success, we've got enough on tape to secure conviction. Well done for getting her to talk.'

'And I'm now ready to speak with Sara.'

'Here, use mine,' Barnes said.

Danny reached over feelingly and made the call.

CHAPTER 33

Danny held the tumbler, glowing amber, and looked down on the dusky schooling grounds. Against the orange of the setting sun, he could make out the shape of Salamanca enjoying a well-earned summer rest out in the lower field, bucking and kicking with rude health.

His attention turned to the front-page headline of the local rag: 'Bookie raiders get total of 22 years.'

He placed the paper on his desk and muttered, 'Cardiff's very own Bonnie and Clyde.'

Beauty about racing, Danny thought idly, however many lows slap you in the face, the occasional highs make it all worthwhile. And, around every corner, there's always hope of striking oil, whether it be plundering a big prize as a trainer, snapping up a rising star as an owner or getting an accumulator up as a punter. A dreamer's paradise.

His phone buzzed. He picked it up and smiled as he read a text from George Evans. *'Told u he was special. Roll on next year!'*

He turned and saw Sara in the doorway, cradling nappies and a plastic beaker. 'Managed to get Jack down, for how long is another matter.'

'Been thinking,' Danny said. 'Perhaps I should get a travelling head lad or lass. Cut down away trips and free up more time to spend round here.'

'Kelly?'

'She deserves it, trust her to do a good job,' Danny said.

'You'll soon see the benefit,' she said.

Danny finished off the whisky.

She added, 'There's something been bugging me ever since you told me what went on in that lock-up.'

'Go on,' Danny said and sighed. He didn't much fancy reliving that evening anytime soon, not while emotions were still raw.

'How were you so sure she'd aim for the body and not the head?'

'Took that risk,' Danny said, 'We had little to lose.' He glanced down at the grainy mug-shot of Ethan in the paper. 'Who dares wins, I guess.'

'Will you say goodnight to Jack? Just got him settled. And then I'll have you all to myself.'

Danny put the empty glass on the windowsill and said, 'Be right there.'

Printed in Great Britain
by Amazon